To Jamie

Basic Black

Merry Xmas 1992

X O

Mum

Also by Arthur Black

That Old Black Magic
Back to Black
Arthur! Arthur!

The Wit and Whimsy of Arthur Black

Basic Black

Arthur Black

Published in 1992 by
Stoddart Publishing Co. Limited
34 Lesmill Road
Toronto, Canada
M3B 2T6

First published in 1981 by
Penumbra Press

Canadian Cataloguing in Publication Data

Black, Arthur
Basic Black

ISBN 0-7737-5516-0

I. Title

PS8553.L3B3 1992   C814'.54   C92-093277-0
PR9199.3.B53B3 1992

Some of these tales have been heard over the airwaves of
CBC or have appeared in the pages of *Lakehead Living*,
Thunder Bay. My thanks to the Corp. and Laurentian
Publishing for permission to have them
reappear in this book. — *A.B.*

Cover design: Brant Cowie/ArtPlus
Typesetting: Tony Gordon Ltd.
Printed and bound in Canada

Stoddart Publishing gratefully acknowledges the support of
the Canada Council, Ontario Arts Council and
Ontario Publishing Centre in the development of
writing and publishing in Canada.

CONTENTS

TO RUBY FRANCES BLACK
THE FIRST WOMAN IN MY LIFE
HI, MA!

CROSS COUNTRY SKIING

I WOULD like to say a few words about a disease. A particular brand of madness that has infested our nation from coast to coast.

Well . . . I don't know that it's *that* far gone. I can't testify for exotic spas like Victoria and Musquadobit Harbour. Perhaps the citizenry of Tuktoyaktuk and Point Pelee have more sense . . . But for the most part, any place in the country that can hold an inch or two of snow on the ground for more than 24 hours will be suffering in some measure from this strange affliction.

Cross country skiing is what I'm talking about. You may know it as touring or nordic skiing. A ruse by any other name. They are all devious euphemisms for the same senseless pastime.

Cross country skiing is basically jogging while wearing lumber. The same personality type that would make mock of a summer morning by donning pyjamas with a racing stripe and 40-dollar sneakers to lurch around a football field until his lungs burst — that's the kind of bedrock lunatic that is the very foundation of cross country madness.

The cross country fanatic is not to be confused with the downhiller. Cross country is kind of the poor-but-proud hillbilly cousin of decadent downhill. Anyone who is rich, beautiful and brainless enough to look comfortable in a Canadian beer commercial usually gravitates toward the downhill scene with its astronaut accoutrements and the après-ski perks of crackling logs in the fireplace, hot toddies and dancing chic-to-chic in form-fitting Eddie Bauer down-filled vests. When all that's going down at the chalet, you can sometimes look out the floor-to-ceiling thermopane and occasionally catch just a flicker of the cross country skier . . . shuffling sullenly among the spruce trees.

Contrary to what you might have heard . . . cross country skiing is easy. You just shuffle with your feet and stab with your poles. Fall down, get up. Shuffle, stab, fall down . . . get up, get cold, shuffle, stab, turn around, shuffle, stab, fall down, get up, shuffle, stab, back to your car. Take off the skis and go home. In cross country, the skiing part is childishly simple. It's the *choosing* you have to do that makes it difficult.

First the skis. You will spend your first ski season fretting over what kind of skis you should have bought rather than the ones you did. There are wooden skis, wooden skis with lignite edges, skis with wooden bottoms and plastic tops . . . plastic skis and finally *really* plastic skis — skis with ripples and dimples on the bottom that are supposed to make the perverse science of waxing unnecessary.

Needless to say, any cross country purist sneers at waxless skis. What? Ski and not wax? It's like asking Glenn Gould to sit down at a player piano.

I'm here to tell you that waxless skis work perfectly. Whenever you achieve a precise combination of sun and temperature and age of snow and condition of track — which is to say, perhaps three outings in a lifetime.

But that's okay . . . because that's about how often you'll hit the right ski wax if you go with the slats that need waxing.

Ever checked out cross country waxes? The sales clerk will tell you you only need three really — green for cold, blue for not too cold and red for warm . . . but then you'll be tempted to round out your kit with a pale green for very cold, a purple for those not quite blue and not yet red days . . . and before you know it you'll have a packsack full of emeralds, indigos, chartreuses, violets and a whole herd of maverick waxes including yellow, black, orange and so help me, silver.

You think I jest? Lemme read to you from a random collection of waxes I have here. Here's a piquant little brown that I think you'll find amusing. Instructions on the tube: 'For dry new snow, 18° Fahrenheit and below . . . thin layer. From 18° to 30° Fahrenheit — thicker layer . . . smooth out well.'

Here's another tube — a zesty cerulean blue. It reads: 'For fine-grained snow from minus one Celsius to minus five Celsius . . . and fresh snow from minus one Celsius to minus three Celsius . . . polish to a fine film, blah blah . . .' I've got an even funnier one in a black tube but unfortunately the instructions read: 'Ranta ja nuoskalin Lempe leppanen, sisu quitos suomi kovisto sibelius' and so on . . . That's one of the features of cross country waxes — they come like lipstick, with the instructions printed on the side — only you have to peel away the container as you use the wax. First peel takes out the English instructions and you are left with Finnish, Norwegian, Lapp and occasionally Russian — but that's a whole other fault report. No ... the point is, by the time you've decided whether the snow is fresh or old, fine or coarse, dry or wet, fluffy or granular ... and decided whether you should polish to a fine layer or lay it on like peanut butter ... by the time you've done all this in the middle of the bush on a midwinter day, your feet are cold, your hands are numb and anyway it's time to go home.

And yet it goes on. Phenomenally. It's more and more popular every year — there are marathon ski tours right across the country that attract thousands of entrants each. The Canadian Ski Marathon held recently in Quebec made tourers ski more than 100 miles in terrible terrain over two days. The wind chill factor on opening day made for a temperature of something like 50 below. Four thousand people entered!

Why? Who knows? I guess it's one way to beat Canada's rotten winters ... Gives you the illusion that you're meeting winter on its own terms and all that Jack London stuff.

Met one marathoner who says he skis every day in the winter to avoid getting cabin fever.

Poor devil. Either his brain is raddled with klister fumes or he's just too far gone to reason.

Doesn't realize that cross country skiing *is* cabin fever. On runners.

SKI

Looking for a challenge? I've got a challenge for you. It is called the North Superior Challenge and it comes around once a year. You just missed this year's North Superior Challenge, but don't despair ... that means you've got an entire year to prepare for next year's version. You can use it.

The North Superior Challenge is a ski marathon, and to

understand why it is the way it is, you have to appreciate a certain reality about Canada. The country can be broken down into two elements: Large Urban Centres . . . and The Rest. For those of us who live in The Rest, the Large Urban Centres can be a pain. The big cities take out primary resources . . . our trees, our hydro electric power, our wheat, our hockey players . . .

And they send us back Kleenex, power blackouts, bread that tastes like styrofoam and Harold Ballard.

Well that's okay . . . but it does create a certain groundswell of resentment in the non-urban areas of the country . . . which sort of explains the North Superior Challenge. It takes place around Schreiber. Schreiber is a little town on the north shore of Lake Superior about 150 miles east of Thunder Bay. Chances are rather good that you've never heard of Schreiber. It's a whistle stop on the CP Line . . . You'd probably pull over there for gas or a coffee if you were driving the Trans-Canada Highway along the north shore . . . It's mentioned in a Murray McLauchlan song . . . but that's about it for Schreiber in terms of worldwide fame. It definitely belongs outside the Big City segment of this country . . . It's unquestionably part of The Rest.

I like to think that one day the town fathers were sitting around the beverage room of the Schreiber Hotel — maybe watching the summer tourists in their Winnebagos stacking themselves up into miles-long traffic jams . . . maybe just listening to the high speed whine of heavy duty tires as the pulp trucks roared through town. I like to think that one of the town elders set down his draft glass and said: 'You know . . . we oughta get together as a town, I mean — and whip up a little somethin' extra special for outsiders. Figger out somethin' that would bring out the folks from Thunder Bay, er Ottawa er Toronto . . . kind o' show them around and show our appreciation at the same time.'

Wicked chuckles sweep the table.

That's how I like to think the North Superior Challenge was born a couple of years back. It's only 12 miles long — 20 kilometres — which is modest as ski tours go. But O my brothers . . . the 12 miles are almost entirely vertical. You have never climbed so high and fallen so precipitously so many times in one afternoon. The crevasses, chasms and black holes of the North Superior Challenge make the Grand Canyon look like an example of mild spring runoff. The peaks, summits and mountain aeries of the North Superior Challenge make the Rocky Mountains look like a series of modest moguls in need of training bras.

Quite simply the trail is designed to reduce the cockiest cross country jock to an amorphous blob of whimpering, quivering jelly. At one point you climb a path that would leave a mountain goat rubber kneed . . . You climb for — I don't know — for half an hour maybe? You climb and climb and slip and climb and curse and climb and slither and rewax and sob and climb and finally you see a sign on a tree! 'Congratulations!' it reads. 'You made it!' So you trudge across the clearing and around a bend, feeling ever so slightly like Rocky Balboa, and you round that bend and suddenly you face . . . a longer? higher? climb?????

You whip your head back to the sign you just passed, and through tear-blurred eyes, you read the fine print on the back. 'We lied,' it says cheerfully.

Another trail sign you could just catch out of the corner of your eye as you plummeted down one of the cliff-face hills reads 'Watch for Tree in Middle of Trail.' You had just enough time to think 'That's an odd siiiiiii.' Blam. Too late.

What a day. What a transformation a mere three or four hours on the North Superior ski trail can make in a person. Oh, we all started out vermillion cheeked and sparkly eyed, our jaunty little ski toques perched on our self-confident little skulls . . . our perky ski knickers just lapping neatly at our colourful water-repellent ski socks . . . Laughing we were . . . exchanging helpful waxing tips as we stood shuffling and champing at the starting gate. All of us came back looking like the shattered remnants of the Mackenzie-Papineau Battalion . . . stockings shredded, hats gone, ski poles fractured, drenched in sweat and hobbling with fatigue.

And I saw you, you learned elders of Schreiber. I saw you smirking and chuckling behind your hands as we hobbled into the Schreiber high school gym when it was all over. 'Well, what did you think?' you asked each of us deadpan . . . 'Did you find 'er challenging enough?'

You may recall O Learned Elders that I was at a loss for words for an hour or so . . . Too busy gasping for air. Well I have words now. I would like to say that the North Superior Challenge is the most vicious and sadistic stretch of 12 miles that I have ever fallen . . . I would like to point out that although the tour finished over a week ago I still hurt in every part of my body. My earlobes ache. I have cramps in my hair. I have spent the price of a good pair of Peltonenn racing skis on Sloan's liniment and blister cream. And I would like to make note of something else.

Somewhere on the North Superior Challenge trail there lies a pair of sunglasses, one gray mitt, one blue toque and a brown sweater with a rip up the back. They all belong to me. I never want to see them again. Right now I wouldn't go back on that trail if there were diamonds in the snow, rubies dripping from the trees and snifters of brandy served by nubile ski bunnies at every checkpoint.

But I won't argue with you. I don't want to argue about anything. I've had my challenge for this year. And that's not a chip on my shoulder. It's a splint.

DIG

ARCHEOLOGY. It's been a lifelong dream of mine. I've always in my heart of hearts wanted to wear a pith helmet over my ear-muffs . . . and to discover a Viking sword on Hamilton Mountain or maybe a fossilized Chianti bottle from the *Santa Maria* on the shores of the St. Lawrence — something romantic like that. So, I signed up for this Beginner's Archeology Course — because it had Field Trips. Last week I went with my class to the shores of a lake that has been a canoe and trading route for thousands of years. It was my very first archeological dig.

Ever been on a dig? Neither had I, until last weekend. Mind you, I knew all about them. A dig was where you scuffed away some surface debris with the toe of your hiking boot and uncovered a Sumerian writing tablet. A dig was where you ran into a small cave to get out of a rain squall, glanced up at the ceiling and discovered a panorama of prehistoric pictographs that proved Phoenicians were in Moose Jaw three thousand years before Columbus was born.

A dig was where you sidled up to the world-famous archeologist on the site and mumbled something like: 'I don't suppose there's anything to it, Sir Gerald, but I found this while I was picking watercress for my ham salad sandwich.' And Sir Gerald looks at your find and says: 'By Jove, young man, this is absolutely incredible — this artifact completely confounds every accepted anthropological tenet since the time of Darwin. I daresay your name will live on in the annals of archeology . . .' et cetera.

That's what a dig is all about. Romance! Adventure! Glory!

I used to think.

I know better now. I've been on a dig.

Even the name is a cruel joke. You don't 'dig' on an archeological dig. You brush. You sift. You scrape. You scrunch yourself down on the cold damp ground and try to get your eyelashes right in the dirt to see whether you've uncovered a Paleolithic adze flake or just circumstantial evidence of a sand flea in need of housebreaking.

Being on a dig is about as glorious and romantic as cutting the front lawn with nail clippers or scrubbing down the patio with a Pic O Pay toothbrush. And it's not just the nit-picking, grit-sifting laboriousness of the it-is-to-laugh 'dig' . . . No . . . you have to *record* the dig too. It has to be all charted and annotated and taken out of a perfect two-metre by two-metre square all marked off with string . . . and you have to shaaaaaave the layers off your square with a tiny razor-edged hand trowel ever so carefully . . . and you have to scoop up all the shaved-off flotsam ever so fastidiously with your little dustpan and tippytoe it over to a discreet pile nearby that won't interfere with anybody else's perfect two-metre by two-metre square, and all of this might be just barely, humanly possible if the area you were excavating was made of onion skins or maybe Gillette Foamy lather, but it isn't — it's made of dirt and rock and tenacious tree, and have you ever tried to shave the roots of a 20-foot spruce?

Anyway. As you may have deduced from the tone of my remarks, there was nothing in my little two-metre by two-metre square. Nope. Yea though I moved enough dirt and rock with my paintbrush and trowel to start my own roadbuilding business . . . Even though I left a cavity that would have brought a lump to the throat of any open pit miner. I found zip-all. And I was tired and sweaty and blistered and more than a little cheesed off about it too.

But you know friends . . . right then . . . at the absolute nadir of my confidence . . . a marvellous thing happened. A young fella in the square next to mine stopped sifting, squinted . . . and then called out the magic words: 'I think I found something . . .'

He had indeed. A beautiful, unmistakable artifact . . . an orange-hued, undeniably sculpted chip of stone that our archeology professor confirmed had come from an archaic spearhead. Oh, I know it doesn't sound like much. It's not the Rosetta stone or the Dead Sea Scrolls . . . but I tell ya . . . When you're sitting down on your haunches there, on a sandy beach by a remote northern Ontario lake and you're holding in your hand a piece of handiwork that came from another human hand, five — maybe seven thousand years ago . . . a fellow human that squatted right where you're squatting now . . . a human who was sharpening his weapon, thinking about bringing down a caribou or a bear — well, I mean . . . five thousand years ago! Stonehenge hadn't been built. The pyramids were just beginning to rise above the sands of the Sahara. Imperial Rome hadn't even risen much less fallen . . . and there you are . . . linked to that forgotten, nameless nomad by that tiny piece of hand-worked stoned. That's the magic of archeology — and magic it is.

I was still thinking about it that evening when I walked down to the lake to watch the sun set. How about that? My instincts about archeology had been right — despite the sweat and the aching backs and the mind-numbing monotony of the procedure, there *is* romance in archeology. Hmmm. Idly I picked up a stone to skip across the water into the sunset. I wound up. I froze. I uncocked my arm. I looked at the stone in my hand. Good . . .God . . . could you believe it? Right there on the shore — a perfect example of a Paleo-Indian projectile point — unmistakably late Archaic. I turned and raced up the bank, skinning my knee, all set to shout . . .

I froze again. No. No, that would not be cool. No, I'd do it just the way I always dreamed I would do it. Suavely. No fuss. Like a professional. I . . . meandered . . . back to the campsite. Nonchalant. Urbane. Trying not to pant. I strolled over to the professor and held out my find offhandedly.

'I ahhh . . . don't suppose there's anything to this,' I said, 'I ahh just picked it up mmmmm . . . down by the lake there.'

Well the professor took one look at it . . . then carefully took it out of my hands and stared. Conversations among the other students died. The whole crew gathered around, bug-eyed and slack-jawed. I stifled a yawn. 'Just . . . found it on the beach there . . .'

The professor turned to me and said, 'Do you realize what you've got here?'

I said, hah hah well I didn't deserve any credit really, just because I'd spotted it out of those thousands, millions I guess of other rocks on the beach — but the professor cut me off. 'This,' he said, 'is a perfect example of a prime Leavit. Some experts call them Dog Rocks.'

Well, I said. Leavits! Dog Rocks! And on my first dig! What culture do they represent? What were they used for?

Not *were* used for, said the professor. *Are* used for. When you find one of these Leavits you got two options. You can wait for a dog to throw it at. Or you can leave it.

I'm thinking of trying Colour Photography for the winter semester . . .

DIGS

KNOW what I want to be when I grow up? An archeologist. Much more romantic than a fireman or a cowboy. Popular too. People respect and admire archeologists. The writer Agatha Christie, who was married to one, said that an archeologist makes the best husband a woman can have. 'The older she gets,' said Dame Agatha, 'the more interested he is in her.'

Fascinating pastime, archeology. 'Frozen history' someone once called it. I thought of that expression one day last summer when an archeologist neighbour of mine invited me on a 'dig' on the shores of a lake not far from Thunder Bay. People don't think of north-western Ontario as exactly a hotbed of archeological potential . . . We have no hidden Mayan temples in the bush here; no sunken galleons laden with Spanish gold; no prehistoric tombs of ancient mummified Kings . . . why even the presence of the white man in this part of the country spans scarcely four centuries. You wouldn't expect to find a lot in the way of cultural artifacts around here.

Ah, but that's forgetting (as we usually do) the fact that humans were living here before those first ratty-looking explorers and fur traders pushed their fearful way into this part of the country. Indians. They'd been here for thousands of years. Which is what drew my archeologist neighbour and me to the shores of Dog Lake that day last summer. He had found, he thought, a likely Stone Age campsite. Sandy shore in a sheltered bay. He thought it was worth a look.

Indeed it was. After some painstaking brushing and digging with trowels, we found the stones of a long-dead campfire. He found the very spot where a long-dead hunter had squatted to sharpen his stone axe head. The chips or flakes were still there in the sand, lying where they'd fallen as he chipped away one similar sunny afternoon probably . . . long ago.

The mind-boggling part of the story was *how* long ago. The campfire we were looking at . . . the stone flakes we saw . . . had been there for somewhere between three and five thousand years.

Granted, stone flakes aren't quite as exotic as Tutankhamen's gold filigree face mask . . . a five-thousand-year-old campfire doesn't have quite the emotional impact of a cave full of Dead Sea Scrolls. But that doesn't detract from the curious little shiver of awe that courses through your mind when you touch something made by a fellow human several thousand years ago.

Besides . . . all archeology is relative . . . I keep thinking of the news story I saw recently from Israel.

Israel . . . where farmers and well diggers and foundation excavators almost routinely uncover evidence of whole vanished civilizations with little more than the turn of a spade. Israel . . . where secretaries eat their lunches on the ruins of ancient battlements . . . where you can find two-thousand-year-old shards of pottery in your petunia patch.

Israel.

You'll never guess what the next great archeological dig in Israel is looking for. It's almost set to go . . . a four-jeep task force, armed with metal detectors and even a helicopter . . . poised and ready to roll through the shifting sands of the Sinai desert . . . looking for . . .

Approximately 180 Mercedes automobiles.

They are stolen. They've been buried there . . . somewhere . . . by an artfully dodging band of Bedouin car thieves. The Mercedes are stored if you will — all carefully wrapped in polyethylene.

The thieves had hoped to leave the cars interred until Israel withdraws from the Sinai in two years' time. Then the cars would be uncovered and put back on the road with new and doubtless non-Israeli owners behind the wheel.

Not surprisingly the legitimate owners of the cars envisage a different ending to the story, which is why the First Ever Mercedes Expeditionary Search and Rescue Squad is set to get under way. It may take some time . . . there's a lot of sand in the Sinai.

I wish them well . . . but frankly I can't get too excited.

Nothing against Mercedes you understand. If you saw the crock of metal and rubber that shivers and shakes me to work each morning you'd more than understand . . . It's just that, as an unfulfilled and forever amateur archeologist, I get more punch from a Paleolithic arrowhead than a hot luxury car. Besides there's probably sand in the gas tanks.

FISHING

I AM going to talk about fishing. I want you to understand before we go any further that I have, in fact, caught fish in my life. Nothing of the order that might inspire a Melville or a Hemingway perhaps, but *fish*, for all that. I particularly remember a chubby little Kamloops trout that collided with my hook one spring afternoon in a set of rapids north of Toronto some years ago . . . and it can't be more than five summers since that memorable moment in a rowboat on Lake Minnitakawiskamonga something or other that, in between retrievals of rubber boots and fragments of beaver lodge, I reeled in some two and a half feet of exceptionally disgruntled northern pike. To the surprise of us both.

So it's not as if I've never wetted a line . . . no, that's not the point . . . The point is, while I have caught fish . . . I've never really caught the fishing bug. The art of fishing for me remains like the dance steps of a fandango or the F stops on my camera — something I'll never really comprehend.

Mind you, it's not for lack of introductions. The world is chock-ablock with the disciples of the rod and reel — only too eager to unveil their secrets to the ignorant.

I once worked with a man in England — an artist by trade, but an angler by inclination. You could tell, because he always went around with a copy of the *Angling Times* tucked under his arm. The *Angling Times* was a strange little British biweekly much given to murky photos of grinning Britons hoisting lately extinct representatives of the piscatorial persuasion.

One day my friend decided I was ready for initiation into the enigmas of Anglo-angling.

The opening day of the season was tomorrow. I would sleep at his place so that we could get an early start. My head had barely touched the pillow when I felt a tap on my shoulder. It was my host.

— What??? Burglars? Fire? Nonpayment of rent?

It was three in the morning, and my host was all dressed in rubber. Either I was about to become the victim of a sex murder bizarre even by London standards, or . . .

'Time to push off, mate.'

'Omigawd we're going fishing!'

We did too. To make a long and miserable story short, we drove through the bone-chilling predawn gloom to a leafy rain-stained grotto where we purchased tickets. Tickets! We then stumbled down to the water's edge to lay claim to a piece of damp shoreline.

When dawn broke I found we were sitting on the edge of what looked like a water-filled gravel pit . . . along with hundreds! hundreds of other fishing persons . . . none of whom smiled, none of whom talked or in any way acknowledged the presence of his neighbours.

We stayed there all bleeding day and my line never quivered once. Not a nibble. Not the merest brush of a fin going by. Nothing. As a matter of fact I didn't see *any*body catch anything. But of course

I fell asleep almost as soon as the sun came up and arrested my shivering.

My friend was undaunted though. He spent the entire day, cheerily immersed to his thighs, casting out and reeling in, casting out and reeling in, catching boo-all. Well, not exactly nothing. He did, at the end of the day, have three minuscule shad-like creatures in a live-bait pail in the water. They were perhaps six inches long each and looked as if they might make decent bait.

I finally persuaded him to quit at sundown. We drove back to his house . . . him whistling, me rediscovering whole litanies of colonial obscenities I didn't know I knew.

His wife greeted us at the door — asked if we'd had any luck. 'Naaaaah nothing!' I growled.

'Wotchew mean, "nothing,"' crowed my friend, splaying out his three fingerlings at arm's length. 'We caught two roach and a rudd.'

Ahhhh well . . . The British eh? It was a relief to get back to Canada where men were men and minnows were minnows.

Or so I thought. Last week I once more allowed someone to try to 'teach me' fishing.

It was my old pal, Edgar. Edgar's a professor of linguistics at the local university . . . and a touch stuffy to tell the truth . . . but he likes to get away for a little fishing two or three times each summer. He always invites me and I always say no, no, I'm no fisherman and he always says, heavens that's not important — the purpose is recreation not competition . . . and well, finally last weekend I decided to take him up on his offer. We drove to a small, secluded lake well north of the city where Edgar keeps an old wooden skiff. I got in the front, Edgar got in the back and we put-putted off to one of Edgar's favourite fishing holes. He threw out a line . . . I threw out a line . . . Aside from the infrequent babble of a loon and the lap of the lake at the boat's hull, all was peaceful. I began to think that there really was something to this fishing business after all.

That's when it started. Suddenly from behind me I heard a hoarse, guttural rasp of a voice that sounded like a cross between Long John Silver and Joey Smallwood: 'Nivir ketch a walleye leave yer line slack like that agin the current with a new moon risin and a north wind afor the first frost, bye . . .'

What? Edgar? Why are you talking like that?

I turned around and Edgar had gone — gone was the pasty-faced, pudgy-bellied linguistics professor from the city. The man in the stern was squinty-eyed, jut-jawed, weather-beaten and frost-gnawed . . . sort of Precambrian Gothic. In the short drive from the city . . . in that tiny boat hop from the shore, Edgar had gone primitive on me.

The rest of the afternoon was too depressing to dwell on . . . Edgar doing weather forecasts based on the number of caws per crow . . . Edgar telling me to cast with my shoulders and to smell the fish on the breeze . . . Edgar telling me how to bait a hook . . . Edgar snorting and hooting at my collection of plugs and lures and spinners and spoons.

'Yer in the north now boy . . . minnahs is the only thing gonna bring in yer pikril.'

Ah well, maybe he's right . . . I didn't catch anything that day . . . but then neither did he. 'Wind wuz wrong,' he claimed.

And neither did my latexed English mentor catch anything that day at the gravel pit if you discounted those three pubescent sardines he brought home.

But I think maybe that's the whole riddle about fishing for us non-fishermen. We think fishing is about catching fish . . . and it's not. It's about dreaming of fishing, and dressing for fishing and planning fishing trips. It's about half-remembered daydreams of Huckleberry Finn afternoons down by the creek. It's about slightly glimpsed glories of Ahab adventures and Old-Man-and-the-Sea struggles.

For some of us it's dressing up in rubber; for others it's going neo-native for a weekend . . . for others it's blowing five or six bucks down at the sports counter at Canadian Tire, buying ridiculous little fluorescent plastic monsters that look like outtakes from the movie *Alien*.

Fishing is about dreaming . . . it's not about catching fish. The dream is all . . . the rest is just tactics. And hardware. As for the art of catching fish . . . it was all said by another Canadian. Back in 1920 a writer (and angler) by the name of W.H. Blake said: 'The weather for catching fish is that weather, and no other, in which fish are caught.'

I'll drink to that. And I'm pretty sure that Melville and Hemingway and even Izaak Walton would as well.

WEATHER

I BELIEVE it was Samuel Langhorne Clemens — Mark Twain — who once complained: 'Everybody talks about the weather, but nobody does anything about it.'

Easy for old Sam to say — he died in 1910, roughly 60 years before the birth of the Canadian Metric Commission — now there's a bundle of bureaucrats who have *done* something about the weather.

I'm sure I'm not the only person who woke up this morning, listened attentively to the weather forecast over the radio — and who still hasn't a clue about what might happen weatherwise today.

Oh I'm pretty much at ease as far as major cataclysms go. I feel reasonably certain that I don't have to move my cot into the root cellar because of impending typhoons, monsoons or twisters. But that's about all I'd make book on. The local weather forecast promised something along the lines of: 'High today plus 8 to plus 10, currently the winds are from the west at 10 with gusts to 24 kilometres per hour and the humidity is 48 percent . . .'

Well, I'm whipped, you see? I only respond to three humidity rates — dry, muggy and raining. A humidity rate of 48 percent is neither here nor there and qualifies as useless information. As for winds west at 10 and gusting to 24 kilometres per hour — lost again. I haven't got a clue what 24-kilometre per hour gust of wind would feel like if it hit me in the face . . . and I'm afraid that for the rest of my poor sad meteorologically muddled life a temperature of plus 8 to plus 10 will be what it was when I was immature and un-metrificated. Scarf-and-mittens weather. Heavy-socks-with-the-felt-liners weather. Prime time for tobogganing and making snow forts.

It's not of course. It's more like bicycle-tire-pumping and oiling-the-baseball-glove weather, but I doubt if I'll ever get that straight.

Not that it's entirely the fault of the Metric Commission. Converting our weather system to Celsius was merely the final straw. I've *never* understood the weather.

Mind you, I'm not convinced anyone else has ever understood it either.

I know . . . I know . . . we have computerized forecasts and satellite photographs and we're up to our isotherms in data-spewing college-extruded climatologists and meteorologists who toothily proclaim each night after the news how many hours of sunshine and snowflakes we can expect in the next 24 hours — but we also have the *Farmers Almanac* and aged Indian shamans and farmers who swear by the prognostications of their pet Holstein, Bessie . . . and to tell you the truth — this is not scientific, but to tell you the truth — based on the number of times I've been dressed for an afternoon in Death Valley and ended up dog paddling for my life . . . on the number of occasions I've started the day in parka and mukluks and wound up being treated for mild sunstroke . . . I'm hard pressed to choose between the forecasts of my friendly teleprompted meteorologist on the boob tube and what some dairy farmer in Dryden says is going to happen. It strikes me that they are climatologically out to lunch just about the same percentage of times . . . which is to say often enough to keep me looking over my shoulder a lot.

But I'm not complaining. As a matter of fact I wouldn't have it any other way. Too many things in all our lives are drearily predictable, boringly foreseeable. As a rather famous Canadian once said, 'The man who is consistent must be out of touch with reality. There is no consistency in the course of events — in history, in the mental attitude of one's fellow man . . . or in the weather.' Lord Beaverbrook said that . . . and I like to remember it whenever that cantankerous, obstinate, contrary phenomenon we call The Weather decides to rain on my picnic or burn yellow patches in my front lawn — or pile waist-high snowdrifts in my driveway, in direct defiance of all the satellite photos and computer printouts Environment Canada can muster.

And on the other hand, when the weather does turn out to be as predicted on the six o'clock news . . . which, let's be fair, it does an uncommon number of times . . . When I'm just beginning to think, by George these meteorologists are getting uncannily good at forecasting the weather . . . then I like to recall the plaque that hangs on a wall in the Winnipeg office of Environment Canada. It's a plaque presented by the Regina Press Club and it reads 'To the newsmaker of the month . . . the Winnipeg Weather Office for accurately predicting a tornado would hit Regina . . . 12 minutes after it did.'

That's the kind of thing that restores a man's faith in the unknown — not to mention the *Farmers Almanac*.

FAT

ONE of the more pleasant and indisputable signs of spring is the shrinking of snowbanks. We get pretty respectable snowbanks here in Thunder Bay — especially after the snowploughs have cruised up and down the streets a few times, furling their cargo higher and higher on what used to be last summer's grassy boulevard. Come about late February those banks are high enough to conceal whole passing cars . . . and driving the streets of the Lakehead after a real late winter storm and ploughing-out with the huge grey canyon walls on either side can seem like a tour of a massive interconnecting bobsled run.

But those walls are slowly tumbling down now. Every sunny day sets the snow to running . . . You can see it oozing in thick creamy gobs off roofs of garages and drooping like syrup from the boughs of evergreens. Backyard fences poke tentative picket tops through the crust . . . but most of all, the snowbanks start to shrink. Suddenly you can see the street again. And more than just the tops of the tassels on the toques bouncing on the heads of schoolkids trying to make the five-to-nine bell . . . Suddenly you can see their whole heads. Ah, it's a wonderful day when the snowbanks start to shrink.

There are of course other winter-caused banks that do not shrink come spring . . . banks a little closer to home. I'm talking about . . . insulation . . . suet . . . spare tires . . . avoirdupois. I am talking about . . . to be brutally frank . . . fat.

Happens to the best of us. In fact scientists estimate that the human body naturally gains two to three percent in weight over the winter. If you weigh 160 pounds that means you can expect to be toting an extra five pounds of yourself around by the time the first crocuses peep through the snow. And that's just average. If you're already predisposed to . . . well . . . chunkiness, you can double that weight without half trying. Why does it happen? Well it's partly due to inactivity. Pretty hard to get out and swat a golfball around after supper when there's half a foot of snow over the first tee and the sun's already been down for two and a half hours.

Part of it is biological. Animals fatten up for winter and so did our ancestors — just for insulation and for those days ahead when you had nothing but your own fat to live off. Unfortunately when our Cro-Magnon forebears forsook the cave for the comfort of thermal long johns and the Esso Home Comfort man . . . they forgot to turn off the biological clock that makes us fatten up each fall along with the bears.

Which accounts for those waist-level flab banks that so many of us have that regrettably don't disappear with the snowbanks.

It's a fairly awesome phenomenon. Doctor Frank Katch is chairman of the Department of Exercise Science at the University of Massachussetts in Amherst. He calculates that there are 50 million American men, 60 million American women and 10 million American teenagers who are overweight . . . Doctor Katch went even further. He estimates that they are overweight to the tune of some one point four *billion* pounds. American figures. I don't have the Canadian ones . . . but given the population spread and the similarities in life styles, it's pretty safe to divide by 10.

I make that five million Canadian men, six million Canadian women and one million Canadian teenagers who tip the scales more than they ought to be tipped.

That's a lot of fat jiggling around, on both sides of the border.

In fact Doctor Katch figures that if you burned all the excess fat Americans are currently carrying around, it would generate enough energy to supply the electrical demands of all residences in Boston, Chicago, San Francisco and Washington for a whole year.

Does Doctor Katch have a solution for all this excess lard? Of course. Was there ever a doctor who didn't? His solution is unfortunately no miracle diet or wonderful aphorism you can scotch tape to the refrigerator door either. Doctor Katch says regular exercise is the key to fat avoidance. And not just deep knee bends on the plush broadloom gym floors of Vic Tanny's. He says if you want to lose

fat, exercise where it's cold. When you shiver, he says, you use 10 to 15 percent more energy. Therefore he says people should exercise some place where it's continually cold. He says they should also wear as little clothing as possible to facilitate shivering.

All of which is, I guess, my way of explaining why you might not be hearing from me for a little while.

It's difficult to predict just how lenient the courts will be on a man arrested for doing 5BX on a shrinking snowbank in the altogether.

CANOES

IT MUST be spring fever . . . but I find myself sitting here, humming snatches of 'Paddlin' Madelin' Home.' Here we are with yards of snow still slung over everything . . . who knows how many feet of ice on the lakes and rivers . . . and I'm getting canoe fever. Got one in the basement you know . . . big old 16-foot Chestnut Prospector slumped kitty-corner across the cement floor sentenced to six months of listening to the furnace click on and off . . . gathering dust. Depressing. Shouldn't happen to a punt, much less a canoe. Canoe. Funny name. Nobody knows for sure where it comes from, but in the 16th century a chap named C. Columbus dutifully recorded in the ship's log that the natives of the island of Haiti got about in a graceful, tapered pea-pod-like craft that he called 'canoa.' It's hard to say. You could paddle from here to Great Slave Lake arguing the derivation of the word. The Dutch have a word for boat that sounds like kaan . . . the Germans have one almost the same.

Even in Latin there's a word 'canna' used to describe small boats.

One thing is for certain, wherever the word comes from — the West Indies, the Netherlands or from the beaches of Capri in the time of the Caesars . . . the canoe now belongs to Canada. We've claimed it. We've earned it. There would be no Canada without the canoe.

Champlain used them . . . Brulé. And for those explorers and trappers and missionaries bent on heading west . . . well once you got to the head of the Lakes — right here in Thunder Bay . . . there

was only one way you were going to move any further west (assuming the joys of snowshoeing to the Rockies didn't appeal to you). Only one way to penetrate the bush country. By water. And only one craft sturdy enough and light enough and manoeuverable enough to handle the white water and the shallows and the portages and the vast distances such penetration involved — only one craft. Barges couldn't make it. Rafts were out of the question. Anything with a sail was silly. Only the canoe would do.

The Indians of course had figured this out several hundred years previously . . . and come up with the most practical and, purists would argue, beautiful canoe ever made — the birchbark canoe . . . an unadulterated, manufactured product of the bush — without a tuppenny nail or a scrap of metal from her spruce-gummed bow to her root-lashed stern.

Nowadays the birchbark canoe is as rare a sight as a Rolls-Royce Silver Cloud. It's been replaced by cedar strip, canvas, aluminum and fibreglass models of different lengths, several depths and various degrees of seaworthiness.

But whatever it's made of, the canoe is still the only yacht within the financial reach of all of us . . . still the only craft that will reasonably take us away from the overused lakes and beaches and into the back country, where few people ever go. I guess that's why you see so many canoes on roof racks and in the backs of campers each spring . . . and I guess it helps to explain that annual piece of Candy Mountain madness that happens here in the Lakehead each March. You haven't heard about the Candy Mountain Canoe Race? Happens the last week of March every year.

Contestants bring their own canoes, haul them to the top of the ski run on Candy Mountain and race to the bottom. Two maniacs to a canoe. The first canoe to reach the bottom still containing its two maniacs wins prize money to the tune of one thousand dollars. Much of which doubtless goes to replacing the canoe they've just dragged the bottom out of.

Sure it's a nutty way to spend an afternoon . . . but as every Canadian knows . . . there is that tantalizingly long, agonizing stretch of time in every Canadian spring when it's too warm to skate or ski . . . but way too early to boat or barbecue.

For canoe fanatics, the wait is unbearable. Not surprising that the weakest among us crack and start hauling our canoes up to the top of a ski trail. Hmmm. 'Paddlin' Madelin' Home . . .'

Now if you'll excuse me I have a chore to take care of in the basement . . .

I have this theory see . . . that if I was to put some cross country glide wax under the bow and stern . . . and maybe just a dab of klister right under the stern seat . . .

UFOs

I'VE got the 64-dollar, 24-carat, all time quintessential cocktail hour question for you:

Ever seen a UFO?

Nah . . . Me neither. But boy do I wish I had. I've heard of a lot of people who have . . . and what an Aladdin's Cave of sagas and visions they have to tell! Bright lights, dim lights, glowing lights and flashing lights . . . not to mention winking, shimmering, dancing, streaking, undulating, piercing and pulsing, searing and soaring lights. Then there are the shapes. Saucer shapes for the classically minded . . . but you also get the refinements: Inverted saucers. Saucers with knobs and turrets and tentacles. Centreless saucers like donuts on a diet . . . Ah jeez I wish I could say I'd seen something indescribably alien zooming across the sky. But I haven't. I think I saw a satellite one starlit night last summer. But I'm not entirely sure it wasn't Flight 735 from Winnipeg to Toronto with stopovers in Dryden and Sudbury.

If I sound like I'm making fun of UFO sighters, forgive me. I'm really not . . . I mean maybe you're one of the sighters and who am I to say that you really didn't see something strange and wonderful and totally un-terrestrial that night in the skies over Lake Wippinickitocky? Yeah . . . *chances* are you're one of the blessed . . . but chances are better that you're not . . . that you're like me — who's never seen anything airborne more exotic than a pileated woodpecker and a Sikorsky helicopter.

The thing about UFOs is . . . it would be so *nice* to believe in them.

It's so irresistible . . . Beings from another planet . . . a whole new fix on civilization . . . Maybe that explains what happened in Rio a while back. Rio de Janeiro. Did you hear about it? Talk about your intergalactic extravaganzas. They knew it was coming you see. The UFO I mean. Knew it was coming, knew when it was coming, knew where it was coming from and where it was landing. They had Brazilian rancher Edilicio Barbosa to thank for that. Señor Barbosa went right on national TV the week before, to announce that at 5:20 A.M. on Sunday, March 8, a flying saucer from Jupiter would land in a farmer's field about 75 miles east of Rio. You don't often get advance itineraries like that regarding the comings and goings of UFOs . . . but then Edilicio Barbosa is not your average Brazilian cattle prodder. He modestly billed himself as a humble messenger from Jupiter with an inside track on Jovian travel plans.

Well. The citizens of Rio are a worldly lot . . . they've seen their share of charlatans come and go. They're not dupes . . . or rubes. Did they buy Señor Barbosa's story?

Only about 50 thousand of them. That's the size of the crowd police estimate showed up on the night of Saturday, March 7 in that Brazilian farmer's field to hold an all-night vigil for the out-of-planet visitors.

And they came bearing gifts. There was a Reception Committee to welcome the aliens. There was a gift-wrapped encyclopedia offering all the up-to-date information about Terra Firma . . . There was even an official Salute Anthem to be played to welcome the tourists.

This was not a carnival . . . Sale of alcoholic beverages was banned on the site. Three hundred and fifty police officers worked all night long, trying to find parking spaces for the four thousand-odd cars, buses and trucks that showed up. There were traffic problems.

There was another problem. Five-twenty A.M. came and went, with not so much as a chirping sparrow darkening the morning sky. No flying saucer from Jupiter.

The 50 thousand faithful took it for about 10 minutes. At about 5:30 A.M. they started to murmur. They wanted to have a little chat with Edilicio Barbosa, the Jovian messenger who'd conned them into standing in a cornfield all night waiting for a space ship. Things got a little ugly after that. The last anybody saw of Señor Barbosa around the no-show space ship site was his benign beaming face as he was whisked away to safety in a police jeep.

Wasn't the last they saw of Barbosa though. He was on Brazilian television again a couple of days later to make it clear why the ship from Jupiter never showed up.

'Too many people on the landing spot,' he explained.

Of course. That's one of the tough things about arguing with UFO believers.

They have an answer for everything.

DEUCES

I WANT you to check your purse or wallet right now — the money part. Assuming you have some paper money of course . . . just riffle your thumb through the bills there . . . yeah . . . you see any of those familiar rusty orange-coloured bills in there? Have you got any twos?

You'd be amazed at how many Canadians wouldn't have a two dollar bill in their purse or wallet . . . not on a bet. Some Canadians are so superstitious about two dollar bills that they won't carry them, spend them or even accept them as legal tender. And the bias is so strong in some parts that it's changed the banking habits in whole areas of the country.

Maclean's magazine ran an article about two-dollar-phobia in Alberta. They said that the fear and loathing of this country's second smallest paper denomination was a Prairie phenomenon. They were wrong. There are strong pockets of the two-dollar-bill haters right here in northwestern Ontario.

I remember when I first came to the Lakehead I kept wondering why I always had so many wads of ones. I'd buy a pack of gum with a five dollar bill and get four ones and change. If I broke a ten, I'd get a five, four ones and change . . . And if they were out of fives, it would be *all* ones. Never twos. I was beginning to forget what two dollar bills look like.

I thought maybe it was just a temporary drought — that the Bank

28

of Canada had thrown a rod or stripped the gears on its two-dollar-bill printing machine or something. But the drought stretched on into months. I began to notice that the cash drawers in the supermarkets and gas stations and liquor stores had piles of twenties, tens, fives — *bales* of ones — but almost never any twos.

And nobody could tell me why. Nobody ever *confessed* to having anything against the two dollar bill. Nobody ever refused to take one from me if I had one. There just weren't very many of them around.

It's a funny thing, this prejudice against the two dollar bill. Nobody knows exactly why it exists. The Americans of course have an even worse case of it. They have an expression, 'That guy's as phony as a two dollar bill,' which might account for it. American prejudice against the two dollar bill was so strong that the government withdrew all such bills from circulation in 1966 — even though they'd been legal tender for more than a century.

In 1977 the U.S. Mint tried again with a new two dollar bill . . . haven't heard how that one is faring, but I'm not optimistic.

This side of the border, well we haven't actually panicked the Bank of Canada into recalling two dollar bills but there are lots of places where you have trouble getting rid of your deuces. That, by the way, is one theory as to why two dollar bills are unpopular. Deuce is a slang term for two dollars. Deuce is also a nickname for Old Nick — the Devil. In earlier times, the theory goes, God-fearing Canadians would be loath to carry pieces of paper associated with Satan in their hip pocket.

But there's one, much more elaborate explanation for Canadians' aversion to two dollar bills. The first time such bills were introduced in this country was back in 1870. Those two dollar bills featured portraits of the two most famous casualties of the Battle of the Plains of Abraham — General Wolfe and General Montcalm — both of whom died in battle. A later edition of the two dollar bill featured the Prince of Wales — Edward the Seventh — who abdicated the British throne for a luckless life as lapdog to Mrs. Simpson. Thus the Canadian two dollar bill (so the story goes) became associated with tragedy and bad luck. Well you can believe what you want . . . All I know is I still see a lot more one dollar bills than two dollar bills.

Still I wouldn't be doing my job as a tough and hard-driving investigative journalist, if I didn't offer some way out . . . *some* solution to two-dollar-bill-itis.

As it happens I have two solutions. One traditional. Folk legend has it that you can bleed all the bad luck out of a two dollar bill by snipping off the top left hand corner.

Ah, ah . . . but before you pick up those manicure scissors, Madame, I must also warn you that performing such surgery, minor though it be . . . is illegal. You would be defacing Canadian currency and you could be fined for it.

Accordingly I offer my second solution. Anybody out there who finds himself burdened with an oppressive number of two dollar bills — Canadian or American, with or without their top left hand corners . . . can simply slip them into an envelope — or a carton if necessary — and ship them off to me. I'll take them off your hands.

Sure, sure, it's a grubby, thankless job . . . but somebody has to do it.

BIRTHDAY

WELL it's our birthday. A good day to talk about words beginning with *can* — like Canada. And canoe.

A man who was once justice minister of Canada and keen on canoeing once wrote: 'What sets a canoeing expedition apart is that it purifies you more rapidly and inescapably than any other. Travel a thousand miles by train and you are a brute; pedal five hundred on a bicycle and you remain basically a bourgeois; paddle a hundred in a canoe and you are already a child of nature.'

I think he was on to something, that justice minister. There is something about pushing your way across the face of this country, using only a flattened-out stick and a craft that looks like a peapod; something about hauling that boat and your backpack around rapids and falls, along rocky portages — something in the late evening campfires and the bone tiredness across the shoulders and the eerie ululations of a loon as you drift off to sleep — something in all that

that tends to rinse away the tensions of 20th century urban living pretty quickly.

I like to think it's because you're seeing the real Canada. It's easy to forget when you're mowing the lawn in Don Mills or watching the regatta in Kingston Harbour or fuming in a traffic jam along the 401 — it's easy to forget that this vast, mostly silent *rest* of Canada is going on behind your back. Going on as it always has. Mostly untouched. Strangely unchanged. Bush and water. Lacy workings of waterways . . . long skinny lakes, great swollen lakes, pothole lakes and crater lakes, all webbed together by veins of rivers and creeks that creep and curl and cascade across the land. And the amazing thing about living in the 1990s is that the best way to see this Canada — really see it — is by blade. Paddle blade. With your knees going numb against the ribs of a canoe. The same way the Indians always knew it and the way the first Europeans saw it.

About the time preparations for Canada's birthday party today were first getting underway, I took a canoe trip. You don't have to travel far from Thunder Bay to leave the pavement and power lines behind. It's not too long before you run out of even bush roads. Then it's wilderness. Canoe country. I took a little canoe trip through that country. Through lakes you never heard of. Strange and beautiful lakes named for forgotten men. Who was the Greer this Greer Lake is named for? This oddly green and slightly haunting lake?

And who was the Melville who sweated and strained over these rocky portages, and how long ago did he pass this way? Where was he bound? Did he know he left behind a body of water — Melville Lake — that bears his name?

And who was the poet of the paddle who paused in *this* great windswept lake with its rocky islands and its sullen shores, and decided to name it after the fall guy in a thousands-of-years-old Greek legend about people who fly too high? Who called this Icarus Lake?

Maybe the loons know. They don't say. They only laugh, as always.

About the time the prime minister and 10 provincial premiers were meeting in the broadloomed halls of Ottawa for the Constitutional conference, I was lurching and swaying like a drunk through a swampy portage, up to my calves in gunk, a canoe on my back, clouds of mosquitoes in my face, praying the next step wouldn't take me in over my knees.

On Parliament Hill they were trying to hammer out a country on paper. Something tangible. In a northwestern Ontario stretch of swamp, I too was looking for something of substance. Something I could stand on.

I guess canoe trips are simpler than creating countries, but there are similarities. In both, you try to get where you're going with minimal damage to yourself or your craft. You try to avoid wrong directions. Blind bays. False creeks. There is, sooner or later, always some swampland.

The great advantage of a canoe trip over a constitutional conference is that a canoe trip allows you to let your mind loose.

Canada. Strange name for a country. Canada. We don't even know where it comes from. Some think the name was bestowed on us by 16th century Spanish or Portuguese fishermen working the Grand Banks off Newfoundland. The Spanish word for nothing is 'nada.' Ca-nada. Nothing. 'Nothing but bush over there amigos, the holds are full, let's sail for home.'

Others believe the name comes from a misconception on the part of Jacques Cartier. In 1535, the French explorer stepped ashore at Stadacona, an Indian village on the banks of the St. Lawrence. He met the chief and in that awkward pantomime of communication that occurs between two people of different cultures and language, he asked the chief, 'How is this place called? . . . Where do you live?' It was a general question. The chief mistook it for specific. He waved a bronzed arm toward the collection of huts at his back and said the Huron word for them — 'Kanatta.' Cartier announced to a crewman coiling lines on the foredeck: 'Chief says this place is called "kanata" or "kan atda" . . . something like that.'

Here we are then . . . four and a half centuries after that little tête-à-tête on the banks of the St. Lawrence . . . here we are, a collection of huts. The second largest collection of huts in the world — four million square miles — and an awful lot of it, thank God, still looks like it did through the eyes of 15th century Portuguese fishermen, through the eyes of Jacques Cartier, through the eyes of the chief of Stadacona.

That's easy to forget nowadays, with our computers and reactors and 60-storey skyscrapers. With our talk of separation and alienation. With our search for the Canadian identity. A canoe trip seems to straighten it all out though . . . especially a trip in the wilderness, through lakes named for forgotten men like Greer and Melville, whoever they were.

That justice minister I mentioned earlier — he wrote something else about canoes and countries. He wrote: 'I know a man whose school could never teach him patriotism, but who acquired that virtue when he felt in his bones the vastness of the land, and the greatness of those who founded it.'

Yup. A canoe trip can do that.

He still canoes that guy, but he's not a justice minister anymore. His name is Pierre Elliot Trudeau.

Funny. Started out talking about canoeing. Detoured for a portage over Parliament Hill. Ended up back in the river.

Canoe trips are like that — full of surprises. Maybe countries are too?

FLOWERS

WELL I don't know about you but I've just about had it. I mean here it is the middle of April, and winter, like a streetwise old tank fighter is still hanging in, slipping punches, using the ropes. Just when you think the brain-damaged old has-been has gone down for the count — wap! A flash storm that hurts more than two head butts and a rabbit punch. But that's it. I've had it. It's time to resort to desperate measures. I *was* going to talk about the economic disparity of Canadian regional units vis-à-vis various third world entities and their aspirations to nation-state status . . . but that's hereby cancelled, due to continuing . . . weather. Instead I'm going to talk about flowers. Because flowers are the ultimate signal that winter is over. When flowers come up, winter is dead. Definitively defunct. Until they do . . . you can never be truly sure.

Okay then . . . flowers. What do I know about flowers? What do

I feel about flowers? Welllll . . . I'd like at this point to wax poetic and come all over faint and tremulous . . . I'd like to sway meaningfully along to the strains of Shakespeare and a rose by any other name. I'd like to tiptoe with Tiny Tim through the tulips and wax nostalgic about the droopy faded pink carnation on my droopy faded white sport coat . . . but the fact is . . . Well . . . I don't really *love* flowers. I respect them all right . . . but I don't love them. I don't think (quite frankly) that flowers are all they're cracked up to be. I mean . . . take away their physical beauty and what have you got? A rather commonplace clump of undergrowth that consorts with bees, is prone to host mites, spiders and other creepy crawlies . . . and likes to keep its feet in the dirt.

Besides, *look* at some of the flowers we love so well. Roses. I know otherwise sane people who have given up their jobs and lost their families over rose bushes. Roses demand total dedication. And perfection. Perfect soil, perfect fertilizer, perfect doses of sun and water and perfectly delicate strokes from their mesmerized keepers. And what do rose raisers get for their troubles? A thorn in the thumb.

And if you want to talk about horticultural hypochondriacs what about the African violet? That is a neurotic plant. You water it, it dies. Don't water it, it dies. Get it out of the sun, it keels over. Give it more sun, it wilts. If African violets devoted half as much energy to living as they spend trying to commit floral hari-kari, they'd probably grow big as a house.

What other plants are overrated? Well, the geranium. Everybody loves geraniums . . . but why? Get up cheek-to-cheek with a geranium and sniff it some time. You'll discover the geranium is the billy goat of the botanical world. Because it stinks and it has hairy legs, that's why.

Well I could go on and on but what's the point? The major indictment against flowers (and I hate to sound crass, but it must be faced) is — flowers are useless. I mean, people cut the flowers' heads off, and put them in bowls. Or in lapels. Because they're beautiful. But you wouldn't do that with a bobolink or a Baltimore oriole — and they're beautiful. That's because birds have other attributes. They can belt out a tune. They gobble bugs. Flowers — their whole routine is just to hang out there with their colourful little faces in the wind, like brainless Hollywood starlets, waiting for somebody to take them home.

Yes, flowers, I'm afraid, are useless, for the most part. But not my favourite one. It's called the scarlet runner and one of the thoughts that sustains me through these last cruel and evil days of a too-long winter is the thought that quite soon now, I will be bent over the flower bed that surrounds my front porch, pushing those big waxy purple-flecked black beans into the soft earth. Each bean will be surrounded by a half-buried tube — a tin can (with the ends out) to protect it from cutworms, which like scarlet runner plants even more than I do. When the seeds germinate and those green shoots bow their way out of the earth, they'll each find a string dangling in front of them . . . and it won't be too many more weeks before they put out little tendrils and grab that string and start to climb. By midsummer they'll have climbed 10 or 12 feet, right to the roof of the porch, putting out huge clumps of vibrant green leaves all the way. Not to mention vivid bursts and flashes of red — the scarlet flowers that give the plant its name. By mid-August the bean pods will be ripe for the plucking — great long green pods that, fresh-picked, steamed, cut-up and smothered in butter, are a meal in themselves . . . and not only that, but my porch will be covered with a most beautiful, very delicate green canopy that I can see out of but you can't see into. Neat.

That's why I'm fond of the scarlet runner . . . Because unlike most flowers, it is not useless. It provides entertainment — you can quite literally see it grow before your eyes; it provides juicy and succulent side orders for dinner; it provides shelter from curious eyes . . .

Ah, you say . . . but that's the *plant* . . . you were talking about flowers before. Isn't the scarlet runner flower just as useless as the tulip or the trillium?

Well . . . I remember one day last July I was standing on my front porch, looking out through my living screen of scarlet runners but not really seeing them — thinking instead . . . prosaic thoughts of death and taxes and perhaps the economic disparity of Canadian regional units vis-à-vis various third world entities and their aspirations to nation-state status for all I know. Or something equally dumb.

When suddenly — almost on my cheek — I saw a flash of green and a blur of feathers — and there was about an eighth of an ounce of ruby-throated hummingbird fluttering furiously, hanging there like a diminutive helicopter while his needle-nose beak siphoned off a little nectar from a scarlet runner flower next to my face.

For some reason I didn't jump. I didn't move a muscle. I tried very much to pass myself off as a hideously mutated scarlet runner plant . . . or at least as a gargoyle. Whatever. It worked. I didn't spook the hummingbird.

And for the next — I guess five or ten seconds although it seemed like ten minutes — I had the unbuyable thrill of watching a hummingbird, so close I could feel the wind from his wings on my cheek.

All because of a flower. The scarlet runner flower.

Now, you can hardly call that useless, can you?

BORES

Oh . . . ahh . . . excuse me? Yoo hoo? Yes? Got a minute? Won't take a second of your time really . . . But did I ever tell you about the time . . . ?

Has that ever happened to you? You're minding your own business at a party, just getting set for a surreptitious assault on the chip dip, when you see him — or her — bearing down on you . . . chopping his way through a forest of elbows and hors d'oeuvre trays . . . never taking his eyes off yours for a second. Nothing will stop him, nothing will deflect him . . . you feel like a lily pad in front of a coast guard cutter. He has seen you and will have you — there is no escape. You are about to be cornered by A Bore.

It's strange. The world is crawling with bores. You would think a planet that could conquer polio, arrange a round of golf on the moon and produce disposable razors cheaper than razor blades — you'd think it could devote an afternoon or so and come up with a spray-on repellent that would turn away bores . . . but no. Science and technology march on and so does the bore . . . unscathed. *Strengthened* if anything. You haven't died until you've been box-canyoned behind a coffee table by a municipal engineer intent on telling about great city sewer systems he has known.

I've been doing a little research on bores this week . . . and I find that although people have been *complaining* about bores for centuries . . . nobody seems to have come up with much of a defence against them.

Not, at least, until a lady by the name of Enid Nemy came along. Ms. Nemy lives in New York, and she decided that she was not going to be held hostage by party bores anymore. But instead of going to the library or writing Ann Landers, Ms. Nemy did an exceedingly simple and sensible thing. She called up all the big-time socialites and party-goers she knew in New York and asked *them* how *they* handled bores. She printed the results in a story in the *New York Times* recently. One of the people she talked to said that he always offers to get the bore a drink. When he comes back from the bar he has three drinks. He gives one to the bore, keeps one for himself, and before the bore can relaunch his filibuster, the escapee murmurs, 'Excuse me I must give this to a friend . . .' and flees.

Another effective anti-bore manoeuvre according to Ms. Nemy is a firm hand on the elbow, a light pivot to the left or right along with the declaration: 'Pardon me for interrupting but I see someone you must meet.'

Still another of Ms. Nemy's bore beaters uses the bore's own weapon. When face-to-face, she would let the bore get out just six words then gush, 'That reminds me of something that happened to me in my childhood . . .' and launch into her own deadly revery.

Well I don't know . . . It may work for Ms. Nemy's friends but I know what would happen if I tried any of those ploys. If I excused myself to get the bore a drink, he'd wave the suggestion away and launch into a monologue about how much better he feels since he's been on a diet of carrot tops and distilled water.

If I tried to take a bore by the arm and steer him on to some other hapless victim, he'd just take me by the other arm before I could gain any momentum. Then I'd try my other arm . . . and then he'd bring in his other arm and we'd eventually end up limbs locked together in the middle of the floor like two amateur sumo wrestlers.

As for trying to beat a bore at his own game . . . hah. That's just silly. Who can out-bore a bore?

I'd have to be as boring as a bore to do that . . . and believe me — if you'd dealt with some of the bores that I've had to put up with you wouldn't even suggest that line of attack.

Did I ever tell you about the bore I met at a press conference for a factory opening in Kenora? Must have been '72 . . . '73 . . . Nope. No, it was '72 because that was the year the spruce budworm was so bad and the summer my sister Helen caught the big lake trout. You haven't met my sister Helen but believe me. She can catch fish in a birdbath . . . anyway where was I . . .

GUNDAGAI

MUST be at least a couple of years since I wrote about the famous Gundagai salute. Gundagai is a town in deepest Down Under Australia, famous for just about nothing, except flies. Millions of flies. Billions of flies. And flies without the breeding we've come to know and expect from the domesticated North American housefly. No, the Gundagai fly is . . . something else. He wants very much to set up shop in your eyes, you see . . . or second best your nostril . . . or at the very least in the corner of your mouth . . . and he won't take no for an answer, your Gundagai fly. No . . . Nor the polite shoo-off. He's very determined, is the Gundagai fly — whence cometh the Gundagai salute.

It's hard to explain on paper, the Gundagai salute. But we'll try. Now raise your right hand, fingers together, thumb tucked under, to the corner of your right eye . . . sort of a Boy Scout, Queen's-Own-Rifles style. Right.

Now, instead of flicking your hand smartly back to your side, the way the scoutmaster and the drill sergeant always taught you . . . let your whole hand sweep across your face, from high on the right temple to the bottom left side of the chin. Right . . . now you've got it. Now when you can deliver that gesture ohhhhh 140 times a minute say . . . then you've mastered the Gundagai salute.

The Gundagai salute you see, is not so much a sign of respect or a mark of military discipline as it is a routine gesture to get those cursed Gundagai flies out of your face.

All of which is a very roundabout way to bring you up to date on the sad tidings out of Eaglehawk, Australia. Now, Eaglehawk is a town not all that far from Gundagai. There is however a certain . . . tension, shall we say, that exists between the citizens of Gundagai and the good folk of Eaglehawk — not unlike the rivalry that lives between people in Calgary and people in Edmonton . . . or between Montrealers and Torontonians. Ask a Gundagai-ite about Eaglehawk and he will smile patronizingly, murmur something about it being a nice little town, but . . . Same with an Eaglehawk-ian. Nothing against Gundagai you understand, some of his best mates, et cetera . . . but well . . . it's not Eaglehawk, is it?

The problem between the two towns is a very simple one. The people of Gundagai, and the stout burghers of Eaglehawk . . . each proudly believe themselves to be living in the most flyblown town on the planet.

Obviously only one town can be right. Gundagai has a strong claim — they have the Gundagai salute for pity's sake — famous throughout the continent — known among connoisseurs of winged pests throughout the world.

And what does Eaglehawk have? Well . . . it has the World Fly Swatting Championships . . . Yes. An annual event. Just set it up this year . . . A tourist draw, it hopes. Something to put Eaglehawk on the map and expose those frauds in Gundagai once and for all.

And so it was set up. Last month (still fly weather in Australia) the Eaglehawk World Fly Swatting Championships held its first swatdown on Main St. in downtown Eaglehawk. And an auspicious beginning it was. Two hundred entrants signed up (including a couple of blowhards from Gundagai). They each were issued a regulation fly swatter and a seat at a long table. With flourish of trumpet and roll of drum, the mayor of Eaglehawk officially declared the first World Fly Swatting Championships open . . . and may the best swatter win. Oh it was all very stirring, all very pageanty and thrilling.

There was only one problem.

No flies.

Hardly any, at any rate.

Cool temperatures and strong winds kept the normally teeming fly population of Eaglehawk battened down.

What could they do? The organizers prayed for a break in the weather — they even extended the one-day championships to two days . . . but the wind kept up and the flies stayed down. The first World Fly Swatting Championships were a distinct flop. Over the whole two days a mere three hundred flies went to the big garbage dump in the sky. That worked out to an average of one point five flies per contestant.

Thank goodness for what was left of Eaglehawk, Austraila's civic pride, the eventual winner was at least a local boy . . . a sharp swatter by the name of John Turner, who managed to bag 79 flies in the two days.

I just hope that the backers of the World Fly Swatting Championshps aren't demoralized by the rather disheartening results of their first effort. I hope there's a Second Annual next year. Because if the idea of fly swatting championships does take off, I think we've got a whole new growth industry here in Ontario's northland.

I'd like to bring a few of those Eaglehawk marksmen and Gundagai gunners over to this part of the world and set them up with regulation fly swatters around a picnic table at a campground on the outskirts of Thunder Bay some warm and humid evening in early July.

In the sub-categories of black fly bashing, mosquito mangling, noseeum nailing and horse fly hammering, I have no doubt we could show those Aussies what persistent pests are really all about.

FISH

I'T's a wired, wired world we live in . . . Wired for sound that is. The bugs are everywhere, and I'm not talking about cockroaches, boll weevils or tent caterpillars. I mean the snoopers. The electronic eavesdroppers. Why, we've seen an American president who secretly taped everything from bungled burglary coverups to the weekly grocery list; we've been exposed to a Moscow microphone buried in the very feathers of the American eagle in the U.S. Embassy in the Soviet capital. We've listened in on long-distance chats between Mafiosi; why even Sergeant Preston and his wonder dog King have been caught in a compromising position — namely with their ear to the keyhole when they were supposed to be out bringing in mad trappers and whatnot . . .

Yep, the bugs are all around us. The pros can plant a microphone in your telephone or in the olive of your martini. A snoop with a superduper shotgun mike can point it at your office window from two blocks away and four storeys down and hear every cough in that private, in-camera conversation you and your cronies thought you were having.

The bugs are all around us. It's hard to know where to go to get away from them.

Which perhaps helps explain why the solitary and largely silent sport of fishing is such a favourite among mobsters, politicians, movie stars and others who have a lot to lose by being tape recorded when they least expect it. After all, you get way out there, a mile off shore in your little outboard. No overhead wires . . . just you, your rod and reel and a six pack . . . You can pretty well count on being out of anybody's earshot — electronic or otherwise, right?

Sorry chum, hate to disillusion you, but there's a good chance the fish are bugged. Naw I'm not kidding . . . this is not an outbreak of piscatorial paranoia here . . . The Ministry of Natural Resources is transistorizing fish even as we speak. Honest. So far just in the Nottawasaga River down in southern Ontario, but it's happening.

The fish are yellow pickerel, or walleye, and they have had tiny radio transmitters surgically implanted.

The reason? So that the fish can be tracked by ministry officials, their movements and habits studied — but mostly so they can find out where the pickerel spawning beds are so that the ministry can protect them. The tiny transmitters emit signals that can be tracked from nearly half a mile away either by an MNR official on foot, or in a plane. How do you talk a pickerel into volunteering for radio duty? You don't. As any walleye fisherman would testify, the fish is an elusive creature not given to co-operative scientific ventures — even ones that are in its own interest.

What happened was, last October MNR officials and a fisheries biologist from the Royal Ontario Museum fired a few volts of electricity into a particular section of the Nottawasaga River. The shock momentarily stunned all the fish in the area sending them floating to the surface. The workers selected 16 healthy looking five- or six-year-old pickerel, performed the necessary and harmless surgery, implanted the transmitters and returned them to the waters.

They're out there now, somewhere, feeding, swimming and beeping along with their transmitterless colleagues. Natural Resources biologists check up on them once a week to see how they're doing and where they're hanging out. They expect to keep doing so for at least another year.

What should *you* do if you're cleaning a mess of pickerel some summer afternoon and you come across one that looks like the prototype for a new TV series called Bionic Walleye? Well, for one thing, the Ministry of Natural Resources would like it if you gave the radio transmitter back — they cost about a hundred dollars a piece. And Natural Resources, like every other government agency, is bucking budget cutbacks so they like to save every cent they can.

That's a good idea I guess. In fact I suppose the whole idea of bugging the pickerel is a laudable one. But, a bug is a bug is a bug. And I can't help lamenting that electronic snooping has invaded this last bastion of inviolability — the honorable pastime of angling.

I guess it's time to update the rules of fishing: keep your line taut, your reel oiled, your beer cold and should the conversation with your fishing buddy turn to income tax fiddles, tax dodges or interoffice extramarital affairs of the heart . . . remember to keep your voices down.

METRIC

THERE are now just five countries in the entire world that have no plans to adopt or use the metric system. Those countries are Yemen, Liberia, Burma, Brunei . . . and the United States of America.

Hard to believe isn't it? A country that's renowned for being in the forefront of technological advances . . . a people that supposedly pride themselves on being innovative and adventurous and eager to change . . . challengers, explorers . . . and look at them. The whole U.S. of A teetering on the edge, dithering over whether to take a chance and go metric.

With all due respect . . . when're you gonna wake up big fella? Europe is metric. Asia is metric. Africa and South America are metric. Australia and Iceland are metric.

Face it America . . . you're up against the wall on this one.

It's late but it's not too late. Heck . . . look at us up here! You may find this hard to believe America, but 10 short years ago, Canadians didn't know their pecks from their hectograms . . . Look at us now.

Now I don't wanna make it sound like we're unusually gifted up here in God's Country . . . Tough, for sure . . . resilient, no doubt . . . brilliant, most likely . . . but that's not what's made metric such a success story north of the 49th . . . No . . .

The secret is . . . metric is a piece of cake . . .

No problem! Couldn't be easier!

Also . . . metric is democratic . . . a real People's system. You know how the ancients determined the length of a yard? It was the distance from some king's nose to the tip of his outstretched hand. A *king's* nose, America! Now compare that to the meter. A meter is the exact distance between two lines scratched on a bar of platinum/iridium alloy that is kept in a vault in a suburb of Paris, France.

Okay, okay . . . a little tricky to check every time you want to buy a bolt of cloth, I grant you . . . but here's the kicker — here's the democratic part: That platinum/iridium bar is just for show . . . for formal occasions . . . A meter is really one ten-millionth of the distance from the North Pole to the equator. None of this royal schnozz stuff. A citizen can get out there and pace it off for himself! Now is that, or is that not, The American Way?

Let's do some simple conversions, America, so you can see what you're missing. Take your weight. Let's say you weigh 200 pounds. Now to go metric we just convert that to kilos. A kilo is 2 point 2046 pounds . . . so all we have to do is divide 200 by 2 point 2046, right? Simple division . . . just move the decimal point of the divider over four spaces in the dividee so that you're really dividing two thousand . . . no, sorry . . . you'll be dividing 22 thousand into . . . let's see . . . four places that'll make it . . . yeah . . . To find your weight all you have to do is divide 22,046 into two million! OK . . 2,000 into two carry the two, bring down 19 and take away . . . Actually 200 pounds is one of the really unwieldy numbers for metric conversion, America . . . Probably the best thing you could do in this situation is deep six your diet, dig into the Skippy and put on exactly 20 point 46 pounds. See, 220.46 pounds in metric is called a 'quintal.' Easy to remember and nobody at Weight Watchers knows whether it's good or bad ('I got my weight down to one quintal now . . .').

Actually let's leave the weight part of metric . . . and do distance instead. Let's do your height. We'll keep it simple. We'll say you are exactly six feet tall OK? Now here's where we're in luck with metric, because six feet equals two yards, right? *And* metric has the meter, which is exactly the same length as the yard! Almost. Actually a meter is a little more than a yard. A yard, as you know, is 36 inches and a meter is . . . 39 . . . point . . . 3 . . . 7 inches. So OK call it a yard and three, three and a half inches. OK, so six feet is really just two meters less three (or three and a half) inches. Times two. Converted to centimeters at 2 point 54 to the inch comes out to point five four move the decimal carry the two . . . and round it off. No. Wait. I had it the wrong way round. It's 2.54 inches to the centimeter . . . Nope. That'd make you 46 feet high.

OK never mind your height . . . let's do your farm. Remember boring old acres, America? Remember 640 divided by 4 and all that? Well, forget it! Metric cuts your farm in half with — hectares! Yes . . . all new hectares! Hectares do twice the job in half the area because hectares are twice as big as puny acres. In fact they're nearly two and a half times as big. Two . . . point four seven . . . times to be . . . absolutely precise.

Let's talk about metric weather. Metric weather isn't called metric weather, it's called Celsius. Don't ask . . . memorize. Celsius. Here, America, is where going metric pays big dividends for you and your loved ones. Celsius, like disco, is where it's currently at in this big loveable lug of a continent we call home. Celsius pays what we in the north like to call 'psychological bonus points.'

Think about your weather reports, America . . . what sort of temperatures do you hear on your old-fashioned Fahrenheit forecasts these days? Two *below* . . . Thirteen *below* . . . Five *below* . . . Okay once in a while it gets above . . . but above what???? *Zero* . . .

North American winters are unpleasant enough, America, you don't need this kind of unlicensed negativity when you're plodding through the nether months of the calendar. And America — when you switch to Celsius, by jingo, you don't *get* it! Want to know what ten below zero is in metric weather? Minus 23. Crisp, clean, clinical and almost cheerfully meaningless. Metric weather delivers big summertime advantages too. Forty-two degrees doesn't sound very oppressive does it? Ha ha . . . don't be fooled. At 42 Celsius you could fry an egg on your forehead. But the beauty of it is, to convert that to something you could appreciate . . . like the Fahrenheit equivalent — calls for arithmetic contortions and algebraic convolutions that make Einstein's Theory of Relativity look like a game of X's and O's. By the time you get even halfway done, a nice Canadian arctic front will probably be settled in over your town, rendering the whole exercise pointless.

Anyway, America . . . I don't want to overload you on this your first introduction to metric. Simple and straightforward as it is . . . Metric can be a trifle overwhelming the first time you taste it. So let's leave it there for now America . . . next time we can get into myriagrams and deciliters and kilopascals . . .

What can you do in the meantime, America? Go to your bedroom window now . . . Throw it open and tell the world what you want! Write to your congressman! Tell him you're mad as hell without metric and you won't take it any more.

And don't forget the ZIP code.

VEG

WELL it's that time of year again isn't it? No getting around it ...
No point in making excuses, or pulling the colour section of the
weekend paper over your face and hoping it will go away. It won't.
It never does. Not until it's had its way with you and left you
mudcaked and blistered in its wake.

Gardening time. That's what I'm talking about. Gardening time.
With all its forks and rakes and spades and hoes ... its mulches and
fertilizers ... its loam mixtures and potassium deficiencies and ni-
trogen needs. Gardening time is here again.

I realize that for the gifted few — for the Ken Reeves and the Bob
Keiths and the Lois Wilsons and the Bert Sitches of this world —
gardening is a sublime experience. But I believe that for the rest of
us — for us modest mortals who are more all thumbs than green
thumbs — I believe that gardening has been inflicted upon us in the
same spirit as fallen arches, traffic jams, dandruff and dead car
batteries.

Let's face it — most of us have as much hope of bringing a garden
to fruition as we do of winning the Nobel Prize for Physics. You
know right now in your heart of hearts that no matter how much
time you spend in the next three or four months down on your knees
doing battle with twitch grass, cabbage butterflies, leaf mold and
cutworms ... you know that despite withstanding a whole sym-
phony of anguish ranging from the fine-tuned torture of indecipher-
able seed catalogues to the rude throbbing cacophony of a runaway
rototiller — you just *know* that come fall your take will be seven
leathery cabbages, half a dozen cigar-butt-sized carrots, a handful
of green, granite-hard tomatoes and maybe a row of onions showing
all the snap and vitality of a line of old skate laces.

That's the way it is. Most of us were simply never meant to handle
produce without an intervening layer of cellophane.

Ah, but we can dream. And we will dream. Despite annual evidence that we'd be better off sinking our energies into stamp collections or Indonesian pen pals.

It's to the dreamers that I want to speak today. I want to give you a horticultural dream to end dreams. Come with me to the three-acre garden of Jose Carmen Garcia, near the village of Irapuato, which is about 250 miles northwest of Mexico City. Before we tour the rows, let me tell you a bit about Señor Garcia.

He is — bluntly — a peasant. No College of Agriculture diplomas grace the walls of his adobe hut. He works this plot with the help of a mule . . . and he works it the way his neighbours work with their land, which is the way Mexican peasants have been working the land for centuries. Nothing unusual there. Jose Garcia buys his seed in the village store — just as everybody else who grows gardens in Irapuato does. He does not use fertilizers, pesticides, herbicides or insecticides. He doesn't know how to.

Thing is . . . Jose Carmen Garcia has an awfully good garden. He has an incredibly, unbelievably, absurdly good garden. Jose Garcia's garden is so good that it has been written about in Mexican newspapers and magazines. It is so bounteous that the Mexican Ministry of Agriculture has been down to study his methods. He is so successful that people from California have made pilgrimages to the Garcia garden to see things for themselves.

Some of the things they see include cabbages three feet in diameter. Collard greens up to five feet long. Radishes the size of footballs. The visitors swear they are as tasty as normal-sized vegetables.

Garcia's secret? As bizarre as his pumpkin-sized tomatoes. He claims that years ago he met a stranger on the road who dressed and talked like a Mexican peasant. The stranger, says Garcia, claimed to have been held captive by a strange race of aliens who lived in a tunnel beneath a nearby volcano. They spoke an alien tongue, the stranger said. And they lived on a diet of gigantic vegetables. The stranger said he had memorized their magic growing formula, which he sketched on a piece of paper. Concentrate on the symbols, the stranger told Garcia, and the message would become clear. Then the stranger walked away.

Garcia says he pondered the scrap of paper for several days, then suddenly the message (whatever it was) came to him. He went out, planted the seeds, and has been harvesting everything from 10-pound onions to 60-pound cabbages ever since.

That's the story anyway. Jose Carmen Garcia is a horticultural legend in Mexico apparently — although I wouldn't know for sure. I mean I haven't seen the garden.

I wouldn't discount it though. A magic growing formula jealously guarded by alien gibberish-spouting humanoids living under a Mexican volcano makes at least as much sense as some of the outlandish theories I've gone through in my miserable gardening past.

I'm thinking of the year I covered my garden with newspapers — 'great mulch' a gardening friend assured me. 'Keeps the slugs out and the weeds down.' Might have too. If it hadn't been for the big windstorm. Didn't get the garden in at all that year. Spent a month and a half mollifying my neighbours and picking newspapers out of their hedges.

I'm thinking too of the gardening season following that, when another gardening expert told me that what I needed around the border of my garden was polyethylene . . . long strips of polyethylene. 'That would keep the twitchgrass out for sure,' he told me.

What he didn't tell me was what colour polyethylene to buy. Black polyethylene might have worked just fine. I got a good deal on transparent polyethylene. It created a greenhouse effect on the twitchgrass undernearth, and I brought in a bumper crop that year. Of twitchgrass. That looked like redwood firs.

No, I'm not laughing at Jose Carmen Garcia this year. I'm not putting in a garden this year either. I plan to spend the summer looking for volcanoes.

ATOM

I HOPE your eyes are good . . . because they're going to have to do a lot of focussing and refocussing in the next few moments. We'll start out easy . . . look at your radio. OK? Now (click) I want you to look at the room the radio is in . . . Now (click) focus on the house of the room that the radio is in. Click. Now, the block that the house is in. Click. Now the town that the block is in. Click, click, click. Now I want you to see the continent of the country that the province that the town that the block that the house that the room that the radio is in. OK? Click. Now fix your mind's eye on the planet that . . . et cetera, et cetera, et cetera, et cetera. Click. I want you to view the earth as an atom. As a paramecium, say — one of those single-celled creatures you can pick out under a microscope with a stomach of sorts and a rudimentary mouth and bloopy little legs and hair-covered skin, grubbing around looking for food in a wee smear of swamp water on a microscope slide.

Can you picture the earth like that?

It's not my idea, actually . . . it belongs to a British scientist by the name of James E. Lovelock — the idea that the earth is not so much a gigantic ball of earth and water and gases whirling around the sun as a creature . . . an organism. Just as terra firma has man and man has dogs and dogs have fleas and fleas have their own microscopic pestilences . . . so our solar system has the planet earth . . . a green, blue and white rotund creature that has its own place in the pecking order of galactic life. 'Gaiia,' Professor Lovelock calls our home planet, purloining the name the Greeks used for their goddess of earth.

It's an intriguing thought. The idea that you and I are spinning out our lives on the back of a creature (earth) that is in turn performing in concert with a number of other spheroid creatures, who are in turn . . . et cetera, et cetera and so on. Click, click and click. I'm no anthropologist, sociologist, geo, bio, zoo or any other ologist . . . but I do like music. And Professor Lovelock's thesis bongs a kind of harmonic chord that I can respond to.

Maybe it's the non-ologist in me. You have to wonder how the caveman explained simple things to himself. Things we take for granted. Like sunrise, sunset, the seasons . . . Did he think because a sabre-toothed tiger blundered into his cave one spring evening that sabre-toothed tigers always visited caves in spring? How many generations did it take him to distinguish Chance from Nature?

What kind of myths did he manufacture for things like . . . frost? Droughts? Heatwaves and hailstorms? Were his conclusions all that less sophisticated than that of renowned British scientist James E. Lovelock . . . who postulates that our whole planet earth is no more than a humble organism, a ball-shaped bug, trying to survive in a cosmic jungle?

I don't know. I do know that when I was numbing my tailbone back in Miss Buell's grade ten biology class many years ago . . . and she was explaining that just as the solar system was made up of little buttons called planets . . . so every living and non-living thing was made up of little buttons called cells, which were made up of very little buttons called neutrons and protons and electrons . . . and it occurred to me that my whole world — my classmates, my bedroom, my red two-wheeler and the corner candy store — could be nothing more than infinitesimally tiny bits of fluff on the handle of some cosmic screwdriver.

I remember too a little kid in a farm field near Fergus, Ontario. I say little, because I was about 17 at the time, and as you can imagine, there really wasn't much that I didn't know.

Well this kid then . . . who couldn't have been more than nine or ten, had been dropped off at the farm I lived on to stay the weekend. And it was my job to look after him. Entertain him. I wasn't that pleased with the assignment. The kid was weird. Did he want to play catch? No. Would he like to go swimming? No. How about grabbing the poles and heading down to the pond to catch some chub? No thanks. Strange. So I took him for a walk. Thinking of all the swell things I could have been doing like hunting groundhogs or patching up the skiff or just going for a walk by myself if I didn't have to be babysitting. The kid was quiet. Walking beside me, drinking in the countryside.

Suddenly — this really happened you understand — suddenly he burst out — 'You know what I think? I think that the earth is God and all the trees and all the flowers are God's arms and hands and fingers.' And then he shut up.

I shut up too. What do you say?

But I've thought about it since. And I'm not sure that the kid's ideas aren't right up there with those of renowned British scientist James E. Lovelock.

I often wonder what happened to him. And I often wonder what he thinks now.

PAPILLON

DID you ever think about how many clichés aren't true? You can't teach an old dog new tricks, right? Then what about the writers Joseph Conrad and Vladimir Nabokov, neither of whom had written a line of English until after they hit middle age?

'Milk For Health,' right? Not necessarily. Many people just don't possess the enzyme that makes the digestion of milk possible. Some experts estimate that as many as 75 percent of the blacks in North America are incapable of digesting the lactose in cow's milk — would become very sick in fact if they tried.

And did you know that the whole idea of somebody 'seeing red' is erroneous? It's based on the idea that bulls are infuriated at the sight of the colour red. Problem is, bulls are colour blind. They can't tell red from yellow from cream-tinted avocado.

The list of bogus clichés and tainted truisms is all but endless. Columbus did not discover America — not unless he had blond hair in a previous life and worked an oar in a Viking Galley.

Ah yes . . . and the limerick does not come from the Irish city of the same name, lightening has been known to strike twice in the same place, James Watt did not invent the steam engine and John Wayne — the Duke — hero of a dozen over-the-top go-get-em two-fisted-Marine-wins-Second-World-War-single-handed

Hollywood movies — John Wayne never even served in the armed forces. Is nothing sacred?

Apparently not. Not even the old cliché about 'honour among thieves.' Remember the book and the movie *Papillon*? The story of a French convict sentenced to a living death in a penal colony on the coast of South America? Ah what a story that was! Papillon was the nickname for the convict, Henri Charrière. He was sentenced to life imprisonment on that hellhole of an island but he would not accept it. He tried to escape. Once. Twice. Again and again. Each time he was punished with unbelievable severity. Each time he gathered his strength and his wits to try again.

He made it finally of course. Against impossible odds. Man-eating sharks. Starvation. Lack of water. Storms. Finally Papillon the survivor washed up on the shores of Venezuela, more dead than alive. But alive by a thread. The rest of his life story was fairy-tale stuff. The Venezuelan authorities allowed him to stay there. He went into business. He prospered. He wrote his book and died in Madrid, a millionaire.

What a story. And a story all the more riveting because it was true. First person. Proving that fact is — to clutch at yet another cliché — indeed stranger than fiction, right? Wrong. It appears now, several years after the death of the celebrated Papillon, that his story was just fiction.

Oh, Charrière did time in the penal colony all right. Thirteen years. It's just that the time he did doesn't bear much relation to the book he wrote about it. If one of his convict colleagues, Raymond Vaude, could get his hands on Papillon, he'd do more damage than Papillon's French guards ever managed. Vaude is paroled now. He lives in French Guiana not far from the island he was imprisoned on with Papillon.

Ask him about his old fellow con Papillon and he spits out one word: 'ordure.' Garbage. He claims that most of the exploits Papillon wrote of never happened to Papillon, they were prison gossip — the adventures of other men. Papillon, it seems, spent most of his time not planning breakouts, but taking notes.

Another — you'll pardon the cliché — idol with feet of clay.

Ah well. So there's no honour among thieves then.

I guess I can live with the disillusionment. I'm not sure I can live with this though. My favourite tombstone epitaph — so favourite that it's become a cliché — is the one that appears on the gravestone of the comedian W.C. Fields. It reads: 'On the whole, I'd rather be in Philadelphia.'

Or so I'd always been led to believe. I find from sombody that's actually seen the grave, that the tombstone actually reads 'W.C. Fields 1880 – 1946.'

What a pity. Anybody who could write: 'I always keep a supply of alcohol handy in case I see a snake — which I also keep handy' deserves a better sendoff than that.

TV

I HOPE you'll excuse me if I sound just a little cocky today, but I'm going through those first insufferable stages of somebody who's just given up a bad habit.

Insufferable for everybody else I mean — surely you've run afoul of the brand new non-smoker. The one who smiles so much his teeth go dry; who usually greets you doing deep knee bends and arm exercises to 'open up the old lungs a little' — whose conversation is limited to up-to-the-minute personal health bulletins and long tirades about people who smoke anywhere more public than their bedroom closets.

Well that's the stage I'm in right now, which is why you might detect a touch of smugness. Except that it's not smoking I've given up. Nooo . . . nothing so simple.

Not drinking either . . . That would be child's play.

Not throwing dice or snorting cocaine. Not betting the ponies or fast living. Conquering such petty vices wouldn't be worth mentioning.

No, the habit I've broken is a good deal more pernicious — infinitely more insidious than that.

It's held me in its thrall for 25 years — a quarter of a century! — but no more. I feel like a born-again human.

I've just thrown my TV set out of the house.

Actually, not 'just' . . . I've been without a televisoin for a little over two months now. It was taken from me by an Act of God. I was just sitting in my living room one evening. Outside a thunder storm was raging with mighty peals of thunder and great jagged rips of lightning providing a sound and light show for the sheets of rain that were hammering the earth. But I didn't see any of that. Didn't see it because I was sitting in my darkened living room in that classic TV posture, the zombie hunch — watching a Blue Jays baseball game (talk about having nothing to do!) on the television.

It was a mediocre game that didn't deserve to be in anyone's living room, and I guess that's the way Fate read it, because suddenly there was an awesome crack, like a Giant Redwood snapping right over-head. The windows lit up and the TV went dark.

And that was it. My TV was dead. The odd thing was, I felt like Sleeping Beauty, or something . . . waking up from a trance. As soon as I figured out that my TV was definitely on the blink, I felt . . . released.

I went over and opened the front door and watched the storm. The ball game had been lousy, the storm was great.

Course I was in that first flush of conviction there — you know, like the first hour or so after you decide to quite smoking? It's easy, and you're all full of confidence and optimism . . . It's the second day that the withdrawal symptoms start to take their toll. The next day I found myself absent-mindedly scanning the TV guide . . . and flicking the TV on and off on and off to see if it had somehow miraculously mended itself overnight. It hadn't. And I felt nervous. I mean, what do you *do* in the evenings if you don't watch TV?

Still, for one reason or another, I never did get around to taking my televisioin in to be repaired for about a week . . . and when I finally did, I just sort of forgot about it. Weeks went by and my evenings gradually transformed themselves into something quite unusual. I found myself listening to records I'd bought months ago but never taken the cellophane off of; I began to read books I'd been meaning to read since high school. I even found myself engaging in conversation with my family. A phenomenon formerly limited to such exchanges as 'Well, whaddya think — Masterpiece Theatre or the Rockford Files?'

The thing about life without TV is — it *is* life. You feel alive!

You're not spending three, four maybe five hours a day sitting passive and quiescent, bathed in the unearthly glow of a TV screen, being force fed on visual Pablum.

'Bubble gum for the eyes' Frank Lloyd Wright called it. Certainly seems like that once you get away from it.

Anyway I decided to get serious about my new life. I cancelled the cable service and I still haven't picked up my TV, even though it's ready and the calls from the repair shop are getting increasingly snarky.

I guess I'll have to pick it up, but I don't know what to do with it. Put it out with the Glad bags on garbage day? Have it bronzed? Bury it in the garden? Stuff it and mount it on the wall?

Whatever I do, I won't be plugging it in.

Maybe I'm in at the beginning of a trend. I've run into three or four people who have given up on TV recently. And Lord knows the new fall TV schedule doesn't offer anything to make you regret the decision.

If you decide you'd like to try life without *Jake and the Fat Man*, the one thing to keep in mind is this: Not having a TV *expands* your life; you're not doing without something. Not having a TV gives you *more* time and more zest to use the time. There are thousands of things to do — read *The Mayor of Casterbridge*, phone up a friend, write some letters, paint a picture, play your harmonica and if you're really lucky — watch a thunderstorm.

You'll never see anything like that on Monday night baseball.

DEODORANT

You know what some millennias-hence anthropologist pawing through the ruins of the 20th century will have difficulty understanding? He'll have difficulty understanding the little cracked bottles of Brut he keeps coming across. The rusted cans of Right Guard, the age-encrusted tubes and vials of English Leather and Old Spice, of Arid Extra Dry and Mennen Speed Stick.

Imagine some future anthropologist trying to fathom the cultural ritual of deodorant. Imagine trying to explain deodorants to a Martian . . . or to any other animal species on *earth* come to that. Dogs snuffle other dogs, cats sniff anything that moves — even elephants lift their great firehose trunks into the wind to monitor beastly comings and goings in the neighbourhood. Most animals depend on their unique scent . . . and the scent of other animals to know what's going on. Only mankind lathers himself with herbs and spices, creams and powders, oils and unguents . . . in a frantic attempt to smell like something else.

Weird. That we would rather smell like a spice stall in Casablanca than give off any aroma of humanity. That we prefer to confuse passing strangers by smelling like a riding saddle or a pine forest rather than let them smell us as we are.

Not surprisingly, our passion for aromatic disguise and deceit has given rise to a multi-million-dollar industry. All over the world platoons of chemists and social psychologists spend their working hours decanting test tubes full of essences and calibrating secretions in a never-ending search for the perfect perfume molecule — the one of which a little dab will tell our colleagues that we are loveable, trustworthy, charismatic and altogether irresistible.

There's a research team galloping along those lines at Warwick University in England. An eight-man team under the control of a senior chemist, one Professor George Dodd. But Professor Dodd's team has taken a rather different tack in the quest for the ultimate deodorant. Instead of investigating the pungent subtleties of ambergris from sperm whales, pollen from rare orchids or the musk from an agitated ocelot, Professor Dodd and the boys have been working from the other end.

They've discovered an amazing thing. The English research team has isolated a substance that is derived from what they call a human pheromone. Now pheromones are a well-known phenomenon in the animal world. That's what dogs and cats and elephants are sniffing about. Pheromones are scent-exuding substances that affect the behaviour of other individuals of the opposite sex. In other words if a male cocker spaniel is making the rounds of the neighbourhood giving off good pheromones, it doesn't matter if he's short and bandy-legged with one eye and a bad case of fleas, he's going to have all the lady cocker spaniels he can handle. Not to mention love-smitten German shepherds, fox terriers and St. Bernards.

Now if you could get a human pheromone — a substance that had that effect on people, you would needless to say have the basis for a rather successful aftershave lotion.

Well . . . guess what? Professor Dodd and the English research team have found a human pheromone. And guess where they found it?

In male sweat. Yes. The very thing that we nervous males have been buying cartons and crates of roll-ons and spray cans to camouflage.

Professor Dodd and his team have temporarily named the discovery alpha androstenol . . . which is not exactly catchy by Madison Avenue standards . . . but if it's as effective in the field and the boardrooms and bedrooms of the world at large as it has been in Professor Dodd's laboratory, they could call it swamp gas and still have a gold mine on their hands.

Imagine though . . . finding out that the most effective male deodorant is actually an *odorant* — something that makes us smell more like ourselves than ever.

That future anthropologist studying the 20th century is going to have enough trouble trying to fathom artifacts like Brut bottles and Right Guard cans. When he uncovers a vial labelled 'alpha androstenol . . . the aftershave that makes you smell like a mud wrestler . . . contains nothing but pure human sweat . . . special introductory price . . . $4.95,' when the anthropologist gets to that, my hunch is he'll take his little shovel, fill in the hole and wander off looking for some other, more sensible culture to study.

SOAPS

I'M WONDERING if the power of clichés comes from the fact that they — some of them anyway — are so perfectly accurate. Let me try one on you. Soap opera. I don't know how long the phrase has been common currency, but what better term to describe those soap-sponsored melodramas that chronicle the ups and downs of Laura and Vince and Sherry and Tom and a whole plethora of cardboard characters that flicker across the TV screen each weekday afternoon wrestling with their middle-class destinies? Never quite winning, never entirely losing. 'Will Phillip forgive Martha for her one indiscretion? Can Allison ever hope to win back the respect of Charles? Does Jonathan really want Cheryl to come back? Can Penelope stick to her diet and still fulfill her duties as judge of the Smithville Black Forest Cake Bakeoff? Tune in the same time tomorrow for the next episode of Search for the Guiding Light at the Edge of Night by the General Hospital as the World Turns during the Days of Our Lives. Brought to you by Grocter and Pamble, makers of Wheeze, the Wondersuds that eliminate static lint forever . . .'

You know the routine. You should. Soap operas have manned the trenches of the great afternoon TV wasteland for — what? A quarter of a century? At least. I remember running home for lunch in grade school . . . partly to tuck into those great baloney and mustard sandwiches my mother used to make. Mostly to find out what that shrew Hazel had done to mess up the otherwise bucolic life of Joanne and Ken on Search for Tomorrow.

And that was a good 25 years ago.

They're infectious, the soaps. You will find otherwise intelligent people sitting slack-jawed in front of the tube day after day, the curtains drawn to keep out the mid-afternoon sun as yet another installment of the tacky twisted lives of their one-dimensional heroes and heroines unfold.

And not — let us lay a common misconception to rest right

here — not just housewives in quilted bed jackets with their hair in curlers. Oh no. Men are right in there with their noses to the screen too. Mary Ellen Sullivan says so. And she should know. She is, after all, the founder of the 'Love in the Afternoon Club' of Cleveland, Ohio — soon to have a chapter in your community. She says 50 percent of her members are men.

And what, you ask, is the Love in the Afternoon Club? I was kinda hoping you wouldn't ask that.

All right. The Love in the Afternoon Club is made up of people who are incurably addicted to soap operas. They get together in Mary Ellen Sullivan's restaurant-sized living room every weekday afternoon in a Cleveland suburb to dab their eyes and nibble their cuticles in the company of similarly afflicted, sentimental individuals.

Why? A silly question to any mainlining soap opera fanatic. 'It's more fun to watch the soaps with other people instead of sitting alone in your home,' says Mary Ellen. 'You can talk about the characters and about what might happen tomorrow. That's what the club is all about.' Yes ... But ... *Why*?

Why would otherwise sane and normal folks immerse themselves in hilarious melodramas that nobody this side of six double scotches could possibly take seriously?

Well the theories are rife. Scott Somers, a night-shift worker at the Ford car plant in Cleveland is a member of the Love in the Afternoon Club and a water-eyed devotee of the afternoon soaps. He's so devoted that when he goes on vacation and can't get to a TV, he telephones family and friends to keep him abreast of developments on his favourite shows.

Paul Bernard is even more faithful. Mister Bernard runs a healthfood shop in Cleveland, but don't expect to pick up any crunchy granola or yoghurt starter from his shop between twelve and four of a weekday afternoon. His shop is closed. He's over at Mary Ellen Sullivan's, watching the soaps.

How is the Love in the Afternoon Club doing? Almost as well as your average soap opera. Membership zoomed from zero to 125 in the first month of its existence and it's still climbing. There's talk at the club meetings now of hiring a Cleveland movie theatre each afternoon to accommodate the crowds.

But still the question looms — why? What's the attraction? You can search me. Forty years ago, James Thurber defined the soap opera as 'a kind of sandwich. Between thick slices of advertising, spread 12 minutes of dialogue, add predictable predicament, villainy and female suffering in equal measure, throw in a dash of nobility, sprinkle with tears, season with organ music, cover with a rich announcer sauce and serve five times a week.'

Forty years ago. He was talking about radio soaps like Ma Perkins and Stella Dallas. But he might as well have been talking about the stuff you'll see on your 21-inch full-colour-works-in-a-drawer fully transistorized boob tube any 1990s afternoon. The formula has remained as immutable and as constant as — well, as soap.

I could go on . . . but I have to make a phone call. See I was out of town for three days this week so . . . well . . . you know. Say . . . maybe you can save me a dime. Now the last time I saw it, Jeremy had finally confronted Cynthia with the letter Mark had showed him. She denied it of course, but she said a funny thing . . . she said that when Andrea came for the long weekend, she'd be able to explain everything. Now personally, I've never trusted Andrea. As far as I'm concerned anybody that would even say hello to that clown Dirk, much less have an affair with him . . .

RINGETTE

OKAY sports fans . . . you think you've got your stats down pat . . . think you're a walking Encyclopedia of Sweat because you know the Blue Jays' pitching staff by heart . . . because you know without looking it up who won the Grey Cup where and from whom in 1953? Because your depth of hockey savvy is so profound you know that Sheldon Kanageiser was an NHL defenceman not an Israeli hors d'oeuvre? Think ya know everything you need to know about sports eh? OK here's a soft lob for you . . . what's Canada's very own game?

Hockey? Hah. If the Russians and Swedes haven't disproved that for you recently, check out a painting by Pieter Brueghel the Elder called *The Return of the Hunters.* Among other things in that painting you will note several rink-ratty looking youngsters scooting around a sheet of ice swatting at a disc with their curved sticks. Not exactly Philadelphia Flyer hopefuls perhaps, but shinny players by any other name. The painting was done in 1565.

Lacrosse? Well you can make a better case for that. Back in the 1700s French explorers noticed that many North American Indian tribes liked to play a game they called Baggitaway with hooped, thonged sticks and a hard leather sphere. They French called it *le jeu de la crosse* and promptly stole it — which as far as I'm concerned invalidates it as an invention belonging to Canada. Lacrosse is an Indian game that was being played centuries before arenas dotted a country called Canada.

Nope. The English have cricket and the Yanks have baseball and the Scots have golf, the Italians have jai alai and the Scandinavians have cross country skiing and Canada . . .

Well, Canada has ringette.

Yup. Ringette. It's ours. Not just Canadian, but northern Ontarian. And young. Invented by a North Bay Parks and Recreation director in North Bay back in 1965. As the suffix on the word would indicate, ringette is strictly for girls . . . and at the moment it's as close as girls can get to the sport their brothers are involved in all winter — ice hockey. Ringette, for those who have never seen a game, is played on ice. The players carry bladeless sticks and use a donut-style ring instead of a puck. Unlike the animal house antics that frequently ruin ice hockey, there is no such thing as goon-style ringette. No body contact is allowed. No sticks can be raised above the shoulder.

Well ringette is not even 20 years old. Is it thriving? Yes and no. Something like 60 thousand Canadians now play the game, more than half of them in Ontario. Sixty thousand participants certify ringette as something more than a northern Ontario eccentricity — as a matter of fact there are ringette enclaves in the U.S., the former Soviet Union and Czechoslovakia. But it's a long way from becoming a regular feature of the Winter Olympics.

Personally I think the game suffers from terminal cuteness. Ringette terminology is patronizing as hell and would give Gloria Steinem or Germaine Greer palpitations. Divisions like Petite,

Tween, Junior, Belle and Debs sound suffocatingly patronizing —
even the name of the game sounds like a Toni home permanent you'd
give your Barbie doll. Ringette.

However silly names have never doomed a sport. Look at cricket.
Spelunking. Squash. Curling. Snooker.

If for some reason it doesn't survive though, I'd like to point out
that Canadians shouldn't feel totally bereft. One Canadian sports
innovation I neglected to mention was the one that's made household names of beanpoles like Wilt the Stilt, Meadowlark and Kareem
Abdul-Jabbar.

Basketball. We invented it. Or at least a Canadian did. Doctor
James Naismith, when he was teaching at the YMCA college down
in Springfield, Massachussetts back in 1891.

I know, I know . . . all you sports stats fanatics out there who can
recite the won-lost-tied tallies of the old Birmingham Bulls before
breakfast — you guys are ready to jump on that one. Basketball
wasn't invented in 1891 you're sneering — the Aztecs were playing
basketball back when Pieter Breughel was painting 15th-century
forwards.

Well not exactly. The Aztecs played an almost unpronounceable
game called Ollamalitzli, which involved throwing a ball (solid)
through a stone ring, which jutted out high on one wall of a stadium.
But the stakes were a little higher than your average NBA match.

The player who put the ball through the ring was entitled to all
the clothes of the spectators. The captain of the losing team was
expected to offer his head for his sins.

I don't think your average multi-million-dollar basketball superstar would much care for stakes like that.

Don't think modern spectators would be too crazy about it either.

It's one thing to lose a few bucks on a match. But coming home
naked?

INCOME TAX

THIS is the time of year when an old Roman cliché gets recycled: 'Render unto Caesar what is Caesar's.' It's Income Tax time — a time when all Canadians conveniently divide themselves into three parts: the frenzied, thrashing segment with the haunted eyes and nervous tics who haven't yet filed . . . the insufferably smug and self-satisfied segment with the knowing smirks who have filed . . . and the third part — the lawyers, accountants and tax specialists who get to work this mini-Kondike every April. The last group is the easiest of the three to spot. The tax form experts are invariably laughing. And they are always on their way to the bank.

The tax specialists have a distinct advantage over the rest of us . . . they understand that bizarre sheaf of commandments, sub-sections and fill-in-the-blanks that make up the Income Tax Form.

Actually they don't. A few years ago the Toronto *Globe and Mail* decided to test the various agencies that fill out your form for a fee. The editors 'invented' a fairly typical taxpayer — wife, kids, job, mortgage — and had his hypothetical tax return computed by a dozen or so top-of-the-line tax-return agencies. The agencies took their fees, filled out the forms and turned in a dozen different results — some said the phantom filer owed the government money, some said he would get a healthy rebate. Only a couple were even close. So it's not that the specialists understand the form any better than you or I . . . it's just that they understand the commercial value of keeping up appearances.

Of course we're all guilty of that. We all feel that we *ought* to understand this preposterous aggregation of fiscal jargon and book-keeping gobbledygook, because it's implied that we're morons if we don't. We see the TV ads of fresh-faced Canadians with toothy grins, cheerfully pocketing large rebates. 'Gosh Dolores, it's a good thing we checked our Interpretation Bulletin 118R in our *Income Tax Guide* . . . now we can send Stanley to summer camp.' Ah yes, the *Income Tax Guide*. My copy has a cover photo of a whole full-colour herd of average Canucks just standing around . . . *hanging* out . . . having a good time . . . smiling . . . remembering great moments they had with their personalized form . . . Makes you feel guilty, stupid and left out all at once.

But I dunno . . . I've been thinking about it . . . and I dunno. My *Income Tax Guide* — this Pollyanna pamphlet that tells me basically that Caesar wants his cut . . . runs to 54 pages. Fifty-four! Now if you were to approach, say, Jesse James, who was also in the business of appropriating other people's money — if you were to approach Jesse and offer him a 54-page brochure to distribute among the passengers and crew of selected stagecoaches . . . I don't think he'd go for it, do you?

I submit that when it takes anybody — Jesse James, Julius Caesar or Jean Chrétien — 54 pages to say 'This is a stick-up' — we have a failure in communication. And the tax guide bears me out I think.

You don't get too far into your tax guide before you stumble over the T-4 form. Everybody knows the old, reliable T-4 . .. . but did you ever ask yourself . . . Why . . . T? How come . . . four? What's wrong with W-13 or N-8? A-1 has a nice, up-beat flavour to it. Now there's a neglected letter! Why not K-7? 'Got yer K-7's yet?' 'Don't forget to file your K-7's . . .'

But no . . . T-4 it is. And not only T-4, but T-4A and T-4A OAS and T-4U and T-5 and T-600TD and TFA-1 and even so help me a T2202A. Look it up for yourself under Education Deductions.

The numbers are a treat too. Under Canada Pension Plan contributions we're told to enter (on line 4) the amount (from box D) up to the Maximum of 169 dollars and 20 cents. Not 170 dollars max . . . $169.20.

Under Unemployment Insurance Premiums we're told to enter (on line 29) the amount (from box E) to a maximum of 187 dollars and 20 cents. One eight seven period two zero.

It's not your average mind that would ask you to compute with figures like 169.20 and 187.20 . . . this reveals sadism on a remarkably sophisticated level . . . which becomes positively inspiring when followed with a paragraph like 'Subtract Total Personal Exemptions on line 45 from Net Income on line 41 and enter the result on line 46. Subtract line 59 from line 46 and you will have arrived at your Taxable Income on line 60. Carry it to page four.' Indeed. Along with two new pencils, a pocket calculator, a cartridge belt full of Rolaids and a triple rye and hold the water.

Why do we put up with it? How come the gnomes of Revenue Canada have never looked over the Bytown battlements to see a howling, torchbearing mob of disgruntled taxpayers bearing down on them?

For two very good reasons. First, we all secretly think we're getting money *back* . . . we all expect in our parsimonious heart of hearts . . . a rebate. Second, we are none of us absolutely certain that we didn't . . . fudge a figure here or there . . . Nothing big you understand . . . no Al Capone evasion stuff . . . but well . . . ha ha . . . why draw attention to ourselves?

Now, it's an absolutely subhuman level of economic rationalization that's going on here. It's as if Jesse James stopped the stagecoach, took all the jewels and money, shot up the menfolk, ravished the womenfolk, but told them they could keep their hats on.

I mean with a rebate the government is giving *you* back a morsel of your own money! And announcing with a generous smile that you've earned it . . .

Ah well . . . never mind. An illusion in the hand is worth two in the bush.

Hats off and a generous cheque of course to those voracious ferrets and tireless terriers of Revenue Canada, who make this time of year far more meaningful for Canadians than the first robin's chirp or the first crocus bloom. Hats off I say! You may not be noble Romans, lads . . . but you have something in common with the noblest Roman who crossed the Rubicon. You've got a lot of Gaul.

BORDERS

I WOULD like to direct your attention to a curious Canadian ritual.

Well it's not exactly a ritual so much as a whole new growth industry. You've probably noticed the salesmen . . . they're thundering all around this dominion right now — self-appointed saviours of the nation . . . beating the bushes, checking under mattresses, peering into attics and root cellars, storm sewers and subway tunnels . . . winnowing out the precious links and nuggets that . . . *hold this nation together.* 'What makes us special?' they ask (usually rhetorically) . . . 'What cuts Canadians apart from the rest of the human herd?'

They come up with all kinds of answers: Ookpik. Anne Murray. The Precambrian Shield. Resdan.

But to my mind, they've all overlooked the most precious and obvious strand of Canadiana there is. What makes Canadians distinct from every other race, creed or nation-state? What cements the incredible tossed salad of nationalities and ethnic strains that make up this great nation of ours?

What indeed, if not that one mind-boggling ceremony . . . that one knee-trembling, stomach-flopping sacrament that every Canadian past toddling age observes . . . sometimes just once, often twice or even several times a year?

The Border Crossing.

Doesn't matter where in Canada you live. You can cross the border at Ogdensburg, New York or Coutts, Alberta; Niagara Falls or New Westminster; Dawson in the Yukon or Calais down in Maine . . . doesn't matter a jot. Point is, you're Canadian . . . so you'll do it. It's just one of the things you're expected to do as a Canadian. Everybody goes 'down to the States.' It's tradition, eh?

God knows why. For many years, when the Canadian dollar was worth a nickel or so more than its American cousin, I think Canadians just went down to the States to feel smug.

Wasn't much reason other than that. True, Havana cigars were

cheaper down there, but our cigarettes were stronger, our beer got you drunk quicker, and if you asked for vinegar with your chips, American waitresses checked to see if you were wearing a plastic bracelet and a hunted look.

And the other thing that made — and makes — going down to the States about as sensible as the lemmings' mass swan dive — is the border crossing itself. Not so much going down to the States . . . as coming *back* from the states . . . when you come face-to-face with the full majesty of Canada Customs. It's eerie. Somewhere between the sign that says: 'Thanks fer comin'. Y'all come back!' and the one that frigidly announces 'Douane Canada Customs' . . . you begin to feel a gnawing uncertainty . . . an uncertainty that swells to a paranoid conviction that you will never actually get to walk on your homeland again. Except maybe in the exercise yard as a convicted felon.

Think about the last time you crossed the border. Have you ever been more terrified? Can you recall a time when any Canadian official was more offhand with you? Or a time when you acted like such a wimp in response?

Ah yes . . . It's always the same with the Border Crossing. What complicates the problem of course is that Canada is a nation of amateur smugglers. Not heroin-in-the-rocker-panel type smugglers. More like Lucky Strikes in the glove compartment.

Now come on . . . don't blush. You're not the only one who ever ran the border with an Omega digital on a flexible Speidel band cutting off the circulation in your upper forearm. And you're not the first one to have his entire life flash before his eyes when the lantern-jawed tight-lipped gent with Canada Customs emblazoned on his bulging shoulder leaned into cast an insolent eye over everything in your back seat.

Where do they get the questions? Where do they get *the delivery?*

Aftnoon . . . you a Cnajun citzen presntly residing wthin borders of which province now . . . youre born where . . . have youever been cnvicted of indictable offence 'r' frany reason rfused pmission tcross border . . . You maam where d'you work . . . This your child carryin any beerwinespirits or firearms ever consorted with known terrorists are you presently employed how many trans border trips 'vyou made this calendar quarter any repairs made to this vee hicle and how long have you been out of Canada?

And just when you were ready to ransom your spouse, leave your firstborn as security and babble a confession about the bottle of bourbon under the car blanket . . . He writes something cryptic on a notepad and waves you through.

What does it mean? Are they waiting to see if your nerve will break? Will Mounties be waiting in your driveway? Will plainclothesmen come to the office six months hence to drag you away? Who knows? It's all part of the larger mystery of The Crossing . . . The crossing of the great undefended border. Ah yes . . . If all the guff that's been written about the magnificence and nobility of that 5,000-mile-long checkout counter was piled in one row . . . we'd have a barrier that would make the Great Wall of China look like a picket fence. Somebody once referred to our border as 'that long frontier from the Atlantic to the Pacific Ocean, guarded only by neighbourly respect and honourable obligations.'

Respect? Honour? It is to whimper brokenly. The somebody who said that about our border was one Winston Churchill, in a speech at the Canada Club in London, back during the Second World War.

Mister Churchill had crossed the border perhaps once. And then with all the pomp and splendour, not to mention brandy and cigars, that go with being the world popular PM of a Mother Country at war.

All the same. Winnie was a canny old codger.

I like to think that when he crossed the border from the U.S. into Canada . . . and the usually supercilious customs people turned obsequious in a flurry of salutes and applause . . . I like to think that if you'd been standing just behind Winnie when he doffed his homburg in return . . . you'd have caught just a flash of a half dozen or so hand-rolled Havanas . . . securely scotch taped to the inside of the crown.

ORANGE

I HAD kinda hoped that after the body language fad died away, that would be the end of it . . . at least for a while. The end of amateur psychology I mean. You remember the body language craze of course? Those were the days when you could be relaxing at a party, just starting to reach for the cheese dip, when some red-faced psycho-sleuth on the opposite side of the room would lunge across the room forefinger all set to impale you to the davenport . . . 'Ah hah!' he'd say, 'Crossed your legs when you sat down *and* adjusted your pant cuff to cover your sock. You're withdrawn! Classic introvert behaviour exhibited by someone who has feelings of inferiority in common social situations.'

I don't know if that guy and all the other freelance psychotherapists suffered a sudden attack of good taste or if they all just moved on to a higher fad — like Zen jogging.

Whatever happened, I haven't had my soul laid bare on a coffee table for some time now — and as I say, I had rather hoped that the whole fad had gone the way of disco boots and edible underwear . . . but that was before I read about the report from Outspan.

Yes, Outspan. Outspan is a British company that moves oranges around the world — like Sunkist and Jaffa. You'd think the threat of late frosts, orange-picker strikes and the latest Anita Bryant offensive would give Outspan enough to worry about. Apparently not. Because Outspan recently commissioned and paid for a report entitled 'Ways of Eating Oranges as a Guide to Personality.' And it's a lulu.

Authors of the report say that the entire orange-eating world can be divided into four categories: suckers, biters, squeezers and chewers.

Biters, reports the report somewhat redundantly . . . bite . . . into the fruit, nibbling the pulp from the peel. They are aggressive, confident and likely to be successful, it says. The report, which

sounds like it was edited by Liberace, goes on: 'These vicious beasts like sport and have a strong moral and rebellious streak.'

Suckers of oranges are airily dismissed by the author as 'classic oral types.' Mind you, orange-suckers are articulate, sensual, imaginative, creative and often work in the performing arts.

Their whole problem is that they crave love.

The report doesn't get a lot more profound as you read on. It tells us that chewers chew and squeezers squeeze. Chewers are ordinary Joes . . . the sort of dull pluggers you ride to work with on the bus and who sit behind you in the movie theatre saying, 'What's happening?' 'What's that he's got in his hand?' 'Did he shoot them?' 'Isn't that Robert Redford?'

Squeezers? Alas. These are the people, says the report, who hold a portion of the orange against their mouths and squeeze with their finger while biting. That's what the report says. Before I sat down to write about this I tried holding a portion of orange against my mouth and squeezing with my fingers while biting. I tried it out. Then I went and had a shower. Because I had orange juice down my arm, all over my typing finger, trickling through my beard and making my eyes water. Only a fool would hold a portion of orange against their mouth and squeeze with their fingers while biting. The report says that orange squeezers squeeze oranges because they were made to feel worthless and inadequate as children. Rightly so. This may be the only portion of the report that I believe.

I've got news for the consultant psychoanalyst that flogged this report to Outspan . . . he hasn't even scratched the outer rind of the weird world of orange eating. I once saw a woman in Spain eat an orange with a knife and fork . . . and I used to work with a disreputable aging cockney sub-editor in London who . . . honestly . . . used to bounce, knead and even softly kick his orange against a filing cabinet before he sucked, bit, chewed or squeezed the life out of it. Every coffee break. 'Mykes it softer dunnit?'

And me? What kind of an orange eater am I? Hah. I'm not. I'm strictly a tangerine man. I like to take my vitamin C neat with no fuss and no shreds of pulp or orange juice stains festooning my T-shirt.

My advice to Outspan? Forget the pseudo-psychoanalytical

reports on orange eaters and plough the money into something ...
tangible ... Like maybe oranges with zippers?

HUSTLE

I WANT you to picture the scene. It is a spring-soaked, sunshiny
day, not too many days from now ... you are walking down the
street on your way to nowhere very ominous ... to a chorus of
sparrow chirps and robin burbles ... It is spring, by cracky ... you
can feel the heat of the sun on your face and already the tedious ritual
of toques and parkas, lined gloves and galoshes are scarcely a bad
memory. *Spring!* The trees are budding ... the sap is rising ... the
earth is bursting ... and you are feeling a good dozen years younger
than you have since sometime before the Christmas shopping rush.
Spring! And there's a devilish what-the-hell lilt in your walk that
tells the world around you that you're younger than you used to
be ... wilder than might be guessed ... and altogether more fascinating than you were yesterday.

That's when you hear it. The voice. More tantalizing than the
sirens who called to Odysseus and his crewmen ...

'*Oh ... Misssssssster ...*'

More beguiling than Vivien Leigh in *Gone With the Wind*; or
Melina Mercouri in *Never on Sunday* ... '*Oh Missster ...*' This
voice is Simone Signoret's eyes and Julie Christie's lips and the voice
of Ella Fitzgerald, Lena Horne, Linda Ronstadt and Donna Summer
all rolled into one mellifluous irresistible beacon ... and she's calling
to *you*.

'*Oh ... Missssssster ...*'

With knees of purest jello and a heart pounding like a runaway
sump pump, you turn to gaze on the source of the murmurous
enticements ... and that's when you hear the rest of the message ...

'*Oh ... Missssssster ... wouldn't you like a Cadmington's Jersey
Nut Brittle Fudge Bar right now ...?*'

The voice is coming from a vending machine and I wish I was
making this up but I'm not. This machine is on the market. It is the

latest merchandising brainwave of the Matsushita Electric Industrial Company Limited of Tokyo, Japan. How does it work? Ahhh, it's drearily predictable once you recover from the cultural insult of being hailed by a vending machine. The thing has an infrared sensor in it. Whenever a person comes close to the machine, the sensor activates a recording that welcomes the customer ... Goes on to list the merchandise available.

Am I the only one that has trouble with this?

I mean imagine! You're walking along minding your own business and suddenly this ... box ... starts *hustling* you! *'Hi ... how are you? Nice to see you. Say a big handsome fella like you could darn-sure use some Elbow Cream. New he-man scented Macho Plus in the dripless dispensered non-aerosol can to protect our ionosphere ... leaves you cooler, drier and with those elbows gals just love to touch'* — I tell you I don't need it.

I have never had what you would call a fruitful relationship with *mute* vending machines — never mind one that talks my ear off ...

I personally have long been of the belief that vending machines in all their perverse variety are nothing short of a bald-faced plot — hatched by whom I'm not sure. Psychiatrists perhaps — worried about shrinking patient loads. The tranquilizer industry possibly — I don't want to point fingers. All I know is that no caring, feeling human intelligence is behind the insane proliferation of machines that take your money and then refuse to sell you chocolate bars, cigarettes, pocketbooks, peanuts, bubblegum or whatever else the machine pretends to be willing to sell to you.

It's not that I haven't tried to be reasonable in my dealings with vending machines. I fully appreciate that a machine can get a little . . . sulky . . . just standing there all day . . . having total strangers insert cold change, yanking at its handles, jabbing its buttons. I could live with a little balkiness . . . a touch of testiness . . . even the odd mistake . . . So what if I get a double cream and sugar when I press the 'coffee black' button? Is it such a big deal that I pull the peanut handle and get a bag of gelatinous jujubes? . . . No. I'm a reasonable man. I know the meaning of the word compromise.

It's when I put my money in and *nothing* happens. Nothing! Just ching ching ching as it takes my money — ka ponk as I push the button . . . then . . . Nothing. That's when the mists begin to move in and I start to slip over the edge. I jiggle the handle. Nothing. I . . . jostle the machine. Nothing. I push the coin return. Nothing, natch. So I . . . sorta *thump* the machine . . . with the heel of my hand. Friendly, you understand. But firm.

Within minutes I am drop-kicking, karate chopping, rabbit punching and half-nelsoning the machine in an all out assault of rabid frenzy. I curse. I whimper. I plead. I *lose*.

I have never — not once — got my money back from a vending machine that refused to deal with me. Sometimes I don't even try anymore.

And now, thanks to the ever-diligent Matsushita Electric Industrial Company Limited of Japan, there's a vending machine on the market that comes on like Irma La Douce. Great. Just great.

Well I'm not falling for this one. I'll take measures. But I'm gonna look mighty dumb walking around wearing earmuffs all summer.

CHAN

I KNOW we're running out of things. I realize that the world is gobbling up its fossil fuels like a vacuum cleaner on overdrive. I recognize that we're ingesting our forests with gluttonish glee, turning them into Kleenex and cardboard and great thick ad-stuffed newspapers that live for one day and then go to the dump. I acknowledge that we're running out of farmland, parking places, trout streams and the ozone layer. These are all serious shortage problems and I don't mean to belittle them in any way. But I think there's a critical run on another commodity right under our noses that worries me even more. I detect a serious, world-wide shortage of A Sense of Humour.

People are losing the ability to laugh at themselves — which, considering the inherent hilarity of human behaviour, is a pretty good guffaw in itself. But we're not laughing. Oh no. Life has become a Serious Business.

Sometimes I get the impression that there's a whole platoon of glowering, beetle-browed commandos scuttling around out there, compiling lists of Things That Are No Longer Funny.

Jokes that mention the word 'housewife' are Not Acceptable — as readers of the *Globe and Mail* are reminded about three times a week. It's funny — the *Globe and Mail* has a feature on its front page called Your Morning Smile — it's a little three- or four-line snippet of a joke that's supposed to illuminate your morning coffee and brighten your day. But the funniest thing about Your Morning Smile, is not the morning smile. It's the letters to the editor *about* Your Morning Smile. Your Morning Smile can go on for weeks printing morning smiles about bad golfers, lazy office workers, kids with poor report cards or shaggy dog gags ... But let Your Morning Smile contain the slightest reference to dizzy blondes or a lousy driver who happens to be a woman — and the letters-to-the-editor column fairly bristles with volleys and broadsides of indignation and outrage about the vicious, sexist stereotyping of Your Morning Smile. I've never seen a funny letter of protest about Your Morning Smile. They're all deadly serious; unblinkingly grave.

The letter writers all sound like they'd like to see Your Morning Smile replaced with Your Morning Lecture on Relative Psycho-Social Attitudes. And they all sound like people I wouldn't want to have my morning coffee with.

There are a lot of old standards it is no longer chic to laugh at. Newfie jokes are no longer funny — in fact any jokes that smack of racial or ethnic stereotyping — jokes involving flamboyant Italians, pinchpenny Scots, French Canadian lumberjacks or brolly-bearing thin-lipped Brits — all ride high on the We Are No Longer Amused list.

It's a long list. And it's getting longer. There's just been a new addition. Down in San Francisco there are picket lines around the film location for a movie. They're trying to ban Charlie Chan. You know Charlie Chan — the portly, unflappable Oriental super sleuth who wears white suits, speaks in Confucianisms and routinely unravels complicated crimes for the American forces of law and order — with the assistance of his bumbling sons, who are numbered for convenience. Charlie Chan is brilliant, gracious and above all a pacifist. He wouldn't dream of resorting to anything so brutish as kung fu or jiujitsu to bring the wayward to justice.

So what's the beef?

Well the Chinese community of San Francisco — the largest Chinese community outside the Orient — doesn't like Charlie Chan. They call him a racist Asian stereotype. They say he gives a negative portrayal of Chinese-Americans. They say they don't want any more Charlie Chan movies made.

Well I say bunk. I say Charlie Chan movies are funny and harmless entertainment and they no more predispose me to think of the People's Republic of China as a nation of 950 million panama-hatted detectives who talk like fortune cookies . . . than a Sherlock Holmes tale makes me think all Englishmen wear deerstalker hats, play the violin and smoke meerschaum pipes.

I say moreover what somebody else said a long time ago. He said: 'It is the uncensored sense of humour which is the ultimate therapy for man in society.'

An expatriate Canadian writer by the name of Bernie Slade put it a lot more simply. He said: 'Laughter is the opposite of a breakdown. It's a breakup.' A point to which I can visualize Charlie Chan inclining his head, smiling inscrutably and murmuring: 'Ah so.'

CANUCK

TIME now to play Canada's favourite quiz game: Just answer the musical question and you can win a colour-coordinated snowmobile, a lifetime supply of Cold Duck from the tropical vineyards of Niagara and an all-expense-paid weekend for two at Minaki Lodge. The question: In 25 words or less — what is a Canadian?

Do you know how long we've been asking that question? Do you know how many wacky and wonderful answers have been put forth?

Back in 1909 one of our northern explorers hewed out a rugged definition of Canadian for what must have been one very puzzled Inuit. Captain J.E. Bernier recorded in his diary: 'I took possession of Baffin Island for Canada in the presence of several Eskimos. After firing nineteen shots in the air, I instructed an Eskimo to fire the twentieth; telling him that he was now a Canadian.'

A U.S. Chamber of Commerce publication back in 1954 said: 'A Canadian may be a mounted policeman, an Eskimo, a French-speaking farmer or Rose Marie. But not necessarily.'

Not so long ago one could be forgiven for concluding that the average Canadian was a silver-haired, fiery-eyed, thunder-voiced senior citizen — John Diefenbaker clones in fact — if one drew the obvious conclusion from the late statesman's characteristic speech opener: 'My Fellow Canadians . . .'

The writer Robertson Davies kind of got weary of trying to explain what a Canadian was. He wrote: 'I am just a Canadian. It is not a thing you can escape from. Like having blue eyes.'

My favourite definition comes from the poet Irving Layton. He said: 'A Canadian is someone who keeps asking the question what is a Canadian?' Well it's almost my favourite. Actually I like Pierre Berton's definition better. He claims a Canadian is somebody who knows how to make love in a canoe.

But somehow the answers are like potato chips — one never seems to satisfy. Still the quiz game goes on. Now it's computer surveys that fill in the chinks in our largely undefined character and etch in the lines in our not-quite-clear face. A New York University professor spent three years finding out how apathetic all North Americans are about crime. He staged robberies — thefts of bicycles, cars and that sort of thing — in different cities around the continent in broad daylight and stood by with a clipboard to see how often average citizens would intervene. He surveyed mostly American cities but he also checked out Ottawa, Calgary, Edmonton and Vancouver. He found Canadians were more reluctant than the average American to get involved — although we ran well ahead of New Yorkers.

So . . . Add a broad streak of apathy to the Canadian makeup. Our own Statistics Canada has not been sitting on its hands in the great What-Is-a-Canadian Contest. Since 1974 it's been publishing, at three-year intervals, an eerie little tome called *Perspectives Canada*. You're in it. So am I. *Perspectives Canada* has documented how we look, what we eat, how much we drink, where we work and even how much exercise we're getting.

It's mostly not a very cheering report. Obesity is a big part of our character it seems. One point six million Canadians are grossly overweight. We drink too much and we smoke too much . . . and only about half of us use our spare time to engage in any sport or recreation. (Watching TV with a can of beer and a bowl of chip dip does not qualify as recreation.)

But it's not all grim, *Perspectives Canada*. Despite our drinking and smoking and overeating, we're living longer. Canadian males' life expectancy has risen by two years. For Canadian women — three and a half years. Canadian children have a much better chance of living through their first year than ever before . . . and we're making, believe it or not, more money — in real dollars — than ever before. That's what it says here in *Perspectives Canada*, although my wallet would contest that vigorously.

Oh yes, and one other piece of good news from this publication. One more brushstroke to add to the portrait of a Canadian.

The most popular leisure activity among Canadians . . . way ahead of jogging or squash or hockey or euchre . . . is lovemaking.

Maybe Pierre Berton was really on to something.

WATCH

Ever noticed how . . . if you really concentrate on pretty well any word, it begins to look and sound stranger and stranger? Take the word watch. Watch. W A T C H. Watch.

Watch out. Watch your step. What time's your watch say? Watch my dust. Watch it! Watch for Cattle Crossing.

Watch. It's an honourable word. Ancient long before the tongue we speak became recognizable as English. Particularly in the military sense. For literally thousands of years soldiers and sailors have been performing that loneliest of all military duties, standing watch. The ancient Hebrews divided the night into three watches. The Greeks into four, sometimes five. The Romans standardized the watches of the night at four. And I still remember one of the most poignant historical artifacts I ever saw.

It was in the basement of a church in downtown London, England — right at the bottom of Fleet Street. The church (I forget the name) had been hit by German bombs during the Blitz and damaged fairly extensively. During the restoration of the church the engineers accidentally unearthed the remains of ancient Roman battlements. The Christian church had unwittingly been built on the ruins of a pagan Roman fortification. But that wasn't the fascinating discovery. The fascinating discovery was right beside the wall. A mound of shells. Oyster shells.

A late-night snack, I like to think. Probably forbidden and thus twice as tasty. Enjoyed two thousand years ago by some lonely Roman sentry who pried them open with his sword or spear blade while the rest of the troops slept and he stood watch. You can see those shells today . . . right where the sentry chucked them probably, burying them under a scuff of sand. His sergeant never discovered the sentry's dereliction of duty. Nobody did. Until 20 centuries later.

And 20 centuries later soldiers and sailors are still getting stuck with sentry duty — standing watch. And many of them draw worse fates than standing on the banks of the Thames for four hours watching for blue-painted savages and eating oysters.

Take the poor devils involved in Operation Sovereign Viking for instance. Sovereign Viking is the code name for a military exercise that took place on Southampton Island. That is absolutely no relation to Southampton, England. If you check your atlases, you will find Southampton Island tucked neatly into the north-western corner of Hudson Bay, just a hair below the Arctic Circle. I don't have to tell you what the outdoor conditions were like on Southampton Island in the middle of winter.

Wretched would cover it. And 90 Canadian soldiers from the Royal Canadian Regiment who made up Operation Sovereign Viking had to endure those conditions for 10 days. Huddled in tents. And not, unfortunately, *always* huddled in tents. Sovereign Viking was a military operation . . . and that means . . . somebody always has to stand watch. And they did. In twos. Armed with automatic rifles and backed up by waist-high trip flares.

With Operation Sovereign Viking, standing watch was not merely upholding an ancient military tradition. Southampton Island, in addition to its bone-chilling ambience, has one more statistic that could get in the *Guinness Book of Records* — the highest percentage of polar bears in the Canadian Arctic. Polar bears have a couple of unusual characteristics. For one thing they are attracted — not frightened — by loud noises.

Thus a convoy of armoured vehicles could be expected to draw them like flies. For another few things, polar bears are perpetually curious, almost perpetually hungry and not inclined to take no for an answer.

To make the situation really bizarre . . . the soldiers were not allowed to shoot the bears . . . only to scare them away. Shooting bears is illegal unless you happen to be an Inuit . . .

Well Operation Sovereign Viking is over now and I haven't heard a thing. And I guess no news is good news . . . we certainly would have heard about it if a couple of sentries had been eaten on duty, I would think.

But I can't help visualizing some poor Canuck on Southampton Island, standing watch while his buddies snoozed, stomping his feet, feeling his nose go numb and his fingers get stiff. With the wind howling unmolested right down from the Pole and the mercury bottoming out of the glass on the thermometer . . . Waiting for a thousand-odd pounds of curious, hungry, ill-tempered bruin to loom up at him out of the Arctic night . . .

Knowing that if it happens, he has the choice of firing a few rounds in the air or running for cover as fast as his army issue mukluks will take him, while yelling, 'Is there an Inuit in the house?'

Unappetizing options, both.

One thing you can be sure of. Any Canadian soldier who took part in Operation Sovereign Viking would have traded watches with that oyster-sucking Roman legionnaire on the banks of the Thames at the drop of a . . . helmet. Plumed or otherwise.

CHISANBOP

I'M A romantic. I admit it. I'm so romantic I like to believe that into every life, at least once, there plops an idea so perfect that is takes the breath away. I like to believe that for me the perfect idea is *Chisanbop*.

You're not familiar with the term? Well that's probably because you don't speak Korean. Don't be surprised though if your kids or grandchildren come home one day Chisanbopping all over the living room — it's the coming thing.

Chisanbop is a Korean word that means 'finger calculation.' It was invented 30 years ago by a Korean mathematician.

And that's the point — Chisanbop is a system of arithmetic that *any*body can understand. Even me!

Maybe you can *do* math. Maybe that doesn't seem like such a big deal to you. But for an arithmetical illiterate like me — Chisanbop is tantamount to discovery of the wheel. Because mathematically, I've been faking it for years. Since grade three as a matter of fact. It was half way through grade three when I got the mumps. Up until my neck started imitating a bullfrog in heat, I'd be sitting in class merrily adding oranges and subtracting apples with the rest of my pint-sized colleagues. When I came back from my sickbed, the teacher was prattling about something called multiplication and division, and I was lost forever.

Oh sure I memorized a few tables. I learned to sound like I really believed that 8 times 12 was 96. But I never really understood it. I could figure three avocados in the left hand added to two avocados in the right hand actually adding up to five avocados . . . because I could *do* that. But three avocados *times* two? I just couldn't master the concept. After that, of course, it was a bewildering whirl of improper fractions, decimals, square roots and integers. Hydra-headed monsters like calculus, trigonometry, geometry and physics loomed out of the mist. '*Let X be the unknown factor*,' intoned my algebra teacher. It was. Still is.

I was still working on three avocados times two.

You can understand the shape I was in when the so-called new math came along a few years ago. I didn't want to hear about it. Especially after hearing some apple-cheeked instructress announce that the new math was just for new people — little kids. That people brought up on the old math would be — she smiled as she said it — hopelessly confused forever.

So for many years I avoided short people with books under their arms who looked like they might be fixing to ask for help with their homework . . . and I resigned myself to the bleak knowledge that I was never likely to understand the rudiments of elementary calculation in my lifetime.

And then . . . Chisanbop. Lovely, splendid Chisanbop. It's sweeping the American school system. It's being taught in both the private and public school systems of Saskatoon even as I speak. In the last year at least 55 schools in Winnipeg had one or more teachers teaching Chisanbop.

I can't believe it. It's so simple. Listen. It works like this. Hold up your right hand. Your index finger is one, your middle finger is two, the ring finger is three, the little finger is four and your thumb represents five.

OK? One two three four five. Now take the same right hand and press the thumb and index finger together — that's six . . . the rest is easy . . . thumb and middle is seven; thumb and ring eight and so on.

Now, the left hand is for 10 and multiples of 10. Ten, 20, 30, 40, 50 — index, middle, ring, little finger and thumb. So to represent the number 55 you hold up the thumb of the left hand (that's 50) with the thumb of the right hand — 55. You can get to 99 that way . . . To show 100 you just touch your forehead.

Now I ask you . . . Is that not the way math ought to be? Kids think so — they love it. In Chisanbop classes, the kids are grinning away as they pop their little fingers on the desk. Winnipeg teacher Margaret Froese says kids find Chisanbop so much fun they don't want to do their other subjects. Well I don't blame them. If I'd had Chisanbop when I was a kid I'd be a different man today. I'd be able to add up my cheque book. I'd understand the deductions on my pay cheque. I'd probably even be able to fill out my own income tax form.

It's so easy! Look — 17 and 14 . . . thumb and ring finger of right hand plus thumb and little finger of left hand equals . . . two left thumbs plus index finger on the right. No. That's backwards — equals two right thumbs plus ring finger on the left . . . No. No . . . that would be 24 . . . I think . . . okay okay . . . two thumbs on the right plus the ring finger . . . no . . . okay left thumb equals 10 right? . . . so two left thumbs equal 20. Or is it 100? Anyway I haven't got two left thumbs . . . Okay okay . . . 17 avocados in the left hand plus 14 avocados in the right hand . . .

BANKS

As far as I'm concerned, Stephen Leacock said everything there is to say about the banking business in the first couple of sentences of his story, 'My Financial Career.' The story begins, 'When I go into a bank, I get rattled. The clerks rattle me. The wickets rattle me. The sight of the money rattles me. Everything rattles me.' Leacock wrote that story more than half a century ago, but I don't think things at the bank have improved . . . As a matter of fact, if *my* financial career is any indication, they've gotten a good deal worse. Banks are more rattling than ever. At least in Leacock's day, a live human being was all that stood between you and your bank balance. You filled out your withdrawal or deposit slip, passed it to a teller, who checked your account, made the necessary written amendments and sent you on about your business.

Those were the good old days. The tellers are gone now. They've been replaced by a covey of Vestal Virgins who smile and take your slip and then line up single file in front of a humming whirring tickety chucka machine that looks and sounds like the control panel from the *Starship Enterprise*. It's a computer of course . . . and well, I remember the soft soap that accompanied their installation 10 or 15 years ago. 'They'll make our banking service faster,' they said. 'So much smoother . . . more efficient . . .'

Well I guess they do provide smoother service . . . When they're not breaking down — a condition they're prone to assume as soon as they hear my footsteps on the threshold of the bank. I guess the computers would be more efficient if it weren't for the fact that there's only one terminal to process all the transactions of that shuffling ill-tempered crocodile line of account holders that I'm always at the tail end of. I guess the computers are more efficient except for those odd times when I get my bankbook back and the print-out of my deposit instead of being in dollars and cents reads like a fragment from a Sanskrit dictionary.

I know . . . picky, picky, picky. It's always better to look on the positive side of things. That's why whenever I have some fast, smooth and efficient banking to take care of, I always make sure to take something along to read. And so it was last week, by a delicious bit of irony, that I happened to be standing in line in my computerized bank . . . reading about Hoare's.

You've heard of Hoare's? Messrs. C. Hoare and Company I mean? Neither had I. But it's a bank. On Fleet Street in London, England. Right out of Charles Dickens.

Listen. You know what you see when you walk through the door of Messrs. C. Hoare and Company? A coal-burning stove. Brass grilles. Top hats and frock coats hanging from coatracks that would give a Yorkville Avenue antique dealer hiccups. Mind you, you wouldn't get through the door. You'd be stopped by a liveried attendant who would — ever so politely of course — inquire if you were a 'client' of Messrs. C. Hoare and Co. No one else is allowed in.

There are no computers at Hoare's. But there are silver snuff boxes at each wicket. And for the eight thousand clients who bank at this, the last family-owned bank in Great Britain that does business with the public — for those eight thousand, a few other perks as well.

Every piece of correspondence that leaves the bank has the signature of one of the seven partners on it — all of whom are named Hoare. One can always get to the boss at Hoare's. And the institution started in 1672 so there must be a certain amount of built-in security, knowing that you're dealing with a bank that's been solvent for more than three centuries.

And don't think for a minute that Hoare's is some sort of a quaint but harmless oversight from an age gone by. They don't talk about profit figures . . . that would be vulgar. But Messrs. Hoare and Co.

do acknowledge the fact that they have some 155 million dollars in deposits. Hoare's is not hurting.

Not cultivating ulcers either. I'm going to quote a bank manager now. Mister Henry Peregrine Rennie Hoare. Senior partner in Messrs. Hoare and Co. — and when's the last time you heard your bank manager talk like this?

REPORTER: 'Tell me, Mister Hoare, why does your bank turn away new business that could be very profitable?'

MISTER HOARE: 'If the bank got really large, we couldn't manage it ourselves. There's really no point, provided it makes satisfactory profits and expands fast enough to keep the staff happy.'

Oh Lord. Royal? Dominion? Nova Scotia? Commerce? Montreal? Are you listening? Did you get any of that?

BLUSH

I WANT you to take a couple of seconds now . . . and try to remember the first time you blushed. And why. Got it? Pretty embarrassing right? Sorry I brought it up. But I've been asking that question a lot of people I ran into over the last couple of weeks. Funny answers you get. One woman recalled that the first time she could remember turning crimson occurred at the beach. She was about five years old. Her mother asked her to take off her sandy bathing suit before she went into the cottage. Just as she was stepping out of the bathing suit the woman remembers her mother crowing, 'Oh darling, you've got the cutest bottom. John! John! Come quick! And bring the camera!' Father John came quick with the Kodak and snapped a picture of a distinctly unenthusiastic kid with a face glowing like a Florida sunset.

Another friend remembers her most humiliating moment in dancing class, circa grade four. There she was enthusiastically pumping out limp-ankled *pas de deux* and the teacher (from France) swooped in like a gull.

'Here to congratulate me,' thought the delighted little girl. 'Just wants to tell me to keep up the good work.' The dance instructress swooped low, hovered over the little girl's ear and said in a thundering whisper, 'Ma cherie you weel nevair dahnce until you lose at least 10 pounds.'

Memories of humiliation. We all have them. My earliest memory goes back to about grade three or so. The teacher, folded piece of paper in hand, summoning me: 'Arthur, I want you to take this note down to the Principal's Office.'

'Sure,' I chirped, abeam with innocence, 'What's it say?'

Well. You'd think I'd asked for a sneak peak at the Academy Award Nomination for Best Actress.

'Never mind what it says, it's none of your business,' sniffed the teacher — to a sympathetic chorus of 'Eeeeews' and 'What a nerve' from my lickspittle classroom colleagues. I was crushed. I carried the note like a burning ember to the principal's oak-panelled lair, and stood there meekly like a serf, waiting for Life's next buffet. I have no idea what the note said. I was convinced at the time though that it was nothing less than a proposal to have me cut off recesses for the rest of my life and moved to the desk at the front of the class.

Probably the teacher was asking for something like more chalk brushes, but paranoia runs deep — even in grade three.

Interesting thing about all the people I asked was that none of them could remember being embarrassed at a really early age. Nobody before the age of five in my 'control' group. That's in keeping with a study done down at the University of Texas earlier this year. A psychologist investigated nearly four hundred children, ranging from babes in arms to 12-year-olds, to try and find out whether embarrassment is instinctive or learned, and if learned, when and how. When you think about it, babies don't blush. In fact the study showed that few children up to the age of five showed any signs of embarrassment. But it's around the age of five that the social roof begins to cave in for kids. By age seven, nearly 80 percent of the kids were reporting frequent bouts of embarrassment... and from there on in, for most of the kids, just as for most of *us* ... life would contain its complement of mortifying moments.

The Texas study does lay one myth about embarrassment to rest ... the folk legend that girls are more easily embarrassed than boys. It just isn't true. Blushing is totally democratic — and of course it's not restricted to the young, either.

Humiliation is one of life's little cherry bombs. It can go off in your face at any time, at any age.

Okay . . . you wanna know the *second* most embarrassing thing that ever happened to me? It happened in an outdoor café in downtown Toronto. My friend Jake and I were having a cup of coffee when up swished a mutual acquaintance with a 'Boys, boys, what luck finding you here . . . I've been trying to reach you all week to invite you out to the cottage next weekend for a planting bee. A few of us are getting together to put in the garden . . . of course there'll be a lunch.' I was proud of myself. I instantly snapped my fingers and moaned, 'Aw, wouldn't you know it Irene, next weekend we have to ahhh help a friend ahh re-shingle his roof ahhh in Wingham isn't that right Jake?' It was feeble but I was desperate . . . I'd been to Irene's little spring planting bees. She had about eight acres and she worked you like a Clydesdale from dawn to dusk. At dusk you got her heartfelt thanks and a paper plate containing two lettuce leaves, an apple and a fig.

It was feeble — but it would've worked. If only I hadn't tried to drive the point home by giving my friend a little jab in the shins under the table with my shoe as I said 'Isn't that right Jake?' I noticed that Irene wasn't listening to my cop-out attempt anymore. She was staring down at the table with a look of mingled horror and outrage. That's when I looked down at the table. And noticed that it had a glass top. And that was my shoe beating out a surreptitious tattoo on friend Jake's shin.

That's the second most blush-inducing thing that ever happened to me. I won't tell you the most embarrassing thing. I don't think anybody ever does.

As Mark Twain said, 'Man is the only animal that blushes. Or needs to.' And I don't think they even had glass-topped coffee tables in his day.

BRIDGE

W HAT does the word Arizona mean to you? Dry, right? Cactus? Sun-baked mesas and squatty little adobe buildings so white in the light of high noon you're forced to squint? Right. So how do you explain the fact that if you rent a car in Phoenix, Arizona, and start driving northwest, and providing your car doesn't boil over and the diamondback rattlers don't get you on your lunch break — providing you manage to drive 200 miles north and west of Phoenix — how do you explain the fact that you wind up in the shade of London Bridge?

Yes, *the* London Bridge. The one that first arched over the Thames, smack in the middle of London back in 1831, the last in a long line of London Bridges that had been taking Britons from one side of the Thames to the other, at or near that spot almost since the time of the Caesars? How do you explain that?

Well there really only is one explanation. A one-word explanation: Americans. What culture but the American one could produce somebody who could walk into an ancient, slightly stuffy city, where form and good manners are paramount. Walk in, shift the hand back to the hip pocket where the wallet is and say something like: 'Nice little bridge ya got there, how much ya want for it?'

Well actually a couple of cultures could spawn feisty folks capable of the grand, slightly crass gesture. Canada's had a couple of tycoon types who might try something like that. Max Aitken, Roy Thomson . . . Australia too. Australia's produced the odd money-heavy mover and shaker who might be grandiose enough to buy a bridge.

Ah . . . but only Americans would buy the bridge, then have it dismantled, shipped and re-erected in the middle of an Arizona desert.

And that's exactly what happened. The McCulloch Oil Corporation of California paid two and a half million dollars for the privilege of buying the London Bridge. Carefully pulled it down, shipped it rock by rock — all 10,000 tons of it — to Long Beach California, then hauled it by truck to Lake Havasu, Arizona.

Mind you a bridge ain't a proper bridge without some water gurglechuckin' under it, so the Lake Havasu city fathers figgered they might 's well cut a channel in from nearby Lake Havasu to run under the bridge. What with cutting the channel and slappin' the bridge up again, the tab went up another seven million dollars.

But there she stands today . . . the bridge that was first opened in 1831 by King William the Fourth; the bridge that Charles Dickens used as a setting in *Oliver Twist*. The bridge that German bombers and blitzes couldn't knock down in two world wars . . . now sits in the middle of Arizona. You can ride across it on — but of course! an English double decker bus. For tennis nuts there's the London Bridge Racquet Club only an easy lob away . . . and at the other end of the bridge . . . an entire English village in miniature . . . which would probably seem a lot more English if the temperature didn't hover quite so close to 100 and fewer of the village folk wore string ties and Stetsons.

Still it's there. And it works. A few years ago nothing stood where London Bridge now stands, save a few cacti . . . Now Lake Havasu City is there, with a population of 15,000. More to the point, some two million rubbernecking, flashcube-popping, dollar-spending tourists visit the place annually to have a look at, and a stroll on, the famous bridge.

Which is a nice way to end a tale. London Bridge after all was only sold because it was sinking irretrievably into the Thames River mud . . . it would have been lost altogether if it hadn't got a second chance in Arizona.

But the hoot of the whole story for me comes in thinking about what happens if somehow the historical records get lost . . . and some archeologist a couple of thousand years hence is faced with the task of rationalizing a 19th-century European bridge rearing its stately arches over the remains of a 20th-century North American tourist town — all in the middle of a desert.

Oughta take them a while to figure that one out.

GOLDFISH

I DON'T remember the first one I ever saw — they were pretty commonplace in those days — but I do remember the first ones I ever owned. Milton and Susan they were. Carried them all the way home on a rocking, rolling city bus while they sloshed back and forth in a cardboard container on my lap. My first investment. Fifteen cents I laid out. For a pair of goldfish.

I called them Milton and Susan because they reminded me of Milton and Susan Friedman who lived down the street. Milton and Susan — the human ones I mean — both wore glasses. But when they took the glasses off to clean them or rub their eyes, they looked a good deal like my goldfish looked all the time.

I'd like to tell you about the love affair that developed between Milton and Susan Goldfish and me. I'd enjoy explaining how I learned to respect smaller creatures and developed a sense of humanitarian responsibility from looking after my finny charges . . . but that would not be true.

The truth is . . . well . . . goldfish are not exactly *dynamic* pets. Once you assimilate the fact that they are more golden than your average fish, you've pretty well exhausted the creatures' charisma. They aren't bright. They won't swim through hoops or sit up and beg. About the most sophisticated trick they can master is to come to the surface when you spread fish food on the water. Houseflies could do that.

All that by way of excuse for the fact that it didn't take me too long to get disenchanted with Milton and Susan. Oh, the first few days it was me that cleaned out the fish bowl. I was the one who bought the tacky little china castle with the arch in it that they were supposed to swim through but never did. I fed them and cooed to them and did all I could to encourage them to make lots of little Miltons and Susans . . .

For about a week. After that I discovered many better things to do, and no amount of parental nagging or sisterly attempts at instilling guilt ('You bought them, and they're helpless, it's your responsibility to keep them healthy . . .') — nothing could make me take on the job of piscatorial nursemaid again.

A pity. I've been reading a bit about goldfish lately. If I'd known then what I know now, I might have respected them a bit more.

I found for instance that the goldfish is a relative of the carp — one of the cagiest and feistiest fish you'll find in Canadian waters. I discovered that the goldfish is a long way from home too. It's native to southern China where it was delighting little Chinese kiddies as a household pet 10 centuries ago.

The idea of keeping a goldfish on the mantel didn't really catch on in the Western world until the 1600s when goldfish began to show up in Britain. It wasn't till the 19th century that someone managed to carry a loaded goldfish bowl across the Atlantic and introduce *Carrasius auratus* to North America.

But I guess the worst thing about being a goldfish is that nobody really takes you seriously. Goldfish are the plough horses of the exotic tropical pet scene. People rave about kissing gouramis and Siamese fighting fish, angel fish, neon tetra — even the humble, homely guppy has more social clout than the goldfish. And why is that? Goldfish are twice as hardy, at least as comely as other tropical fish, and if allowed to grow to their full size — which can be over a foot — goldfish could make a whole platoon of Siamese fighting fish look like a bunch of draft dodgers with mononucleosis.

So why doesn't the goldfish get more respect?

Why, even the name is a patronizing dismissal. Goldfish aren't just gold — they can be red and yellow and white and black — or any combination thereof. They can have short fins or fins that flow and billow like chiffon scarves. And there are strains of goldfish with names as exotic as anything you'll find by a Caribbean reef — fantail, blackmoor, comet, lion head, celestial, shubunkin — names that can more than tread water with the humdrum likes of mollie, guppy and tetra.

Oh yes, I can talk glibly of the goldfish now. I can speak boldly of championing goldfish rights and fin power — now that it's too late for Milton and Susan.

My mother found them one morning, their little white bellies bobbing on the surface. Disease perhaps. Boredom very possibly.

I've long harboured suspicions about my younger brother and his penchant for testing potions whipped up in his junior scientist chemistry set, but I said nothing.

Milton and Susan were gone, and no amount of bickering or haggling would bring them back. I remember dimly that I consoled myself with the thought that somewhere up there Milton and Susan swam free of their little goldfish bowl and were happily speckling their celestial aquarium with thousands of little Miltons and Susans. I would have felt a good deal more consoled if I'd ever learned how to tell boy goldfish from girl goldfish. I was never entirely sure that Milton wasn't a Susan . . . or Susan a Milton.

FOX

YOU want adventure? I've got a real-life adventure for you. It could come right out of an episode of that old TV series, *The Fugitive*, with David Janssen . . . Or it could be cribbed from one of the more exciting chapters of *Uncle Tom's Cabin* . . . You have the man — the fugitive — gasping for air as he lurches and stumbles through the underbrush . . . staggering, reeling against branches, caroming down unseen hollows . . . and always the wide-eyed glance over the shoulder . . . towards that ominous, relentless baying of a pack of hounds on the scent. The quarry staggers through a stream to try to throw them off, scrambles up the far bank, slips, rolls, falls to his knees and slumps . . . It is too late . . . The lead hound has just charged into view. It's all over.

Right out of the movies. Except for two things. First, those movies seem to always take place in the swampy bayous of the deep American South . . . with gators lurking and Spanish moss streaming from the trees. This one's happening in the rolling domesticated green fields of England . . .

The second thing that's different is that in the B grade movies and second-rate novels . . . what happens next is that a stereotypical Deep South sheriff red of neck and swollen of paunch . . . with a little bitty stump of a cigar in his jowl and a double-barreled shotgun in the crook of his arm . . . Comes waddling down to the fugitive with an evil little grin that shows off his bad teeth, tips back a sweat-stained Stetson and says something like, 'Prewitt, Prewitt . . . I'll be danged if yew ain't jes the most headstrong ole con-vict I ever did see. Yew goan get whupped fer this boah . . .'

After which an interlude of stock violence involving boots, gun butts and near asphyxiation in swamp muck unfolds . . . well you've all seen the movies . . .

But that doesn't happen in my scenario . . . in the English variation I'm talking about, what happens is the pack of hounds rush up to the guy in the water, start licking him and frisking around in joyful abandon, and a gentleman in a red coat and jodhpurs gallops up, dismounts and says: 'Jolly good show, Prewitt, best hunt of the year. Your cheque will be in the post.'

It's the latest thing in the best circles of Britain: human hunting. Fox hunting minus the fox — and minus the grisly finale that usually accompanies what is called a 'good' fox hunt.

I suppose it had to happen. Too much of Britain has been paved and subdivided. Too many non-fox-hunting Britons have been outraged by the hunt for this centuries-old tradition of barely bridled barbarity called 'The Hunt' to survive.

Ten years ago the very suggestion of substituting bloodhounds for foxhounds and a jogger for the fox would have been sheerest heresy, but times change. In the last few seasons anti-blood sport groups have been doing their best to disrupt the hunts — everything from throwing themselves in front of horses, to playing tapes of baying hounds to lashing pepper on the trails. The substitution of runner for Reynard would seem to have left them without a mission.

And who's to complain? Certainly not the fox. And there's never been what you'd call a groundswell of public support for foxhunting. To most British the hunt has always been a bizarre fetish exclusive to one exceedingly eccentric segment of the upper classes. To the farmers whose crops were trampled, fences bowled over and livestock stampeded, the fox hunt was something between an inconvenience and an unnecessary catastrophe.

Oh I suppose there'd be a contingent of florid-faced bluebloods who would fulminate about the destruction of a tradition and the debasement of a noble sport . . . but they would have made the same snorting noises about bearbaiting and preschool chimney-sweeps a couple of generations ago.

As far as I'm concerned, Oscar Wilde said all there is to say about the fine tradition and venerable nature of the fox hunt.

'The unspeakable,' Wilde called it, 'in pursuit of the inedible.'

I'll drink a stirrup cup to that.

KITES

I WENT to somebody's house the other day and found my friend and his eldest son in the living room. They were not talking. They were not smiling. They were not looking at each other. They each held something in their right hand that looked like pocket weapons left over from *Star Wars* and they were watching TV. Well, they weren't exactly watching TV — not a program anyway. They were watching two phosphorescent dots float around on the TV screen. The dots would drift over to the sides of the screen and make a little 'blip' as they caromed back off in some random direction. It was a computer game and somebody was losing and someone was winning but I couldn't figure out who or how. Or, come to that ... why. For 10 minutes I listened to 'blip,' 'blip' 'blip' then I helped myself to a beer from the fridge, drank it and went back home. They didn't hear me leave. I'm pretty sure they didn't hear me arrive.

I think I could've been a burglar and stripped that house down to the broadloom and — as long as I didn't walk in front of the TV screen they'd still be there. Grim as fighter pilots, staring at the TV, going 'blip' 'blip' 'blip.'

Games sure have changed in my lifetime. Remember kites? That's what all kids used to be doing at this time of year. Flying kites. Or more likely preparing to fly kites — up to our ears in balsa wood strips and glue, yards of string and tissue paper — or the lightest, thinnest cloth we could manage to cajole our mothers out of.

Then it was out to the schoolyard or some broad flat meadow where we'd try to get our contraptions up in the air. To catch the brisk fall breezes and watch them soar and wink and dip at what was probably only a few hundred feet in the air but looked and felt like it was three miles high.

For such an essentially frivolous way to wile away a Saturday afternoon, kite flying has an extremely venerable past. The Chinese were flying kites three thousand years ago and there was nothing frivolous about kite flying then. Kites figured largely in Chinese religious ceremonies. They were also used for sending military signals.

In the 18th and 19th centuries, the use of kites was appropriated by serious-minded men of science in Great Britain, Western Europe and America. Ben Franklin, of course, with his famous, if somewhat damp, kite flying sortie in the middle of a thunderstorm to find out if natural electricity (in other words, lightning) was the same as man-made electricity. He discovered it was — to his shock. Other scientists in Scotland and England were using kites to carry thermometers aloft and to work out principles of aerodynamics that eventually led to the development of the airplane.

Along the way, the scientists established some pretty impressive records. You want to know the record height for kite flying? . . . 28,000 feet, accomplished by Professor Philip Kunz of the University of Wyoming back in 1967. And don't ask me who was holding on to the string.

The longest recorded flight for a kite is just over a week . . . 169 hours. That marathon was pulled off by a *team* of kite flyers in Fort Lauderdale three years ago.

And for all of us who remember too well that balky kite that just wouldn't get off the ground no matter how fast you ran with it . . . or even tugged it behind a bicycle — take heart. The heaviest kite that ever flew was built in Naruto, Japan, back in 1936.

It was made up of thirty-one hundred panes of paper and weighed in at nine and a half tons.

Ah, but statistics . . . that's not what kite flying is about. An instrument as simple and joyous and downright playful as the kite can never become the exclusive property of the scientists and the record busters. Kites are for fun. What else can you do for entertainment these days that gets you out of doors, doesn't cost a dime, won't strain your back, doesn't pollute the air or the eardrum, won't

burn a drop of petrochemicals and fills the eye and heart with delight?

Sure beats watching 'blip' 'blip' 'blip' on the TV screen.

Next time your kid comes home whining about how 'Johnny's daddy bought them a Digital Derby Pro Am Computer Game that plugs right into the TV . . .'

Tell him to go fly a kite.

ETIQUETTE

I THOUGHT I better get on the air to explain about that giant reverberating thump you heard a few days back. No, you didn't imagine it. We all heard it. What it was, was a footstep. A small step for man; a giant step for womankind. There's a brand new gaping breach in that long winding wall of indifference and misunderstanding that separates the sexes . . . and coming through that hole on our side, guys, are . . . flowers.

Yep. Flowers. Story in the *New York Times* says that florists are beginning to notice a strange and delightful new trend in their customer profile. *Women* are beginning to send flowers to *men*. A lot.

The florists are reporting that something like 20 percent of their business is now made up of orders from women, addressed to men. Women's Lib? Flower power? Nobody knows exactly why it's happening, and the florists are too busy punching up their cash registers to ask.

Well that's nice . . . but I don't think I'll bother clearing away any space on the mantel to make room for the influx of bouquets, sprays and wreaths for a while yet. Even if women turn out to be *twice* as thoughtful as me in the flower game — I still only figure to rate about one dog-eared clutch of half-dead daisies maybe once every seven years. I'm . . . not good . . . at sending flowers. For one thing I never remember birthdays, anniversaries or the like. Oh I dutifully record birthdays, wedding days and other anniversaries. I've got special genuine naugahyde-covered, alphabetically-indexed little anniversary books just for that. Dozens of them. Somewhere. I lose the books just a shade faster than I can buy them and fill them out. Which means I almost never have one.

Yeah, I'm not good about flowers. Come to think of it, I'm not exactly what you'd call subtly cosmopolitan at anything smacking of the social graces. I'm a walking *faux pas*. I'm the kind of guest who admires your new broadloom and forgets to take off his galoshes; who uses the wrong fork and mops his plate.

I'm good at drinking though. I remember practising for a big dinner once, in front of my mirror with a goblet. I'd seen this movie with Errol Flynn . . . and I was enchanted with the way he twirled his goblet.

I practised in front of that mirror for hours. Letting my fingers splay elegantly around the glass, rolling the wrist just so as I tossed off *bon mots* and one liners from the side of the mouth. I was very good. Came the dinner and time to take our seats. I was just finishing one of my better stories about my days as a cattle prodder in the Toronto Public Stock Yards. In the hush that followed the punchline, I suavely reached for my water glass, twirled it expertly with a look of calculated insouciance, then tossed it off in a gulp. Perfect. Didn't knock over the salt shaker; didn't dribble it down my tie. Errol Flynn would have applauded.

Although if Errol had done it, he probably would have drained the water glass, rather than the finger bowl. Small talk? Not good at that either, I'm afraid. I'm still trying to get it through my head that Pablo Casals is not a matador and the Group of Seven has never been an insurance syndicate.

Ah well . . . so I'll never be mistaken for Cary Grant. Still I *am* getting better. I didn't have to look up the date for Valentine's Day this year. I was only two days late on my mother's birthday — and the other day I even held a supermarket door open for a young woman struggling along with an armful of parcels.

Actually that last move — totally well-intentioned — was a bit of a gaffe.

The woman was light years ahead of me in etiquette . . . there I was, observing a quaint 19th-century notion of gentility. She was an expressive proponent of manners 1990s style.

She launched into a two-minute spontaneous denunciation of me. Over the peaks and ridges of her parcels, she told me I was sexist.

She called me a male chauvinist pig. Vocally she went up one side of me and down the other using phraseology that caused bubbles in my Old Spice and employing language that I haven't heard since I accidentally stepped on a sailor's toe in a Halifax bar.

Story of my life. I finally master one small shard of public behaviour, only to find out that it's gone out of style.

Still I wished she'd slowed down long enough to tell me her birthday.

I might have sent her some flowers.

SIESTAS

SOMEBODY once described a Canadian as 'someone who drinks Brazilian coffee from an English teacup and munches a French pastry while sitting on his Danish furniture, having just come home from an Italian movie in his German car. He picks up his Japanese pen and writes to his member of Parliament to complain about the American takeover of the Canadian publishing business.'

Yep, we're a great nation of carpers, not to mention borrowers . . . but while we were cruising about the far-flung flea markets and discount houses of the world . . . it really is a pity that we didn't pick up one bargain-basement buy . . . the siesta.

The siesta . . . what a thoroughly civilized idea. You know how it works? Actually, 'works' is the wrong word. Siestas are about *not* working. A three-hour break in the middle of the working day, when the hard, harried, jangling world of commerce and industry screeches to a halt and everyone . . . *relaxes*.

A delicious bite-size chunk of the best part of the day reserved for rest and recreation. No scurrying to banks or haring around the aisles of a supermarket either, because the people that make the banks and supermarkets work are taking a siesta too. Bank managers take siestas. Checkout girls take siestas. The siesta is nothing if not democractic.

And we don't have it. They have it in Spain. They have it in Italy. They have it in Portugal and parts of South and Central America.

But we don't have it here. And it's our loss. Think of what you could do with three uninterrupted quiet hours in the middle of the working day. Next time you're levering open your lunch box to get at those cold baloney sandwiches, or lining up beside that squalid little lunch wagon in the parking lot — the one that sells pressed cardboard sandwiches and plastic-wrapped honey buns and styrofoam cups of mud with cream and sugar . . . reflect for a moment that your counterpart in Spain or Italy . . . The Madrileño and the Venetian and the Roman worker . . . is sitting down at home to a sumptuous midday meal, with a glass of wine and bambinos gathered round . . . secure in the knowledge that work is three full hours away. Must be nice. Mind you it might not be nice much longer. Indications are that the fine old tradition of the siesta is under serious assault in Rome right now.

There are a number of prongs in the attack — rising gas prices and horrible traffic congestion make it more difficult and expensive to get from plant or office to home each midday . . . then too siesta-takers have noticed that their habit has an unavoidably inflationary effect on the waistline. Trade unions are clamouring for a shorter workday, and the easiest way to make it shorter would be to squeeze out that little three-hour vacuum in the middle of the workday sandwich. But most serious of all, it seems that Rome has caught a fairly severe case of the Anglo-Saxon disease.

That's the one you and I suffer from. Nine-to-five-ism. Efficiency. Productivity. All those horrible words that cost-effectiveness types keep throwing at us . . . words that should never have been applied to anything more animated than a Husquevarna chain saw or a Massey-Ferguson combine.

But I'm not worried. The siesta has been under siege for centuries. Ever since some peasant in the dim and distant past drew the obvious conclusion that only an idiot would work in the heat of midday, tilted his sombrero over his nose and went to sleep . . . there have been petty tyrants and would-be foremen nattering at him to wake up, shape up, roll up his sleeves and get on out there and win one for El Gipper. Newspaper editorials in Spain have railed against the siesta almost as long as they've railed against bullfights.

Successive Italian governments have promised that one of their first reforms would be abolition of the siesta. I have a theory that's why there've been so *many* successive Italian governments. People don't want their siesta messed with.

And rightly so. The siesta is a People's Movement in the purest sense of the word. Or non-movement I suppose.

Siestas are for us. For families. For lovers. For reading good books and eating fine meals. For good conversation. For a glass of wine. For looking at trees and for listening to birds.

Remember the line: 'A loaf of bread, a jug of wine and thou ...' You think that was written in the measly hour between blasts of factory whistle? Uh uh. That's siesta talk.

Remember too the lines: 'Mad dogs and Englishmen go out in the midday sun?'

So do Canadians. And more's the pity.

CRACKER JACKS

REMEMBER when you first discovered *funny*? I do. I don't remember how old I was — six, seven maybe ... Standing outside my favourite corner store with probably a seven-cent bottle of Pepsi and a five-cent Crispy Crunch in my hand. It was a true corner store ... at a crossroads ... one through-street intersecting with a gravel road that sported the familiar lollipop-style stop signs. That set the scene for the coming 'funny' ... Some car didn't bother to stop at the stop sign ... just oozed out onto the through-street. There was a screech of brakes and a blare of horn as an oncoming pickup veered and sideslid into a cumulo-nimbus of dust on the shoulder. The offending car hovered uncertainly half way across the road as the truck driver got out, furious. He stood with one leg hooked up on his running board and roared:

'Wheredja getcher driver's licence ... inna box o' Cracker Jacks?'

Boy, I howled at that. My first introduction to wit: savage and biting division. I bet I used that line a dozen times in the next few days. On kids that fell off their bikes: 'Hey wheredja getcher licence — inna box o' Cracker Jacks?' On my oldest sister when she dinged the garage door trying to park the car 'Wheredja getcher licence — inna box o' Cracker Jacks?'

I got a lot of mileage out of that dumb line.

I don't want to analyze it too much because it isn't that funny . . . but I guess the humour (such as it is) derives from the fact that in those days, a driver's licence was one of the few things you couldn't get in a box of Cracker Jacks.

Remember Cracker Jacks? Remember the crazy little doodads and trinkets you used to find in every box? Plastic put-together toys . . . tin whistles . . . key chains . . . charms for bracelets . . . rings and brooches . . . tiny yo-yos . . . little tops that would actually spin. Not to mention all that gooey popcorn gorp that were the Cracker Jacks proper. To tell you the truth, I never liked the Cracker Jacks much . . . but I loved the prizes. Me and millions of others apparently. I found out some details about good old Cracker Jacks recently. I found out that they've been putting trinkets and gewgaws in boxes of caramel-covered corn since long before I dug my chubby little fist into my first box at that corner store.

They've been doing it since the beginning of the First World War. Sixty-eight years ago the first Cracker Jack munchers found hand-painted metal and wooden toys — even porcelain miniatures. In an odd sort of way, what was happening outside of Cracker Jack boxes was often reflected in what you found inside them. In the 30s . . . Cracker Jacks became embroiled in a minor scandal. One of the Cracker Jack prizes was a miniature old sailor with a pipe. And a mustache. Thousands of outraged patriotic Cracker Jack consumers wrote to the company to complain that the sailor bore an uncanny resemblance to one Joseph Stalin. The sailor was hastily withdrawn.

And in the 40s with the world at war, Cracker Jack prizes took a distinctly militaristic turn. The magnifying glasses, the puzzles and the riddle books were replaced by miniature fighter pilots and thumbnail-size howitzers and tanks.

I found out something more about Cracker Jacks and Cracker Jack prizes that surprised me. They're still going strong.

The folks at Cracker Jack (now a division of Borden Inc.) are still popping prizes into Cracker Jack boxes, and Cracker Jacks are still selling like . . . well, Cracker Jacks.

Every year kids of all ages manage to snap up 400 million boxes of Cracker Jacks. And if you want to get some kind of visual idea of the volume involved there . . . that's enough to fill the entire Sears Tower in Chicago from basement to top floor with sticky popcorn.

Times have changed things of course. For one thing, the boxes are smaller and the price tag is bigger. And the prizes have changed too. Miniature pin ball games are buried in the popcorn these days. And instant tattoos. And stickers and denim patches . . . They're the latest in some 10,000 different registered and licensed official prizes that have found their way to the bottom of Cracker Jack boxes over the past seven decades.

Some people never grow up . . . they're still buying Cracker Jacks, still ripping the top off and stuffing their hand in deep to feel for the magic buried treasure. There's a man in Fontana California who has some six thousand Cracker Jack prizes. He keeps them in a safety deposit box.

Me . . . I don't buy Cracker Jacks anymore. Didn't even know they were still being sold. Still have that terrifically witty line on the tip of my tongue every time I get behind the wheel though . . . Just waiting for some other driver to cut me off, or turn without signalling or do something stupid enough to allow me to roll down my window and sneer majestically: 'Hey! Wheredja getcher licence . . . inna box of Cracker Jacks?'

Yeah . . . it's not great wit. But it's got a certain aura of nostalgia about it, okay?

Besides . . . you know what the very first Cracker Jack prize was . . . way back in the pre-World War, post-Boer War days of 1912?

It was a joke book.

Sample joke: 'Why don't the Boers wash themselves?' Answer: 'Because they are waiting for the British to give them a good licking.'

I'll bet that was a real howler in 1912.

SURVIVAL

Lᴇᴛ's talk about worries. Are you worried? Worried about earth-quakes, volcanoes, typhoons, monsoons, inflation, depression, urban riots, rural droughts, war and peace, gold and PCBs, high rises, low productivity, right-wing crazies, left-wing loonies . . . are you . . . worried?

Well, not to worry. Near as I can figure, mankind has always been worried . . . always been nervous about something. When we didn't have carcinogens in the bacon we had sabre-toothed tigers in the vestibule. Before air pollution indices we had black plague, inquisitions and operations without anaesthetic.

We've always worried about something. And someone's always profited from our concern. When wild animals were the major fear, somebody had the franchise on hickory clubs; when black plague was the problem, you can bet there was a whole platoon of agents running door to door, selling slivers of the cross, bones of the saints, prayers of the holy — something double-your-money-back guaranteed to stave off the horror to come and the terrors about to descend.

Which is what brings us to Survival Incorporated. Survival Inc. is a company that operates out of Carson, California. It looks sort of like a sporting goods store . . . but with a subtle difference. You won't find those silly looking hunter's hats or fluorescent vests here. No picnic hampers or bathing suits. The product line at Survival Inc. is not given to frivolity. It's serious. Deadly serious.

Instead you will find things like gas masks. Radiation suits. Cylinders for burying valuables underground and bomb-proof two-thousand-gallon storage tanks for water and fuel. At the front desk you can sign up for seminars on self defence, survival skills and farming and canning techniques.

Well, is Survival Inc. just another one of those nutty off-the-wall fly-by-night enterprises that we've come to expect from the fruit-cake state — California? Not exactly. Survival Inc. is a business. Big business. William Pier, the man who runs it, serves more than three thousand customers a month, most of them out of state. His monthly retail sales volume is half a million dollars and rising.

Customers? They come from all walks of life. Bankers, brokers, schoolteachers, truck drivers, secretaries and sales clerks. People who have finally peaked on a steady diet of nervous apprehension over urban riots, power failures, foreign threats and the rollercoastering economy, and decided to try to do something about it.

Survival Inc. customers have one other thing in common — money. They need it. Things don't go cheap at Survival Inc. A gun vault that will store a dozen firearms sells for 1,500 dollars. A radiation suit goes for 90 dollars. And if you suffer from a combination of extreme neurosis and an overweight wallet, you can carry away a year's supply of pre-packaged food for a mere 1,525 dollars. The company has no trouble moving its merchandise at such prices. No half-price sales at Survival Inc.

But what does it mean, this surge of Future Dread? Not too much I reckon. Humans have always been fairly prone to Future Dread. When a comet appeared streaking through the atmosphere in 1531, Medieval Europeans went mildly crazy. The end of the world, they told each other. God's wrath. The return of Lucifer. When a comet did the same thing in 1607 . . . the same reaction, and 75 years later, another comet visitation — another earthly outbreak of weeping, wailing and gnashing of teeth. One person who did not lose his head was the British physicist Edmund Halley. Halley thought he recognized some striking similarities between the accounts of the comets of 1531, 1607 and 1682. He was pretty sure it was the same comet. In fact he was so certain that he predicted the comet would reappear in 1778.

It did and it's been reappearing at roughly 75-year intervals ever since. Now that humanity knows that Halley's Comet is benign and predictable do they handle its appearance any better? Well . . . the last time it passed this way — back in 1910 . . . a half dozen The End Is Nigh cults were formed; some entrepreneur made a fortune selling special Comet Viewing Glasses and many people took the precaution of dousing themselves with a special and expensive Anti-Comet Elixir. Guaranteed to protect the consumer from the physiological ravages of comet watching.

Moral? Well I don't want to moralize. I will pass along a couple of tips though. The first tip is that Survival Inc. takes MasterCard — so it's not worried about the future.

And tip two: Don't worry so much about tomorrow. As somebody once said: 'I have seen the future and it is very much like the present — only longer.'

MANATEE

QUICK now . . . what's the ugliest creature on God's green earth you can think of? I guess some of the more common nominations for the Oscar Award for Odiousness might be the toad . . . the buzzard . . . the rather aptly named Gila monster perhaps . . . I suppose the tomato worm, the tarantula and the long defunct pterodactyl, which looked like a knobby flying leather satchel, might get a vote or two.

But ugliness is relative, isn't it? I mean I can't help speculating about the opinion your average iguana holds concerning you and me — large, clumsy, pink and hairless shuffling bipeds with vestigial teeth, pathetic claws and not a feather or a patch of decent fur to our name.

I think we humans judge shades of beauty on how far they're removed from Robert Redford or Bo Derek. Which is laughably presumptuous when you think about it.

In any case . . . all these maundering meanderings are by way of working myself up to comment on the plight of a creature, which — well he's not ugly . . . but you'd have to say he's one of the homeliest fellow tenants on the planet. His name: Manatee — and he's pretty hard to describe. If you took a large — say, one-ton bulbous bag of gray blubber, fixed a couple of rudimentary flippers port and starboard, added a large flat tail the size of a doormat at one end . . . Orphan Annie eyes, and grey whiskers over an apologetic looking grin at the other . . . then you'd have something resembling the manatee. The manatee isn't seen at all in these parts . . . you have to go 'way south to find them — West African rivers, the Amazon basin . . . and along the shores of the Caribbean.

The only ones you'll find in all of North America are in Florida. The manatee lives in warm waters, munching weeds and grasses, basking in the sun and minding his own business. He is totally and utterly gentle. Young manatee nuzzle each other and even humans. The manatee quite literally wouldn't hurt a fly. Unless he rolled on it.

The manatee lives, as I say, in warm waters. And sad to report, he dies there too. The victim of a technological absurdity. The manatee is being wiped out by outboard motorboats.

It's not a case of wanton vandalism. Nobody wants to kill a manatee — it'll cost you a thousand dollars and a year in jail if you're caught doing it — nobody wants to hit them with boats either. The problem is, they're hard to miss. One of the manatee's great pleasures in life is basking just below the surface of the water with only its nostrils showing. Florida has half a million outboard motorboats. Not hard to see the conflict.

The sad thing is, the manatee didn't need propeller pressure on its population. There are only about a thousand or so left in the whole state, and female manatee give birth only once every five years or so — and then usually only one calf at a time.

The population of Florida manatee is already below the critical level. The state is doing its level best to give the poor beast a boost. There are now enforced speed zones for boats in manatee populated areas, there is a state-wide toll-free hot line you can use to report any manatee in trouble. And the protection laws are so stiff that you can do time just for bothering a manatee, never mind abusing him.

The sad irony of the manatee's plight is, the *only* thing that's driving him to extinction is the boat propeller. The manatee has no natural enemies. Its food supplies are plentiful. Hunting manatee is forbidden.

Poor manatee. Poor sad dumb gentle unsuspecting unimposing manatee.

Contrary to the biblical homily, the meek are not always remembered in the will.

One more argument for canoe power.

SALOP

I DON'T know exactly what happened. I was out of the country at the time. All I know is, when I came back somebody had stolen three towns right out from under me. Yeah I was in Europe for a couple of years, and when I came back and drove down a stretch of the 401 I thought I knew, I came to a city I had never heard of. Cambridge, the sign said. Population such and such. Cambridge? What happened to Galt, and Hespeler? And Preston? Well, they had gone. Been amalgamated into the brand new city of Cambridge. Part of the local reorganization of Ontario. There was a lot of it going around at the time.

It happened all over the province. About the time Galt and Preston and Hespeler were being phased out like out-of-favour Russian commissars or urban Edsels . . . about the same time, the twin cities that I live in — Fort William and Port Arthur — were being renamed Thunder Bay North and Thunder Bay South.

And a couple of years earlier, in the same spirit of streamlining and improved efficiency, the towns of Cooksville, Clarkson and Malton were struck out of existence and replaced by an instant town called Mississauga. Population 105,000. Area 123 square miles and a total figment of some bureaucrat's imagination, for who ever heard of a town without a main street?

In the late 60s and early 70s there was a lot of that local government reorganization going on. Had to move with the times, they told us. Had to shake out the old systems and bring 'em into line with the electronic age.

Wasn't just happening in Ontario either. Same thing was going on in Britain apparently.

Take the case of Salop. You probably knew it better as Shropshire. Shropshire is a county that lies along the border of Wales. It's been called Shropshire for more than a thousand years, since before the Norman invasion, but suddenly a number of years ago, the British

112

Parliament announced that as part of the Local Government Reorganization Act, Shropshire would henceforth be referred to as Salop.

That might have been all there was to it too ... it there hadn't been a Colonel J. F. Kenyon, retired, around. Colonel Kenyon was a Shropshire lad, born and bred. One day he noticed that the old slate county marker that had peeped out of a hedgerow for all of his lifetime was gone — replaced, as he put it, 'by a hideous metal object protruding from the ground, reading "Salop."'

Colonel Kenyon immediately declared bloody, all-out take-no-prisoners war. He started petitions, he wrote long and furious letters to the editors. He besieged his member of Parliament. He button-holed everybody who could possibly have had anything to do with the name change and he asked them one thunderous blood-curdling question: 'Why?'

He found out an interesting thing with all his letters and telegrams and petitions and phone calls.

Nobody *knew* why.

Nobody could come up with any reasonable explanation for having changed an ages-old name without even asking the people the name belonged to.

One official said it might have been a mistake. Another guessed that perhaps Salop was easier to spell than Shropshire. An answer that did nothing for the Colonel's blood pressure.

The Colonel isn't the only one up in arms. Christopher Booker has been leading a campaign in the British magazine *The Spectator* to throw out the many iniquitous and arbitrary name changes wrought by the Local Government Reorganization Act. He condemns the whole sorry movement which has churned up countless traditions and landmarks as 'typical of the wholesale flight from reality that characterized the late 60s and early 70s.'

Hmmmmmm. Maybe that's what it was. Maybe it was a worldwide virus, like a flu bug that whipped bureaucrats into a frenzy of renaming and reclassifying.

Whatever it is ... it seems to have subsided. And left us with a few mementos ... like Mississauga and Cambridge on this side of the water. And Salop over in Britain.

That may be temporary though. The people in uhhh ... Salop don't think all that highly of their new name. The editor of the

Shropshire (not Salop) *Star* took a poll recently . . . Asked his readers which name they preferred. Results: Those in favour of Shropshire, 1,138. Those who liked Salop, 30.

Another interesting sidelight. Salop *is* an old name within Shropshire. It's the slang name for one of the towns within the county and it appears in the title of the county council. As near as anyone can figure out Salop is the name Normans bestowed on the place back in 1066 because they found Shropshire too hard to pronounce.

What chance do a handful of bureaucrats have of making the name stick when an entire invasion and conquest of Normans couldn't do it?

And the Normans didn't have a Colonel Kenyon to deal with either.

DAYDREAMING

I GUESS one of the lines I'll never get used to is: 'Not feeling too good today — the old war wound's acting up.' I don't have any old war wounds, and I probably won't get any. I'm too old to be called up . . . and I don't have any from World War Two for the very good reason that I wasn't around when World War Two was. I was too young for Korea and fortunate enough to be living in a country that didn't have a dance card when Vietnam broke out. So I never get to complain about my war wounds. I do have battle scars of a sort though . . . a searing throbbing pain that flashes across the knuckles of my right, sometimes left hand, every so often — usually completely without warning. Sometimes I even imagine I can still see the cruel white line that used to run across those knuckles — shortly to turn an angry flaming red — every time Miss Huff laid into me.

Miss Huff was in charge of Grade Three, and I mean In Charge. She was a bony angular unsmiling six feet of austerity, complete with regulation Board of Education bun at the back of her head. And she was death on daydreaming.

What she would do, Miss Huff, when she detected that glassy stare and slack-jawed look of the student who had strayed into the realm of mental adventure — what she would do when her eyes lit on one such miscreant, is smoothly begin to angle toward her desk, never ceasing her chainsaw monotone. At her desk, one crab-like hand would slide out and noiselessly palm the yardstick from her desktop. Then, her voice still droning on, she would edge to within striking distance of the aforementioned woolgatherer and then, suddenly, in mid sentence — *Ahhhhhh Sah*! A vicious arcing overhead broadsword chop. Right on the knuckles. It was an avalanche of emotion for the culprit . . . the humiliation of being the centre of attention; the confusion from being yanked out of a world of fanciful illusion to the harsh reality of the classroom . . . but most of all the pain of that ruler swat right cross the knuckles.

I was thinking of Miss Huff and her samurai-style sorties the other day, while I was looking at a book called *Mind Play*. It's a study of daydreaming . . . and among the other conclusions it comes up with that I would like to track Miss Huff down for and wave in front of her bleak face . . . is the conclusion that daydreaming is good for you. Yes. More than that — essential to good health. A short list of the things that daydreams do for us includes: solving current problems, preparing for future events, warding off tension, relieving boredom (that's you Miss Huff), dissipating anger and pulling us out of depression (you again Miss Huff).

We all daydream. According to this book 30 to 40 percent of our waking moments are spent on the pastime. Most of the daydreams are just flashes — 5 to 14 seconds long. A daydream that lasts for two minutes is considered a long one.

Many athletes use daydreams to psych themselves up for better performances. Musicians too have discovered that dreaming a perfect performance of Beethoven's Concerto Number 5 in E-Flat Major, Opus 73 can actually lead to a superior rendition of Beethoven's Concerto Number 5 in E-Flat Major, Opus 73.

And artists? It doesn't take a lot of imagination to figure out the importance of daydreaming to sculptors, painters and potters . . .

As for science . . . it was daydreaming in the tub that gave Archimedes the clue to his great principle. It was woolgathering under an apple tree that led Newton to muse on the McIntosh that conked him . . . and come up with the law of gravitation.

Of course I didn't have any scientific data to fall back on back in

Grade Three, when Miss Huff was gliding down on me with malice aforethought. I thought I was just having a good time dreaming about open meadows and pirate ships, cowboys galloping through the draw, facing down a seedy dishevelled looking gunman on the dusty main street of a sleepy western town at high noon . . . or else maybe just . . . Owwww!

Have to go now. My old war wound's acting up.

ARCH

I KNOW too much today. I know way too much. I've only been out of bed a few hours and already I know about civil strife in Brazil, industrial problems in Great Britain, crop disasters in the American southwest and what the NDP Energy critic thinks of the government's latest oil price arrangement. I also know what the weather's going to be today in the northern White River and Geraldton area, the Kenora Whiteshell and Lake of the Woods area and the Rainy Lake-Sioux Lookout-Atikokan area. I can't remember the forecast for where I live. I know too much. I know the price of gold in Brussels this morning. I also know who won what last night in the NBA, the CFL, the PGA, the NASL and the local Lob Ball League.

I don't need all this information. But I get it, every day. We all do. Throw away the newspaper and there's the great one-eyed monster in the corner of the living room, spewing out videotaped reams of film clips and commentary.

Pitch an ashtray through the TV screen and after the tinkles and pops of exploding circuitry have subsided, you hear the radio chattering in the background, talking of triumph and heartbreak at the 40th Annual All-Invitational Peachtree Roadrace.

Of course, I should talk. I am. Here on the page. And I'm here to bring you some more news you don't need. Just when you thought you could relax and bleed off a little information overload. Just when you thought you might not have to digest something new and strange and vaguely threatening for a few minutes. Forget it, slackers. You know what scientists have been doing while your back was turned? Invented a whole new science is what. Yes. And a science with the tongue-torturing title of archeoastronomy.

Actually, it's not a new science — it's an investigation of an old one — an ancient one in fact. Astronomy. Scientists are just beginning to appreciate how sophisticated many long-dead cultures were regarding the study of the stars. Twelve hundred years ago — about the time Vikings were pillaging the north of France, scientist-priests of the Maya Indians were charting the motions of the planet Venus and unerringly predicting eclipses.

More than five centuries before Columbus made his famous voyage, a whole host of cultures around the world were routinely making celestial observations of the most complex kind. Incas, Polynesian Islanders, several North and South American Indian tribes and ancient long-dead European peoples were charting the heavens, plotting the stars, figuring out complex relationships of planets in a way that modern man never got around to until long after the invention of the telescope. Indeed there are some who believe that prehistoric astronomers unlocked heavenly riddles we still have to crack. They certainly left a number of earthbound structural riddles behind to befuddle and bemuse us. There is little doubt that the great pyramids of Egypt were used as astronomical observatories. There's no reason to suppose that the pyramids of South America and Mexico weren't put to the same use. Scientists have only recently confirmed that the great slabs and monoliths at Stonehenge in England were actually rigidly engineered to reflect changes in seasons, phases of the moon, even planting and harvest times and animal migrations.

Such things of course were much more important to our prehistoric ancestors than they would seem to be in a 20th-century world of pavement, moonshots and telecommunications.

But it's funny that we've always taken for granted the fundamental brutishness of prehistoric cultures. We dismiss them as savage. Take it for granted that the people led nasty, unenlightened subsistence lives of scrambling in the dirt and chasing down supper. We never think of them as . . . well, thinking. Pondering the universe. Gazing off toward Venus and speculating about its travels across space.

Archaeoastronomy should change all that. This fledgling science has already taught us what a mistake it is to date astronomy from the invention of the telescope back in 1608.

Maybe it will teach us more. Maybe archeoastronomy will teach us to have real respect for people and cultures we dismiss as primitive because they don't drive Ranch Wagons, watch Johnny Carson or sizzle steaks on a backyard hibachi.

If so archeoastronomy will be a good thing to know. And a lot more useful to know than the morning price for gold in Brussels.

WEATHER

THOUSANDS of years ago, the ancients used to have a charming routine for dealing with bad news. Especially bad military news such as a defeat in battle. What they would do to the poor soul who'd just come puffing up the path panting out the news that General Phillipidiestra or whoever had just blown the game plan and lost half his army . . . what they would do to this poor jogger who'd run like the Pony Express all the way from the scene of the battle, whose only sin was that he carried bad news . . . what they would do is blame him — the messenger — for the setback. And put him to death. On the spot.

Well that was thousands of years ago of course, deep in humanity's barbaric past. We've come a long way since then. Nowadays we just *fantasize* about snuffing out the bearers of bad tidings. Particularly when they're weathermen.

Come on now . . . own up. Have there not been Saturday afternoons when you've fired up the barbecue in the backyard, plopped the steaks on the grill, secure with the promise of last night's TV forecast that today would be sunny, hot and dry . . . and then heard a hiss . . . then a plop . . . then another hiss . . . and felt raindrops the size of half dollars begin to pound your fluffy chef's hat flat to your skull . . . And did you not then (for just the briefest moment) indulge yourself with lewd and murderous imaginings of turning a 10-pound roast brisket of meteorologist on that selfsame spit?

Of course you have. We all have. When unexpected rotten weather hits, we still murder the messenger — if only mentally.

Poor weathermen. The job must rank right up there with dentistry and bill collecting as one of the most thankless jobs of the 20th century.

Think about it. Imagine the tension in a job where you have to measure, extract and collate so many unknowns . . . barometric pressure, cloud formations, satellite photos, warm air masses over Flin Flon, troughs moving in from South Dakota, reams of wire, copy data, scan dials, meters and decipher charts and maps, mull it over with your colleagues . . .

You have to make sense out of all that . . . and *still* know that you'll be reviled and cursed by the community if you don't deliver three straight days of tropical perfection for the coming holiday weekend.

Yeah, we don't think much about the weatherman as a fellow human . . . and it can't go on much longer. It's, well, inhuman to expect any group of professionals, however dedicated, to go on doing their job when the only reward they get is widespread abuse for every weather system that interferes with a picnic, a rock concert or a ski tour. Sooner or later meteorologists are going to crack.

As a matter of fact there have already been occasional hairline fractures. What you are about to read is an actual wire copy transmission that went across the wire service of North America a few years back. It came from the U.S. Weather Bureau in Los Angeles and it was fairly routine stuff for the first couple of lines — the usual recital about a persistent cold front moving in on the California coast. But then suddenly the telex machine chattered out the following: 'Thursday evening, storms produced a massive orgy in southwestern Georgia and northwestern Ohio. Elsewhere around the nation, active Americans were indulging in almost every kind of normal activity except for some reports of S and M in California and western Oregon with some heavy whips and chains at higher elevations . . .'

Well the report goes on, but I can't — not in a family book.

After a few more lines that you'll never hear Knowlton Nash read, the report subsided into conventional accounts of temperatures and conditions . . . and the machine stopped. All was silent. Then after a discreet few seconds, it tapped out the following message:

'Please disregard the above weather summary as it is not . . . current.'

It was a little late for that of course — newspapers, radio and TV stations across the continent had received the story hot off the wire. Reporters deluged the L.A. Office of the U.S. Weather Bureau. The Bureau eventually issued a statement that the report was the work of an employee who was 'experimenting' with a new computerized system and accidentally sent his doodling onto the wire.

Well they can try to float that one if they like, but I'm not buying it. Sounds more to me like the work of a browbeaten, terminally hassled, battered-down and fed up weather forecaster who'd had it to here with civilian abuse and who wasn't gonna take it anymore.

I admire his courage and I'm sure he got the silent backing of 10,000 ghosts of murdered messengers past, but I can't say I'm very optimistic about his future with the U.S. Weather Bureau.

I have to suspect that the forecast for our mad meteorologist in Los Angeles read 'cloudy, with widely scattered pink slips.'

ABACUS

I DON'T know how you feel about arithmetic, but I know how I feel. 'Uncharitable' would cover it. Which is not entirely unrelated to the fact that I'm completely useless at it. Born out of my time, that's what I am. I belong back in the age when multiplication meant how many kids you had; division was an obscure military term and square root was something you occasionally saw on a radish. I should have lived in times when people couldn't count past 10 without taking off their sandals — as a succession of armflailing eye-rolling geometry, algebra and trigonometry teachers in my past would be only too willing to testify.

I'm rotten at arithmetic — and I live in the wrong age for that. I see little kids blithely unravelling insanely complicated numerical problems using something called the New Math. The New Math. I didn't have a prayer with the old math.

I've looked at the New Math. I've also looked at a telephone directory printed in Arabic. I had better luck with the phone book.

And as if throngs of knee-high, cherubic masters of the New Math calculating circles around me wasn't humiliation enough . . . the little beggars use *pocket* calculators too. Their pudgy little fingers flying over the buttons and knobs in a blur as they routinely work out the Gross National Product of Somaliland or the fuel-to-air ratio for A.J. Foyts Indy 500 Road Racer.

I bought a pocket calculator, back when they were just becoming faddish. Thought I should be in on the leading edge of a trend. Figured its magical powers might just be the ticket to lift me out of the depths of my mathematical illiteracy.

Took me 15 minutes to figure out how to turn it on.

I'd give up hope completely if it wasn't for a story I saw in the paper the other day. It's about a product that's making a big comeback in Japan. You know Japan — silicon chip capital of the planet? World nerve centre of transistor technology, computer components and other murky matters of electronics? Well you'll never guess what's making it big in Japan right now. The abacus. Yes.

That primitive, rudimentary calculating device that Japanese shopkeepers have used since the 15th century; that you find in shops in South America, in Africa, the Middle East . . . The device the Chinese have been using to work out sums for eight thousand years. The abacus.

The thing about the abacus is it's childishly simple. Just a little wooden frame with rows of beads that slide on rods. There are variations, but the Japanese abacus has two sections to each rod — four beads on the bottom section, one bead on the top. All mathematical problems are solved by breaking numerals into units of five. Is it fast enough? Ha ha. In the hands of an expert it is. Each year in Japan they have competitions. An abacus expert takes on all contenders with electronic calculators. The abacus-user has never lost.

Which maybe helps to explain why traditional craftsmen — abacus makers — in a small western Japanese city called Ono, suddenly find themselves sitting on top of a 10-million-dollar-a-year industry — turning out abacuses for an abacus-hungry world. Yes, world. A full 10 percent of their production goes overseas. Brazil buys them by the carload, South Korea is a big customer . . . but more than half the total exports end up in the United States and Canada.

Yep. If you enroll at the University of California or the University of Hawaii, you can now take a course in the abacus. Several other American states have incorporated abacus calculation into their elementary school curriculums.

The abacus is definitely making a comeback . . . the only thing nobody's yet got around to explaining is — why?

I can think of a couple of reasons: the abacus is made of *real* components — actual wood and glass beads — not high impact polystyrene . . . which means the abacus feels authentic. Then too, the abacus is guaranteed not to click, whirr, hum or fall flat on its elegant face during power failures, brownouts, or pooped out batteries.

But most of all the abacus is simple . . . the only moving parts are the beads . . . and they work on gravity.

The abacus is so simple that I think even I could master it.

Mind you . . . I wouldn't count on it.

FORGE

I WANT to introduce you to a nice man. Real gentleman. An artist. Elmyr de Hory his name is. Hungarian-born and extremely successful as a painter. De Hory paintings hang in some of the finest homes of serious art collectors around the world. Some of those paintings were bought for hundreds of thousands of dollars apiece. Mind you the painter, Mister de Hory, didn't get those hundreds of thousands of dollars. And the art collectors who paid it are for the most part blissfully unaware that they have de Horys hanging on their walls. They think they have original Cézannes and Matisses and Renoirs and Picassos. They don't. They have fakes. Because aside from being a gentleman and a consummate artist . . . Elmyr de Hory was one other thing. He was a fraud. A forger. He specialized in the Old Masters. Until a few years ago Elmyr de Hory lived on the Mediterranean island of Ibiza. He had to. He was dodging extradition orders from France.

The French government very much wanted to treat Mister de Hory to an all-expenses-paid trip to Paris to answer charges of falsification and fraud. Mister de Hory preferred the sunny climate and easy pace of Ibiza.

Mind you there was a time when Mister de Hory could have been the toast of Paris — or any other city big enough to boast an unscrupulous art dealer or two. Shady art dealers loved Elmyr de Hory. Because for a few hundred dollars and a couple of hours at the easel, Mister de Hory could crank out a Monet or a Degas that would bamboozle the most critical eye — and which the art dealer could then turn around and sell for many thousands of dollars.

He worked cheap and he worked fast. De Hory in an uncharacteristic fit of bragging once said that he could turn out a Matisse in the time it took to smoke a cigarette.

Sadly, that's *all* de Hory could do — imitate. There are dozens of de Hory paintings around the world. Paintings that critics swear were done by this or that master. But de Hory was only a master forger. A master of the styles of the masters . . . but there is no de Hory style. He became so good at copying that he lost the original.

In any case, the bubble burst about 15 years ago, when somebody blew the whistle on the de Hory industry.

Collectors started checking the backs of their original Gauguins and van Goghs and Manets and discovered that the canvas was too new and the paint too fresh. And they knew they'd been had.

That brought the kind of fame no artist needs — notoriety. And de Hory retired to his small cottage in Ibiza to weather the storm of protest and outrage and to shadow box with the blizzard of summonses and extradition orders that began to descend upon him.

Elmyr de Hory died in Ibiza a few years ago. Under mysterious circumstances. The cause of death is listed as suicide, but friends suspect murder. De Hory had long hinted that an art world mafia was after him . . . and was the real force behind the extradition orders.

Ironically, de Hory was on the verge of real fame at the time. A Spanish art gallery had just hired him to turn out Impressionist paintings in his own name for a large annual fee.

In his own name. That was one of the classy things about de Hory. For all the Cézannes and Renoirs he turned out, he never truly *forged* them — he never signed a painting with another artist's name. The people who bought them were too greedy to own an original master to wonder about this obvious mystery. They just assumed the artist forgot. Besides. The paintings were so perfect they simply had to be originals.

He fooled the best of them, Elmyr de Hory. And to tell the truth he did sort of take part in a forgery once. In the 50s he met Pablo Picasso, superstar of the art world, at a reception. De Hory had a Picasso nude with him and asked the master if he would sign it. Picasso took the painting, held it at arm's length and broke into a lusty reflective smile. 'Ah yes. I remember painting her. Mind you it didn't take me long. Only an afternoon. I had to hurry, because I couldn't resist making love to her.'

De Hory got his signature. Plus an unmistakable glow of satisfaction. It had only taken de Hory two hours to finish the painting the day before.

GEORGE

I WANT to tell you about the weirdest pet in northwestern Ontario. That's no small chore ... because this part of the province is pretty well wall-to-wall with weird pets. Drive through Kenora and you'll be accosted with a statue of a monstrous leaping muskellunge. That's Huskie the Muskie, patron saint of fantasizing fishermen everywhere.

At the other end of northwestern Ontario down near Wawa, tourists have been known to drive off the road babbling about a vision of a gigantic steel goose. It's not white line fever. There really is a stainless steel goose outside Wawa. Wawa is the Ojibway word for goose, so what did you expect?

Here in Thunder Bay the pet fetish rages unabated. The 1981 Canada Summer Games were presided over by a felt-covered Flintstonish cuddly confection of a mascot with a big nose and bigger antlers.

His name is — wait for it, now — Chocolate Mousse.

Weird indigenous creatures all — and there are others. Consider the black fly. Tiny enough to sneak through a pinhole in a safari jacket. Big enough to leave you with lumps and welts that look like the aftermath of 10 rounds with Sugar Ray Leonard.

Yes, unusual animals are nothing — well, *unusual*, here in north-western Ontario . . . but they're all pale compared to George of Kenora. Now that makes him sound like a hairdresser; George is nothing of the sort. As a matter of fact George is quite hairless. He is also five feet long with short stumpy legs and a long spiky tail. And teeth? George makes the Osmond family look like refugees from a Polident commercial. George of Kenora has two gleaming rows of wraparound teeth that stretch all the way from here to there. Most alligators do. And George of Kenora is an alligator.

Now you probably don't have to be told that George is not a native Kenora-ite. He's a transplant. A pet in fact that Thelma Harris bought for her son some 13 years ago. George was not quite 12 inches long then . . . and cute as a button. He is now 62 inches long . . . and when George swivels that tooth-studded, scaly head around to check you out . . . the expression 'cute as a button' does not leap to mind.

As a matter of fact, some visitors never get by that first deadpan, Clint Eastwood stare from George. A man who came to install Mrs. Harris a carpet took one look at George basking on the chesterfield and backpedalled all the way out to his truck in the driveway. The carpet company sent around someone else to do the job . . . but they had to ask a few before they found a carpet layer who didn't mind being watched by an alligator while he worked.

George doesn't mind northwestern Ontario winters because he doesn't see much of them. Most alligators hibernate for the winter, like bears. George just takes December, January, February and March a little easier than usual . . . dozing in the warm water of his six-foot aquarium or curled up on top of the hot air register.

If George finds our weather a bit uncivilized, he's far too much of a gentleman to let on. In fact he seems to be quite happy. And why not? He's got his own private swimming pool plus a whole family of human servants who serve him up his favourite meal of raw stewing beef garnished with fresh crayfish in season.

Sure the winters are long, and the flies are tough in the summer,

and it's rather a yawn watching these northeners whoop and gasp and bulge their eyes out at their first sight of an alligator.

But it sure beats George's other options. Being a weird pet in Kenora sure beats being a pair of shoes in Schenectady. Or a handbag in Honolulu.

SPARROWS

Don't get me wrong. I love birds. I think they're charming and decorative and beautiful and melodious and an integral part of our environmental matrix and all that stuff. I believe life without birds would be a cheerless, gray-on-gray experience not worth living. I adore the little critters — from peregrines to parakeets, from pelicans to penguins, from yellow-bellied sapsuckers to rose-breasted grosbeaks — mad about them I tell you.

But to tell you the truth . . . I'm not crazy about sparrows.

Oh they're cute, and they're tiny and sort of melodious if you go for a steady musical diet of chirrup chirrup chirrup . . . But it's not their looks or their repertoire or their size that troubles me.

It's their personality.

Sparrows are rude. They're pushy. They're grabby. They're noisy and they're quarrelsome and pretty well altogether without class.

Ever watched a group of sparrows descend on a bird feeder? It's like watching the Mongol hordes under Attila the Hun. Or Benny and the Jets trash a restaurant. One minute you've got elegant cardinals and charming little chickadees peck-pecking away at the sunflower seeds and caraway balls. The next moment — the sack of Rome, as hordes of boiling, boisterous, swarming, swearing sparrows shoulder their way in like a pack of Hell's Angels at a Strawberry social.

I've heard them referred to as English sparrows or house sparrows. What a joke. There's nothing remotely British *or* domestic about them. The English are renowned for their reserve, good manners and sense of decorum. The sparrow? Don't make me laugh. And as for 'house.' Sparrows don't need houses. They'll nest in a pigeon coop, a chicken shack, a mail box, an abandoned dog house . . . A glove compartment if you leave it open too long.

And they take over. Wherever they are, they take over. Your backyard. My backyard. Schoolyard. Farmyard. One sparrow finds it and phhhhhht! There goes the neighbourhood. They take over birdhouses. Fences. Scarecrows. Anything. They're the original squatters. The spoilers of the bird world. Bluebirds, house wrens, tree swallows, chickadees, nuthatches, woodpeckers, purple martins . . . as soon as they see a sparrow in their midst they're already packing their bags.

They might as well. The sparrow, if he is to be admired for anything . . . can be held in awe for his relentless ability to take over and ultimately kick out just about any other native bird species we have.

And the ironic thing is, the sparrow isn't native. He's a transplant, introduced to North America back in the middle of the last century by European immigrants homesick for the sound — any sound — of the life they left behind.

Well, the sparrow doesn't need a lot of encouragement. Give him some new turf . . . some effete feathered neighbours to bully around and pretty soon he's established. Never to be removed.

There's a man by the name of Don Grussing, down in Minnesota, who's been carrying on a war against sparrows for three decades. For 30 years, Grussing has been trying to attract native North American bird species to feed and live around his home. For 30 years he's been foiled. By sparrows. Sparrows that take over his purple martin houses. Sparrows that bully their way to the front of his bird feeders. Sparrows that in the last resort have been known to kill both the adults and the young of other birds.

Mind you, he's had a measure of revenge on the birds he calls 'feathered thugs.' Don Grussing's written a book. A book called: How to Control House Sparrows.

For what it's worth. Because after 256 pages, Grussing's conclusion is: 'The battle [against sparrows] cannot be won. There is no way, at least at present, to eliminate the bird from the North American continent.'

Harsh words . . . elimination of a species.

Scary too . . . I keep thinking of the words of another American —

one Benjamin Franklin. In 1784, in the wake of America's decision to go with the bald eagle as the emblem of America, Franklin wrote:

'I wish the bald eagle had not been chosen as the representative of our country; he is a bird of bad moral character; like those among men who live by sharping and robbing, he is generally poor . . . and often lousy.'

Franklin would have done well to stop writing there. Unfortunately he didn't. He went on to write: 'A much more respectable bird, and withal a true original native of America is . . . the turkey.'

Can you imagine the turkey as anybody's national emblem?

That's what worries me about my dark thoughts about the sparrow. Maybe I'm wrong. Maybe Don Grussing's wrong. Maybe the sparrow's a noble little piece of life that deserves his place in the sun along with the pheasant, the cockatoo and the peacock.

But somehow . . . as I watch a gang of sparrows trash a trio of self-respecting evening grosbeaks in my bird feeder . . . somehow I doubt it.

LIMEY

I LIKE the British. Not everybody does. Or has. They've been dismissed as a nation of shopkeepers. The French for centuries have regaled themselves with droll stories about British rigidity and stuffiness. Americans with their renowned friendly puppy approach: 'Hi how are ya, I'm Bill Smith from Tulsa, I'm in copper tubing' . . . Americans have been alternately baffled and charmed by British standoffishness.

And Canadians? I think we're just spooked by the British. It's 125 years since we formally snipped the apron strings . . . and we're still dithering over whether or not the time is right to demand our official certificate of independence — to repatriate the constitution.

Yes, we all have attitudes about the British . . . and interestingly enough, it's also 125 years since one of the most prevailing attitudes toward them was formally codified by a British Act of Parliament.

In 1867, about the time Sir John A. et al were waiting for the ink to dry on the Confederation Bill, their colleagues in Westminster were passing The Merchant Shipping Act . . . one of the provisions of which made obligatory the supply of lime juice to all sailors, to prevent scurvy.

The rest of the world's tars looked on this as yet another example of British eccentricity . . . and dubbed Englishmen (forever more) 'lime-juicers' or 'limeys.'

And the name has stuck. An Englishman today — be he a bowler-hatted banker tapping his way down Threadneedle Street, or a wisecracking cockney in a leather apron . . . a bluff Yorkshireman with a complexion like red bricks or a Somerset farmer given to 'ooo arrrs' and other Long John Silverish expressions — no matter where he hails from he is, once he leaves the shores of Blighty, a limey.

Considering the epithets that are applied to other nations and races, 'limey' is rather gentle — gentlemanly even. But there was nothing gentle about those first shipments of lime juice on British ships. There was only one way known at the time of preserving fresh lime juice for long voyages — alcohol. Rum of course.

Needless to say, those pioneering British sailors lined up for the 'scurvy shots' with a certain amount of uncustomary British enthusiasm. The officers however noticed that their work suffered somewhat. The splices on the mainbrace were not all they could be, and there was an unwonted amount of giggling around the poop deck. Then another British invention came to the rescue. A Londoner by the name of Laughlan Rose came up with a system of preserving lime juice by means of a sulphur method, eliminating alcohol. For the British sailors, a bit of a letdown, but for the world . . . the birth of the first 'soft' drink. The wag who came up with the term limey must not have been paying attention, because nobody ever suggested rechristening limeys as 'softies.'

In any case, I see that in a recent yacht race to Australia, the British clipper the *Great Britain II* formally celebrated the origins of limey-dom by taking aboard huge quantities of lime juice for the excursion. Foreign competitors in the race were also offered complimentary kegs of the juice, accompanied by the promise that they could be honourary limeys for the duration of the voyage. The foreign competitors declined ... so only the crew of the *Great Britain II* got to observe the fine old tradition.

Only on the *Great Britain II* you say ... Pity.

ELM

I REMEMBER when I first fell in love with them. It was the first time I drove into Beeton ... a little country town about, oh, I guess 40-odd miles north and west of Toronto. This would be back in the late 50s and there was a dusty gravel road that took you into Beeton. It was one of those hot, hot summer days when the cattle stand stock still with their heads down and the fields kind of shimmer and you soon learn to keep your bare arm off the metal window frames of the car. We were driving along and the sun was beating down and the dust was rolling out behind like great brown clouds of cumulus. It was hot. Conversation was mostly sighs and dreams were of ice cold sweating bottles of Coke and ginger ale. Suddenly there they were in front of us. Lined up like elegant soldiers on either side of the road as far as the eye could see ... their great fernlike arms stretched out and over the road. Interlaced above to form a huge dark green cave.

Elm trees. For about a half a mile outside of Beeton this ... bower of elm trees — 50-, 60-, 80-footers — formed a leafy tunnel that was a good 15 degrees cooler inside than out, and as welcome as an oasis in the middle of the Kalahari.

Ah, the elms. There was a time when the elm was the most common piece of natural architecture in much of North America. Nearly every main street of nearly every town seemed to have elm trees fanning out above it. Farmers usually left at least one towering elm in any land they cleared for pasture. The shade of the elm gave the cattle and horses a place to doze away the steamy August afternoons.

There was a time before *that* when huge elm forests covered much of the eastern U.S. and Canada.

All that's changed now. It started to change 50 years ago with a single load of logs unloaded at New York. The logs were from Europe. Why New York was buying logs from Europe is a puzzler. The tragedy was that somewhere in that load of logs, lodged under the bark of one of the trees, was a tiny, unnoticed fungus. Plant pathologists call that fungus *Ceratocystis ulmi*. We have all learned to know it by a simpler more chilling name: Dutch elm disease.

It's a sad story, what Dutch elm disease has done to the face of North America. Plant pathologists in Holland first unmasked the malady back in 1919, but nothing anyone's been able to come up with in subsequent years has had much success in stopping it. There are treatments you can give an elm that has caught the blight. But the treatments are complicated, expensive and extremely iffy. The experts still advise that once your elm's leaves begin to curl and yellow . . . once the tree's crown begins to thin and brown streaks appear under the bark . . . the best thing you can do is chop it down to save other elms from its grisly fate.

Biologists are mounting other attacks. In Montana they've discovered a bacteria that attacks and destroys the killer fungus . . . they've had limited success with that. Other experts are trying to replace the famous elm with other hybrids that are resistant to Dutch elm disease. But they don't look like the glorious elm of old.

In the meantime the filthy fungus continues its march across our continent. It claims nearly a half million new victims in the U.S. alone each year. The city of Milwaukee has lost 80,000 elms within its municipal borders in the last 25 years. The city of Urbana, Illinois had 14,000 elms at the end of World War Two. It now has 220.

The story is no prettier on this side of the border. A drive through the countryside shows all too graphically how we're doing in the Dutch Elm Disease War. Those beautiful, towering, fan-shaped trees are mostly gone now. In their place, blackened, naked trunks and branches clutching arthritically upward. Many of them have disappeared entirely. Long since felled and cut up for firewood.

And the town of Beeton? With its heart-gladdening leafy tunnel of elms? I don't know. I haven't been back. And if anybody has been there . . . and if what I think has happened, *has* happened . . . please don't tell me. I don't want to know. I want to remember it the way it was.

STRONG

THIS country's had its share of strongmen you know. Angus McCaskill, the Cape Breton giant who was given to carrying fishing dories on his back and massive beer kegs with one arm. Louis Cyr, the 19th-century Montrealer who once lifted 18 men sitting on a platform into the air. And who also once hoisted a 535-pound weight off the floor using a single finger . . . And another Montrealer, Arthur Dandurand, who once carried a 455-pound engine block a distance of 84 feet and put it down on a table as if he was palming an ashtray.

This is about another Canadian strongman . . . not so well known. Practically forgotten in fact. Even though he was once called the strongest man in the world. He lives in Olha, Manitoba. And his neighbours always thought he was nuts.

His name is Mike Swistun . . . A Ukrainian Canadian farmer, and if he was ever the strongest man in the world, he isn't any more. But that's okay, because he's 80 years old. His heyday was in 1923 when the Ringling Brothers Circus sought out the legend of tiny Olha, Manitoba (you won't find it on the map. It has a population of 50) — sought him out and signed him up as the Strongest Man in the World. He was pretty strong all right.

He could hold five men aloft on his rib cage. He held two straining automobiles together with just ropes attached to their bumpers and his arms. He used to hold an eight-foot iron bar while three men on either side of him used all their strength to bend it into a 'U.' What was remarkable was that Mike Swistun was holding the bar in his teeth.

He might have got himself into the *Guinness Book of Records* except that his career as Strongest Man in the World was extremely short lived. Thirty days. After one month with Ringling Circus, Mike went to his boss, and in broken English explained that he'd have to leave the circus. 'What? Leave? Are you crazy? Big money, fame . . . why do you have to leave?'

Mike Swistun had a crumpled letter from his father back in Olha,

Manitoba. It was harvest time back there. Mike was told to leave the international tour and come back home to help bring in the wheat in Olha.

And he went. And he would have been forgotten too. Known only as Crazy Mike the hulking giant to the other 49 residents of Olha, Manitoba, had not a filmmaker by the name of Halya Kucmij come along. Somehow she heard the story of Mad Mike Swistun, and for some reason she decided to make a film about it.

She didn't seem to notice that Mike Swistun was just an over-the-hill prairie farmer or that Olha, Manitoba was no more than a wide spot in the road. She seemed to think she had a hero on her hands. She made the film and then she called Orson Welles to narrate it. That didn't work out. So she called Peter Ustinov to narrate. That didn't work out either. She called the agent for Jack Palance. He laughed at her. Told her the paltry fee she could afford was out of the question. Halya Kucmij didn't give up. She called Jack Palance himself. And he said yes. Yeah, I'll be proud to narrate the film about Mike Swistun.

And so it came to pass that the residents of Olha, Manitoba — population 50 — got to host the world premiere of a film called *The Strongest Man in the World*.

And there up on the stage was their oddball neighbour Mad Mike Swistun, the man who didn't even have an indoor toilet, signing autographs. With Jack Palance, a Hollywood movie star.

How did that happen? Well it happened because a filmmaker, Halya Kucmij, wouldn't settle for second best. And it happened because it just so happens that nobody — not even Halya Kucmij — realized that Hollywood film star Jack Palance — happens to be the son of Ukrainian immigrants. And his father had worked as a circus strongman. Just like Mike Swistun. Ms Kucmij didn't know that when she called him. She just called.

Yeah. Canada's had her share of strongmen all right. Angus McCaskill. Louis Cyr. Arthur Dandurand. Mad Mike Swistun.

But sometimes we forget that we've had our share of strong women too.

Like Halya Kucmij.

BINGO

M<small>AYBE</small> it's because I never won the Jackpot. Maybe it's because I've watched the disease spread like leprosy across whole towns and cities, gobbling up arenas and movie theatres and community halls. Maybe it's because I can almost always find better ways to spend an evening than pushing corn niblets around a sheet of squared off cardboard . . . I don't know exactly *why* it is . . . but I don't like Bingo.

I remember when I first began to dislike it actively. It was when I was living in London, about 10 years ago. A Canadian can get to feeling very lonely, living in England. People keep inquiring about what part of the States you come from and asking if you want your coffee *'bleck oah whoite, luv?'* Everybody thinks you talk funny and act crudely and you begin to long for something . . . just anything . . . that would remind you of back home.

I discovered that in London that year there was one thing I could do that was quintessentially Canadian. I could go to a live hockey game. Yes. Ice hockey in London. There was a league of about six teams, some Scottish, some hinterland English, and once a week on Saturday nights, they would take to the ice at Wembley Arena to play the London team . . . The Wembley Lions. They weren't very good. Their lineups were sprinkled with a clutch of pudgy, balding, overweight, expatriate Canadians and the games were scrambly, erratic and played at somewhat less than supersonic speed. But it was hockey. And it was something.

I'd seen about two games when a notice appeared in the *London Standard* that hockey would no longer be featured at Wembley. They were taking the ice out. To put in . . . Bingo tables.

Bingo. Do you know it's a century old, that game? Invented back in the 1880s in Britain. Most things that are 100 years old are creaky, or at least venerable. Not Bingo. It's never been more robust. There are six million regular Bingo players in Britain alone.

And it's not much better on this side of the Atlantic. In fact, it's not better at all. It's worse. Come with me now to Hollywood, Florida.

To the brand-spanking new million-dollar Hollywood Bingo Emporium. We won't be alone. Twelve hundred people will take seats in this hall tonight. Twelve hundred people show up every night . . . to play Bingo. They come in cars and trucks, in taxis and chartered buses, from as far away as Tampa, clear across on the other side of the state . . . to play Bingo.

Mind you, if you like the game, it's worth the trip. You win the super jackpot at the Hollywood Bingo Emporium and you can take home as much as 19,000 dollars. Which isn't bad money for an evening of filling out Bingo cards.

Not only that, you get valet service, friendly waitresses at your table and an armed escort to your car after the game if you need it.

Ah me. Bingo as big business. The best thing I know about the Hollywood Florida Bingo Emporium is that the profits go to Florida's Seminole Indians.

The Seminoles were driven into the swamps by invading whites in the early 1800s. Since then they've been forced into the traditional Uncle Tomahawk roles . . . making trinkets, dressing up for rain dances or wrestling alligators while tourists snap their Instamatics.

But not the 400 Seminoles who live on the 480-acre Hollywood reservation. They have the Hollywood Bingo Emporium. They also have a clever lawyer who discovered that as Seminoles they were exempt from many state laws — one of which restricts the prize money in Bingo games.

In the rest of Florida, the most you can win at Bingo is 100 dollars. In the Hollywood Bingo Emporium, the top prize is 19,000 dollars.

Not that that hurts the house. The house never hurts. The Hollywood Seminole tribe will make one and a half million dollars this year from Bingo fanatics. The money will build two gymnasiums, a swimming pool and a centre for senior citizens and children. And next year looks even better. This month the Hollywood Bingo Emporium moved into afternoon games as well as evening games.

What was it the Indians sold Manhattan for? Twenty-four dollars?

They're making it back. They're making it back.

SHAGGY DOG

Is THERE anybody out there who hasn't been the victim of a shaggy dog story? You know shaggy dog stories. My dictionary defines them as: 'humorous stories whose humour lies in the pointlessness or irrelevance of the punch line — or any joke involving talking animals.'

Yeah that's another thing about shaggy dog stories . . . There may not be a dog in it. Example: a shaggy frog story.

Man walks into a bar, slips onto a barstool in front of a bartender, takes off his hat to reveal a frog sitting on his head. Bartender's seen it all . . . Deadpan he asks the man what he'll have. Man doesn't reply. Instead he whips out a pad and pencil and writes: 'Martini — extra dry.' Bartender plays it cool, serves up the martini. Man drinks it, puts on his hat and leaves. Next day, same thing. Man comes in takes off hat, frog on his head. Writes request for martini. Drinks it. Leaves. One whole week this goes on. Finally the bartender can't stand it. Throws down his towel, yells 'OK . . .OK . . . you win. Mister I can't stand it. Do you know you've got a frog on your head?' Bartender looks at man. Man looks at bartender. Frog says: 'No, but can you believe this wart on my behind?'

That's a shaggy dog (or frog) story. But I've got a better one. Better because it involves a dog. And better because it's true.

Ladies and gentlemen, I would like to introduce you to Bruno — the all time shaggiest dog ever to sniff a fire hydrant.

Bruno is real. He exists. In the Swiss Alps as a matter of fact, where he is part of an elite canine corps famous around the world for its feats of derring-do and errands of mercy. Bruno is a St. Bernard . . . and he is one of those St. Bernards about which legends are spawned and stories told round the fire. Bruno is one of those mountain rescue dogs trained to brave the fiercest gale, the deepest snow drifts and the most bone-chilling cold, to ferret out skiers and other mountaineers lost in blizzards, avalanches and other high Alps catastrophes.

At least . . . that's the way it's supposed to be. The sad fact is, Bruno's performance on the trails and mountain passes has been something less than sterling. As a matter of fact, in the last two years of mountain rescue work Bruno has been sent on rescue missions eight times. And eight times Bruno has failed to come back. He gets lost. They had to send human teams out to rescue him.

Can you imagine? It's like having a near-sighted guide dog or a vegetarian foxhound or a Doberman that believes in nonviolence.

Not surprisingly, Bruno has been retired from active rescue work. They had to retire him. He was the laughing stock of the mountains. Now when the alarm bells ring and his colleagues spring from their kennels, ready to trudge on out into the icy blasts to search out lost skiers, poor sad dumb Bruno gets left behind. In . . . the kennel . . . where it's warm . . . and dry . . . and there's lots of food . . . and the living is easy.

So . . . while his brethren are ploughing snout deep through snow swept canyons and crevasses, hauling half-frozen humans out of drifts and waiting shivering to get back to their kennels . . . Poor? Sad? Dumb? Bruno is already *at* the kennels. Lolling around, no doubt tapping his out-of-service brandy keg and catching an extra forty winks whenever the spirit moves him.

Reminds me of another shaggy dog story (or shaggy gorilla story) . . .

Seems this very famous gorilla in a large American zoo passed on one day, leaving the zoo officials in a bit of a dither. A delegation of foreign dignitaries was to visit the zoo and the ex-gorilla was the star attraction of the zoo . . . with him gone, the zoo didn't have much to offer. What to do? The officials couldn't hope to find or afford another gorilla like the deceased. In desperation they decided to hire a zoo janitor to dress up in the dead gorilla's skin and pretend to be the gorilla. All went well. The man learned to move around in the gorilla suit, developed a taste for bananas, even learned a few of the tricks his predecessor had been famous for.

One trick he couldn't quite master though, was the triple back flip off a swinging rubber tire. Which was too bad because the ex-gorilla was world famous for that particular trick. So the man in the gorilla suit practised and practised . . . and by the time the delegation of foreign dignitaries arrived he figured he had it down pat. Up he

climbed onto the rubber tire and back he flipped. Unfortunately he miscalculated. He flipped himself right over the top of the cage into the lions den next door.

There was dead silence as the circle of lions gazed balefully at the hairy intruder . . . The largest of the lions padded up to the ape and stared right in his eye. The phony ape's nerve broke. 'Get me outta here,' he screamed. 'I'm not a gorilla, I'm a man . . . get me outta here!' The lion's eyes closed to slits. His ears flattened against his head, he opened his huge cavernous tooth-studded maw . . . and whispered. 'Quiet, idiot . . . you wanna get us all fired?'

I think Bruno would've liked that shaggy dog story.

SOLITUDE

W HAT do *you* think kids want most? Their own car? A girlfriend or boyfriend? The latest album by Rush? Nope. They want exactly what they keep *telling* you they want, if only you'd listen. You know what they say every time you ask them why they don't go outside or read a book or shovel the walk or do some homework. You know what the answer is, some variation on the theme: 'Aw fer cryin' out loud will you leave me alone?'

That's what they want — to be left alone. Solitude. Who'd have guessed it?

But it's official now — if you accept the results of a study just completed by researchers at the University of Chicago. They monitored 75 high school students and discovered that the kids spent more than a quarter of their waking hours . . . *by themselves*. By choice.

Quite a monitoring job it was too — for one whole week, the kids went about their normal daily lives, going to class, watching TV, hanging out with their pals in the school halls and the shopping plazas . . .

With one significant difference. The 75 teenage guinea pigs were each wearing one of those electronic pagers on their belts. Every once in a while (roughly every two hours on average), the pager would beep and the kid would have to say something like 'Oh hang on guys, I gotta fill out a report here . . .' And he or she would whip out a small booklet and answer questions like: What are you doing? Where? Who's with you? Would you rather be somewhere else? Questions like that.

It also asked the students to grade their moods from happy to sad, alert to drowsy, cheerful to irritable.

The Chicago University researchers ended up with nearly five thousand self-reports this way . . . and one conclusion they drew after analyzing all the entires was that teenagers want — and need — a fair amount of solitude. A full 25 percent of their waking hours on average.

It's a bit sad . . . because if there's one commodity this planet's running out of faster than fossil fuels and fresh air . . . it's solitude. The elevators are full of Muzak, the airwaves are full of round-the-clock chatter and it's getting harder and harder to find a hiking trail that doesn't sport little cairns of Coke cans and sandwich wrappers along its shoulders.

But if it's tough here, it's a nightmare in Japan. Imagine. A hundred and fifteen million people squeezed into a necklace of islands (many of them uninhabitable . . .) the square mileage of which is less than Newfoundland and Labrador. Solitude is really at a premium in Japan.

They took a survey of school kids in Tokyo and you know what three things the Japanese kids craved most? Number three was more free time; number two was more money to spend — no surprises there . . . but number one . . . the thing they wanted more than anything in the world — was a simple, small room of their own. A place, in other words, where they could be alone.

Seems awfully ironic when you live in a place like Ontario's north. If there's one inexhaustible commodity up here, it's room to be alone.

Northwestern Ontario is big . . . about 20 thousand square miles bigger than all of Japan. Japan has 115 million people. We have 224 thousand.

Solitude.

I guess about the nicest lines that were ever written about solitude came from the pen of an Irish poet by the name of William Butler Yeats. He wrote:

I will rise and go now, and go to Innisfree,
And a small cabin build there, of clay and wattles made:
Nine bean-rows will I have there, a hive for the honeybee,
And live alone in the bee-loud glade.

Solitude.
We're short on clay and wattle cabins up here. The growing season
is a bit harsh on bean gardens . . . but if you substitute the whine of
black flies for the drone of bees . . . I think we in the North have
pretty much what William Butler Yeats could only dream about.

BIRD SONGS

You know what bugs me about Spring? The fact that I'm already
used to it. It was just a couple of weeks ago that I got all dewy eyed
and jelly kneed on hearing my first robin. This morning at dawn
there was an entire Glee Clubful of them doing four-part harmony
outside my bedroom window and I wanted to throw my alarm clock
at them. Talk about ingratitude. Talk about short memory.

Still, you've gotta wonder what it is that makes a robin want to
warble his head off at the crack of dawn on a nippy spring morning,
when the sensible thing to do would be to hunker down in your nest,
bag a few extra winks and wait until the sun has warmed things up
a bit. What urgent little bulletin is so important that the robin, or
the rooster, or the chickadee or the sparrow can't wait till a more
civilized hour to get it off his downy little chest?

Poets and songwriters of course have always claimed — or at least
intimated — that it's a case of pure unbridled joy . . . that our little
feathered friends are so delirious about the rising sun and the
plenitude of dew worms that they just can't contain themselves . . .
and the little melodic trills and arias tumble unbidden from their
chirpy little beaks as spontaneously and naturally as the sun rising
in the east.

Scientists in their workmanlike, unromantic way have pretty well
disproved all that. They have painstakingly charted and photo-

graphed and recorded and banded virtually all of the world's eight thousand, six hundred different bird species. They have discovered that about half of those species are songbirds; that it is almost invariably the male who does the singing; and that the songs, far from being the bubblings of a heart bursting with happiness — are warnings and advertisements.

Some of the songs define nesting territories. Others proclaim wife wanted: must be prepared to assume domestic chores, bear and raise young, and live in. The songs of birds, the scientists tell us, are about as romantic as no trespassing signs or the honk of a Yellow Cab looking for a fare.

If you want to look at it that way.

I don't.

I guess it's all very logical to look at life scientifically and not to accept anything until it's been proven with flow charts and test tubes . . . but when it comes to bird songs I always remember a tale a neighbour of mine — not a neighbour that I was particularly fond of — told me once.

He showed up in my driveway one fall evening looking rather smug. Been sitting out by a duck pond not far from his place, waiting for mallards or blacks to come in on their way south. Suddenly he'd heard the sound that duck hunters dream about — the tell-tale singsong slightly neurotic sounding honk honk honk of high flying geese. Coming down.

There were four of them he said . . . They circled the pond twice and then came in. He nailed three of them before they had time to realize the terrible blunder they'd made. The fourth one climbed like mad to get away from the pond where her . . . colleagues . . . floated in crumpled heaps of feathers. She didn't have to. My neighbour had already emptied his gun. You're only allowed to carry three shells in a shotgun. He never could've reloaded in time to bring the fourth bird down.

She was safe enough.

Or she would have been. Except that Canada Geese have this funny, unscientific, terribly romantic habit. They tend to stay with their mates for life.

And the mate of this surviving bird was lying down there on the water in a welter of goose down and pond ripples. Strangely still.

Oddly . . . crooked. She didn't know what to do, that fourth goose. So she circled the pond again, high at first, then lower, and lower. 'You should've heard her' my neighbour said. 'She was honking and honking . . . calling for her mate you know. Kept getting lower and lower. About the fourth time around I nailed *her* too.'

My neighbour always thought I was a bit of a sop because I didn't want to go duck hunting with him — and he had a point. You can definitely get too romantic about such things.

But I think you can get too scientific about such things too. And I don't need any biologist to explain the lyrics of the song that last goose was singing.

MALE

MADE your vacation plans yet? No? Great! 'Cause have I got a place for you. I mean, face it. The Caribbean is ruined. You have to win a lottery to afford Europe. Florida is coast-to-coast rhinestone sunglasses . . . all the good places have been packed out by plump, pink, oil-smeared get-away-from-it-alls like us.

Ha ha. Not *all* of the good places. I've found one . . . entire . . . country that is so unspoiled . . . I . . . well . . . look . . . let me just tell you a bit about it . . . you be the judge.

It's right next to Greece, rises to nearly seven thousand feet above the unearthly blue water of the Aegean. It's small . . . about 40 miles long and 4 miles wide.

But there are 12 towns in that 160 square miles . . . and if that sounds a little too crowded for you — relax. There are only 900 full time citizens. Nine hundred!

And getting away from it all? Hm hmmmm . . . Brother, have you come to the right place. Listen. No newspapers. No telephone, no telegraph — in fact there's only one vehicle in the entire country. You want to get out of the rat race? — this is hands-down the place.

The food is great. Some of the places you stay are actually wineries, so the beverages are fine . . . and listen to this . . . you can have a belt-busting meal of lentil soup, fish, salad, home-baked bread, vintage wine and or water all for the one low price of — absolutely nothing.

That's right. Nothing. If you're cheap. If you feel like making a modest contribution in dollars, drachmas, dinars or the currency of your choice, that's fine. But nobody in this entire country will ever ask you for money or even suggest payments of any kind for food or lodging.

This is not Oz or Utopia or Shangri-la or some other fantasy island I'm talking about you know. This place exists. It's real. You can look it up in your atlas right now. It is precisely 150 miles east of Salonika . . . juts right out into the Aegean Sea and it's called the Holy Athonite Republic. Or Mount Athos.

Talk about dream vacations! All you have to do is visit the Greek Ministry of Foreign Affairs in Athens, pick up a card for about four bucks which entitles — entitles! — you to free room and board . . . and presto! You're on your way to the Holy Athonite Republic. Gorgeous scenery . . . fine wines, great food . . . a priceless collection of rare Byzantine art and artifacts if you like that sort of thing — even the preserved hand of John the Baptist — if you like *that* sort of thing . . .

Language problem? Don't worry about it. Many of the country's 900 inhabitants are scholars — quite a few of them speak English and are happy to practise it with visitors.

There . . . is . . . one . . . small thing about visiting the Holy Athonite Republic . . . A trifling thing really . . . hate to even bring it up . . . 'cause it kind of casts a pall over this dream world. But I suppose I have to well . . . *mention* that ahhhhhhhhmmmmmm well actually . . . there are no . . . women allowed.

Yah . . . no women . . . Hasn't been a woman in the Holy Athonite Republic since, well heh heh — the No Women Law was passed six years before the Normans invaded Britain — in 1060 it was. So there haven't been any women in the Holy Athonite Republic for just about a thousand years.

The 900 residents of the Republic are monks — members of the Greek Orthodox Church . . . and not only are women banned but also female dogs, cats, even parakeets.

The female gender is definitely out in the Holy Athomite Republic, as is smoking, horseback riding, transistor radios, cassette players, all musical instruments and even singing.

Because this is the only monastic state in Europe . . . the only theocracy — a country literally ruled by God — in the world. So the rules are a little strict. Many of the residents, brought here soon after their birth, have never even seen a woman.

A reporter by the name of Nino Lo Bello — a man of course, visited the Holy Athonite Republic — and wrote about it for the *Globe and Mail.* That's how I heard about it. He asked one of the monks about the no-female rules. The aged monk replied: 'The life here is good, it is quiet, it is rewarding. We live longer in Athos than people do anywhere else in the world. Why do we need women here??'

Hm. Hmmmmmmmm. Intriguing. Unfortunately I think I'm kind of too hooked on women to enjoy the Holy Athonite Republic.

Besides. I suspect the men there don't really live longer without them. I suspect it just feels that way.

RUNNING

I KNOW it's way too early to start getting all jelly-brained and prattle-mouthed about the coming spring . . . but a funny thought just occurred to me. Do you realize that now, thanks to the 70s, we have a whole new harbinger of spring to anticipate each year?

Oh we can still look forward to spring breakup, the first crocus to poke through the snow, the returning robins and buds on the lilacs . . . but something new has been added as well. The doggedly jiggling, determined stride of the roadside jogger. Oh I know that there are some runners who go all winter — even here in Thunder Bay you see them, swaddled in scarves and warmup suits, huffing great clouds of carbon dioxide as they skirt the snow banks and try not to slide under the wheels of passing buses. But these are terminal exercise junkies . . . They're not enjoying themselves out there, sliding on the ice and ploughing through the snow in their Adidas . . . they're just trying to bleed a little frenzy off their addiction. If they didn't go out and run they'd probably be beating their spouses or organizing radical terrorist groups to liberate Third World vegetarians.

But a little bit of melting . . . a little more spring sun and it won't be long before all the runners — crazies and only mildly demented — will take over our streets again, plodding up boulevard and down avenue as their lungs labour and their minds dream of the day when they enter jogger's Valhalla — a real, full-fledged 26-mile, 385-yard marathon.

That's what they're all training for you know — oh they won't admit it — *'Nah I just liketa run a coupla miles inna morning, clear the cobwebs out* . . . Bunk. All of them secretly see themselves staggering exhausted over the finish line to tumultuous cheers in Boston or New York or Toronto or any other place that hosts a bona fide Marathon.

It's got to be the oldest jock dream in history, the Marathon. All the way back to 490 B.C. when the Athenians and the Persians got into a little dust-up in a Greek valley. The Athenians, though vastly outnumbered, outmanoeuvered and outhustled the Persians and proceeded to make mincemeat out of them. Final casualties: Greeks 192; Persians 6,400. Sorta like the Washington Capitols drubbing the Moscow Selects 21 to zip. Anyway, the Athenian general was afraid that the city of Athens might surrender to the Persian navy through ignorance of the Marathon Valley upset. Athens was 26 miles, 385 yards away. He called for his best runner, a long-legged lad by the name of Pheidippides . . . and told him to hotfoot it to Athens with the news. Pheidippides ran the whole 26 miles even though he just finished running to Sparta and back. He had the Jimmy Cagney Hollywood ending too. Pheidippides staggered into Athens, called out 'Rejoice we Conquer' and pitched over dead in the street.

So remember the next time you pass a jogger on the street or spot one plodding around the cinder track at the high school — that he or she doesn't see him- or herself the way you do. The jogger does not hold a self-image of a chuffing, boysenberry-complexioned, flabby-thighed and jiggle-paunched North American painfully trying to hold on for one more block as he dodges the dog dirt. No, in the jogger's eye his chin is out, he is covered with a fine sheen of sweat, the long cables of muscles in his thighs are snapping and rolling in perfect cadence . . . And Athens City Limits are just over the next hill.

So have a little respect. Don't honk at them, don't splash them or crowd them or curse them for making your driving a little trickier.

And take heart. Soon they'll be out all over the place.

Just like the robins.

HEARING EAR DOGS

THE heaviest one ever on record would have to be old Schwartzwald Hof Duke I guess, who lived down in Oconomowoc, Wisconsin. Wasn't easy to coax him onto the scales but they did manage to, a couple of months before he went to the great kennel in the sky. Old Schwartzwald tipped the scales at 295 pounds . . . and earned himself a line of type in the *Guinness Book of Records* doing it. He'd be the heaviest . . . and I guess the title 'most valuable' would have to go to Caversham Ku-ku of Yam, a British blue-blood. An American offered 10,500 pounds sterling for Ms Ku-ku of Yam. Disdainfully rejected of course. The richest one in the world? Almost certainly Viking Baron von Heppeplatz. The Baron spent most of his life in service to a Munich landowner named George Ritt. When Mister Ritt died he left his land to the Baron. About a quarter of a million dollars worth.

Lots of other titles remain unsung. Most prolific . . . probably the slightly absurdly named Low Pressure — a Londoner, made Don Juan and Casanova look like underachievers. Low Pressure was the father of 2,414 duly certified offspring . . . and according to the *Guinness*, at least 600 other freelance littluns.

And the strongest? That title would go to one of our own — a Newfie by the name of Nelson. Nelson only weighs 168 pounds but 10 years ago down in Washington, Nelson pulled more than two and a half tons — 3,260 pounds — a distance of 15 feet, without any help from anybody else.

Thing that's especially interesting about all these titles and accomplishments is that the title holders — all of them, Schwartzwald Hof

Duke, Caversham Ku-ku of Yam, Viking Baron von Heppeplatz, Low Pressure and Nelson the Newfie — all of them . . . are dogs. Dogs. St. Bernards, Alsatians, Greyhounds, Pekingese and of course Newfoundland . . . but dogs by any other name.

The *elite* of dogdom no doubt. Don't think for a moment that your humble Fido and my peasant Angus would ever nibble kibble from the same dog dish as Caversham Ku-ku of Yam . . . but dogs nonetheless . . . with a furry paw in each corner, a tail at one end and a bark at the other.

We take them for granted, dogs. And not just the champions but the also-rans as well. The non-pedigree, un-blue-blooded mongrel hordes that sniff fire hydrants, chase cats and sleep in front of the fireplaces and heat registers of hundreds of thousands of homes. There are signs that maybe we should stop treating them like . . . like . . . well . . . dogs.

We all know what a boon seeing-eye dogs are for the blind . . . but down in San Francisco the first graduates of a hearing-ear dog course have been placed in the homes of deaf people. What do these dogs do? Well they're trained to get the attention of deaf people . . . to let them know that the phone is ringing, that someone's at the door or that the smoke detector upstairs just went off.

They've also been trained to respond to unusual noises — rattles in the plumbing, thumps from the furnace . . . and signs of distress from children or others in the house.

The San Francisco Society for the Prevention of Cruelty to Animals has been training these hearing-ear dogs — the training runs at about 2,500 dollars per animal. The trained dogs are made available to anyone over 18 who has profound deafness and no one with good ears living in the same house.

But the best part of the story as far as I'm concerned is the pedigree these hearing-ear dogs can boast.

There isn't one. They're all strays. Abandoned curs fresh out of the San Francisco SPCA animal shelter. They're selected for their temperament, alertness, intelligence and reliability — beyond that it doesn't matter if they're fifth-generation Arabian gazelle hound or nondescript, kinky-tailed back-alley mutt.

Personally I don't know if this represents a breakthrough for humanity . . . or a smooth public relations move on the part of the canine world. Because not far from San Francisco ... in a place called Sunland, California ... some guy has trained two pets by the name of Sylvester and Jo-jo to take a blindfolded trainer around obstacles, to ring bells and pull straps — even to stop on red and go on green.

Pretty standard stuff for a German shepherd seeing-eye dog. Except that Sylvester and Jo-jo aren't dogs ... they're birds. Macaws to be exact.

The fella that's training them says that seeing-eye birds have a lot of advantages over seeing-eye dogs. For one thing they can live 50 or 60 years compared to around 15 for canines. They don't have to be walked and they eat like ... well ... birds. Blasphemy to generations raised on the likes of Rin Tin Tin and Lassie.

And I'll bet Nelson the Newfie isn't the least bit impressed.

FRANGLAIS

W ELL, international invasions seem to be the order of the day — anything from American Embassies to full-scale countries like Afghanistan. So I guess it's fitting that I blow the lid on yet another international invasion that's underway right now. Relax ... no Russian tanks or Moslem pseudo-students in this one. The invasion is taking place in France. Paris to be exact ... and the invaders? You and me.

In a manner of speaking. As a matter of fact it is precisely the manner of speaking that constitutes this invasion. Parisians are being assaulted squarely in the larynx ... they are beginning to be overrun by English.

Actually it's not even English — not British English anyway. It's international English — the kind you can speak in Birmingham or Burlington or Biloxi and be understood.

In Paris this English takes on a little French garnishing and *voilà* — you get a tongue that features a little English and a *morceau* of French — a mongrel tongue that the French call Franglais.

The first French beachhead for English came in the world of technology. It's tough to translate words like radar and sonar, stereo and computer input relay terminal into French . . . and somewhere along the line, somebody decided not to bother trying.

But the English incursion has gone a lot farther than technological hard- and software. Walk down the Champs Élysées in Paris today and you may be tempted to have 'le quick lunch' in 'un snack bar' which you may want to pay for with 'le cash' or 'les travellers cheques.' You might want an aftersnack smoke in which case you might pick up a pack of the newest French cigarette on the market — just call the garçon and ask him to bring you a package of 'les Rich and Lights.'

A lot of Franglais comes from the same source kids pick up slang from here — from Sam the Record Man and the popular songs and albums of the day. French radio plays about the same gamut of music you hear in Canada — you can twiddle the dial and pick up 'le rock,' 'le pop' and even 'le country' believe it or not.

Heard, of course, through 'les best speakers' you can afford to buy with the money you make on 'le job.' If your job is 'super' you probably have a stereo . . . otherwise you're stuck with an old-fashioned hi-fi — except in Paris it's pronounced hee-fee.

Newspapers abet the invasion. French headlines scream of hippies, beatniks (there's a chestnut), punks, rockers, gangsters, pickpockets and even les holdup men.

The purists of course are appalled. After all France is the only country I know that actually has an appointed body to oversee and rule on what new words will be allowed entrance into the French language. They're appalled. Outraged. Infuriated. And powerless. Despite editorials in *Le Monde*, hysterically tinged letters to the editor and all the knuckle rappings France's grammarians can administer, the invasion rolls on, remorseless and unchecked.

But it's a bloodless revolution for all that. Nobody's getting bashed over the head or having a foreign tongue rammed down their throat (le English kiss?). The French seem to be taking what they like of our language and leaving the rest. French has been around as long as Anglo-Saxon. They'll both be around for a while yet.

The great Franglais battle in the streets of Paris does raise funny feelings in somebody who lives in the north of Ontario though. In the streets of towns like Geraldton, Longlac, Nakina, Timmins and Kapuskasing some folks have been speaking something like

Franglais — Frangloontarian maybe? — for decades. Far as I know neither the Anglos nor the Francos have felt conspicuously endangered by this situation.

As for the Paris invasion? Well it may not be . . . *chic* to say so. But as an Anglo I feel a little smug. All those years of having Parisians sneer at our accents, our cooking, our fashions, and our architecture . . . and now . . . *Mon Dieu* they're singing our song. *C'est la guerre.*

ABSENT

DID you hear the one about the absent-minded professor who went to the drugstore and said to the druggist 'I would like a box of prepared tablets of the monacetic acidester of salicylic acid?'

Yeah you probably have . . . and if not, you've heard a dozen variations on the theme. The absent-minded professor is one of the rocks upon which 20th-century conversational humour is built — along with the shaggy dog, the travelling salesman and the dumb blonde.

But if you think you've taken in all the absent-minded-professor jokes you can handle . . . spare a tear for Doctor James Reason. He's head of the Department of Psychology at Manchester University in England. And for the last two years, Professor Reason has been making an exhaustive study of . . . you guessed it . . . absent-mindedness.

How . . . do you go about studying something as fleeting and intangible as absent-mindedness? More to the point — why would anyone bother? Well Professor Reason thinks it could turn out to be a very important field of study. He says one of the big problems is that we've always treated the phenomenon as a kind of a joke . . . a sort of slip on a mental banana peel.

But it all depends what's going on when the pratfall takes place. If it's a funny-looking physics professor who picks up the telephone and hollers 'Come in' into the receiver — that's funny. But if it's a commercial airline pilot who mistakes the dashboard lighter for the switch that lowers the landing gear — that's not so funny.

In fact, Professor Reason's interest in absent-mindedness came out of reading about aircraft accidents. The more he studied them the more it seemed to him that many air tragedies and collisions came out of tiny errors — misreading instruments, hitting wrong switches — that we all make every day around the home and the office and in the car . . . make and chalk up to simple absent-mindedness.

To kick off his study, Professor Reason asked 35 people to keep a running diary of their slip ups . . . their 'nonplanned actions' as the professor called them . . . for a 14-day period. The people did so . . . and the professor ended up with a surprising list of 700 individual slips, or instances of absent-mindedness if you will. Which means the average person surveyed, 'messed up' 20 times in two weeks, or one point four times each day.

Now again . . . that's not too bad for most of us . . . probably even charitable. But when you think of brain surgeons or police officers or locomotive engineers or taxi drivers having a mental lapse one and a half times a day . . . well, it begins to look like Professor Reason is on to something.

From his study, the professor has been able to break absent-mindedness down into four categories. One: selection failures . . . when you substitute the wrong action for the right one . . . such as yelling 'Come in' into the telephone. Number two: errors in discrimination . . . such as trying to start your car with the house key. Number three: what the professor calls test failures . . . finishing a sequence of action too soon or too late . . . such as dressing up for a night out and feeling quite impeccable in your best suit and your 12-dollar tie and your favourite shirt . . . and oh my God you forgot to change out of your running shoes.

The fourth category of absent-mindedness is one that I'm good at — 'storage failure' the professor calls it. That's where you find yourself standing over the coffee pot in the morning saying to yourself 'Now have I put four spoonfuls in? Or one? Or will this be six?'

Actually I'm not all that discriminating when it comes to absent-mindedness . . . I feel perfectly at home in all four of Professor Reason's categories . . . and I take little solace in the professor's prediction that absent-mindedness will be ever with us. Chimps aren't absent-minded he says. Foxes and falcons and pheasants and fish don't misplace their glasses on top of their head, or wander down to dinner with no pants on. 'It's the penalty we humans pay,' says Professor Reason, 'for having so much cerebral equipment.'

Hmmmmmmph. Small consolation. It's like that absent-minded professor that I started out telling you about. The one that walked into the drug store and said to the druggist: 'I would like a box of prepared tablets of the monacetic acidester of salicylic acid.'

The druggist screwed up his forehead for a bit, then said 'Do you mean aspirin?'

'That's it,' cried the professor. 'I never can remember that name.'

That's the other thing about absent-mindedness.

Even the jokes about it aren't that funny.

BLUE EYES

You hear a lot of talk these days from people who are sorry they've grown up. Lamentations of lost innocence. Moanings and groanings about those long lost days of freedom and joy.

Bunk. I'm an adult . . . but I'm still young enough to remember what childhood was really like. I recall too well the Don't-Do-Thises and the Mustn't-Do-Thats. I remember the chuckings under the chins and the patronizing pats on the head from distant relatives who demanded to know what I was going to be when I grew up. 'I'm only eight years old Mister . . . what do I know?' I remember what it's like to quake in mortal terror at the sight of a shortish middle-aged man wearing bifocals as thick as the bottom of Coke bottles . . . whose only connection to me was that I had to serve detentions with him and receive guidance instructions once or twice a school year.

I remember my childhood as not idyllic or bucolic or all that splendid.

The childhood I remember was composed of equal parts of fear and ignorance and anxious wonder at what could happen next. Mostly I remember the tests. Remember all the tests? Remember how you'd be sitting there, minding your own business, peacefully defacing the heroes in your history book . . . when suddenly the public address speaker would crackle and pop and there would be the voice of the vice principal: 'Attention . . . attention . . . all grade nines are to report to the auditorium immediately. All grade nines . . . to the auditorium . . . immediately.'

And off you'd troop in bedraggled twos. No stopping at the water fountain, no you can't go to the washroom, keep those lines straight, no *talking*.

You knew when you got to the auditorium it would be another test. Something with an incomprehensible name like SATO or GOOT or Stanford-Binet. Another test with diagrams to complete, figures to match up, series to figure out, problems to solve. Another multiple-choice maze to work your way through with the special electrographic pencil for computer scoring. A test which nobody troubled to explain the worth of to you . . . but upon which your entire academic future probably hinged. We weren't a sophisticated lot, we students . . . but I think we all saw these tests for what they were: a gross invasion of privacy. That's probably why I and the kids I went to school with used to sabotage the tests deliberately.

'Draw a house' the test would order . . . And we'd draw a twisted blasted shack with the windows broken and the roof caving in. Knowing instinctively I think that somewhere some not-too-bright clinical psychologist would look at the drawing and solemnly intone something like: 'This student exhibits strong feelings of rejection and hostility toward society as a whole.'

Nobody ever told us what happened with the test results. You couldn't 'fail' the tests of course . . . because they were supposedly just measuring your abilities, your Intelligence Quotient . . . your aptitudes. Chances are you'd get a call into the Guidance Office in a month or so and old bifocals would tell you that 'The Tests' showed that you should become a forest ranger, a lifeguard or a travelling salesman. That was it.

I don't know. I suspect that those tests were the academic equivalent of LIP grants, Senate appointments and most Royal Commissions — just make-work projects to keep sociologists off the streets.

I can't prove it of course. But I take great comfort in the results of experiments that have just been completed down at the Pennsylvania State University.

Researchers there have been conducting a whole series of complex and exhaustive tests at the university's Motor-Behaviour Laboratory, acknowledged as one of the most advanced in the world. They were trying to explore the parameters of human reaction time — how rapidly people respond to physical stimuli . . . and what factors *affect* that response time.

The researchers extrapolated all the known variables . . . sex, race, socio-economic status . . . no doubt they went back and examined the subject's high school SATO and Stanford-Binet results too.

Know what conclusion they came to?

They concluded that brown-eyed people react more quickly than blue-eyed people.

That's it. The fruit of all the sophisticated gadgetry and computer blanks of sociological theory and practice is that brown-eyed people hit the brake pedal quicker than blue-eyed people.

The man in charge of the project, Professor Daniel Landers, said, 'It's such a bizarre idea I didn't really believe it at first . . . but I've become more of a believer.' The test results are stark and irrefutable . . . They show that subjects with darker eyes have a reaction time that is anywhere from 12 to 22 milliseconds faster than subjects with lighter eyes. Period.

Why this should be, the researchers can't say — oh they speculate that perhaps the melanin — that's the dark grainy pigment that gives eyes their colour — they think perhaps the melanin could be genetically related to the amount of neuromelanin in the nervous system — but that is just speculation . . . they really don't know.

And me? I really don't care. I just wish I could find that wretched guidance teacher from years gone by. I'd screw my face up into a most un-adult nyah nyaaaah. And give him a big brown-eyed wink right into those bifocals.

Behind which, if memory serves, glared two myopic orbs of deepest cerulean blue.

DANDELIONS

A MAN named Gerard Manley Hopkins, who lived in the last century, once wrote a poem, part of which goes:

What would the world be, once bereft
Of wet and of wildness? Let them be left,
O let them be left, wildness and wet;
Long live the weeds and the wilderness yet.

Poems can tell you a great deal about the people who write them. One thing I know for dead certain about Old Gerard Manley is he never owned a *lawn*.

You don't catch folks who own lawns singing the praises of weeds and wildernesses . . . because people with lawns know only too well how tenuous man's grip is on that fragile patch of clearing that separates the driveway from the front walk.

The threat of a crabgrass invasion lurks constantly . . . not to mention incursions of plantain, burdock, twitchgrass, thistles and corruption from within by May beetle, cutworm, mole, vole and each spring it seems some new unheard of exotic infestation with a name like Afghanistani figwort palsy or Bohemian bulb blight — something robust and lethal, that sneers away all attempts at chemical containment.

But those are the big battles, best left to botancial commandos and herbicidal alchemists who get their jollies from major confrontations. Me, I've just got a small, reasonably healthy patch of green that any self-respecting major infestation is bound to pass by as unworthy of occupation. Which leaves me to fight the little battle — the one I never win. The battle of the dandelion.

I've mounted enough springtime offensives against the dandelions in my lawn to qualify as a Roman legionnaire — except that legionnaires *won* some of their battles . . . I have nothing to show for my pains but grass-stained knees and a jaundiced yard. I started off as all gardening naifs do . . . I guess . . . simply cutting the dandelions off with a lawnmower or a sickle. I think this treatment actually stimulates dandelions into a frenzy of procreation. The next time you look you find five little yellow heads standing sturdily in the remains of the decapitated parent.

Next came attempts to pull the dandelions out by hand . . . Fruitless . . . the plant would invariably break off just below the surface leaving a healthy root intact. And pregnant.

Next came the major excavations. Armed with trowel and fork and gardening gloves . . . I decided to dig the beggars out in their entirety. That's when I began to develop a respect for this humble little nuisance . . . a respect that approaches awe. Because beneath that cheerful bright delicate little plant in the grass . . . there's a fibrous tawny grey tap root that's as tough as nails and has at least a foot and a half long death grip on the underside of your lawn.

I never did find any satisfactory way to control the dandelions on my lawn . . . By the time I began to make *some* inroads in their ranks their yellow heads had mostly turned to grey . . . a grey which of course on close inspection proves to be thousands of little wind-borne seeds . . . the paratroopers of next spring's invasion.

Ah but this year I vowed things would be different . . . This year I promised myself I would spend some time in the winter learning all I could about my foe. Probe its weaknesses, list its faults . . . and come spring . . . banish it from my lawn once and for all.

So I did . . . I read everything I could lay my hands on about the dandelion. And I discovered some interesting things. It's a perfect Canadian name . . . because it's both English and French . . . Dandelion is an Anglicization of *dent de lion* . . . which means tooth of the lion . . . a reference to the plant's jagged leaf.

But Canadian as the name might seem, the dandelion is not native to Canada or North America . . . It was probably brought here in the pant cuff or hat band or steamer trunk of some early pioneer. Those wispy grey paratroopers *do* get around.

I learned that the dandelion is considered a culinary treat in many parts of the world. The young leaves can be boiled like spinach and sprinkled with oil, lemon and salt. Dandelion wine is another by-product of the plant.

And dandelions more than merely taste good. Listen to this from a turn-of-the-century tome called *Doctor Chase's Recipes*. 'The dandelion has a direct action in removing obstructions of the liver, kidneys, and other viscera. It is particularly valuable in many liver complaints, derangements of the digestive organs, . . . and in dropsical affections.'

All of this began to alter the image I had of my arch enemy. I began to see the dandelion not as a tiresome affliction but as a valuable and attractive plant. One other quote that I came across turned the tide completely. It was by the American philosopher Ralph Waldo Emerson — 'What is a weed,' wrote Mister Emerson, 'but a plant whose virtues have not been discovered?'

Right on Ralph Waldo. And it explains why my lawn and I have finally signed a treaty of perpetual peaceful co-existence. No more attacks from me — chemical or physical . . . ever.

I swear the grass looks better already now that the threat of force has been permanently removed. But don't take my word for it — drive by the house and have a look for yourself.

It's easy to find my place. It's the one with the yellow lawn.

MOOSEMEAT

Two things keep tumbling through my mind this week: moosemeat and electric toothbrushes.

Not, I think you'll agree, any immediately obvious connection between the two . . . and I'm not sure why they keep rattling around in my skull like lumps of gravel in a hub cap. I guess I have to take them one at a time . . . to figure out the connection.

The moosemeat is easy. I spent one evening this week in the kitchen of an older Finnish couple who live nearby. Charlie and Lempe are in their 60s I would guess. They've lived in the bush of northwestern Ontario all their lives . . . were born here . . . but they're still as Finnish as the mayor of Helsinki. As a matter of fact they both have Finnish accents and sometimes when they're talking to each other they'll lapse into Finn just as easily and naturally as you or I slip into our favourite slippers.

Charlie is, as I said, in his 60s, tall, ruddy-faced with a build like an over-ripe jack pine. He says he's getting to feel his age now because when he goes out hunting moose he finds himself puffing and panting up the hills. He shot a moose this year ... just as he does every year. It took him four days in the bush, and after he killed it, he had to butcher it right on the spot because his pickup truck was two miles away. He got two hundred pounds of meat off the moose ... and he got it to his pickup in three trips. That's how old and out of shape Charlie is. Anyway, steaks from the moose that Charlie shot were on the table that night. I had never tasted moosemeat before. I'm not a hunter but I'm glad Charlie is ... I've never tasted such meat in my life.

So that's how the delicate aroma and texture of moosemeat came to be floating through my mind. Electric toothbrushes? Well they're connected to that night at Charlie and Lempe's place too ... After dinner we all sat around with glasses of beer and watched logs burn themselves up in Charlie and Lempe's fireplace. It was shirtsleeve warm and I suddenly realized that there was no forced air furnace in this place. Just the wood stove in the kitchen and the fireplace in the living room. 'This keeps you warm through the winter?' I asked. They looked at me as if I'd said something foolish. And I had. It was already well below freezing outside and warm as toast within.

I have another friend up here — not an oldtimer — a newcomer like myself. He decided to 'Live Better Electrically' when he bought his house a few years ago. He is not much fun to talk with nowadays ... All that seems to be on his mind is the incredible amounts he has to shell out every time he gets his hydro bill.

I can still remember that same 'electrically enlightened' buddy showing me the newest gizmo in his house ... electric toothbrushes for the whole family. That was a couple of years ago of course, back in the days when Ontario Hydro spent a good deal of money on commercials that crooned at us to 'Live Better Electrically' via electric lawnmowers, electric blankets, electric heating, and of course electric toothbrushes.

Ontario Hydro's changed its tune since then. Now we get solemn, Voice-Of-Doom messages on the radio and television telling us that the days of unlimited electricity supply are gone forever, and would we please turn out the lights. Quite a turn around in just a couple of years. Kind of makes you wonder who's minding the store.

Me, I've moved into a nice warm modern farmhouse for the winter . . . and though it's not electrically heated, it's got the usual electric accoutrements . . . Lights, stove, freezer and an outlet in the garage for my car. My hydro bills are pretty whopping too . . . which makes me wonder: is Living Better Electrically a philosophy? An anachronism? Or just an example of black humour?

But I find it a wee bit encouraging that to Charlie and Lempe . . . it couldn't matter less. They'll go on chopping wood and burning it, talking to each other and their friends in the language of a country they've never seen while the rest of us fret over brownouts and blackouts and backbreaking hydro bills. Charlie will go on shooting his one moose a year, Lempe will go on cooking it up into the most delicious steaks and roasts and stews you can imagine.

And neither one of them would know an electric toothbrush if they stepped on it.

PARANOIA

YOU'VE noticed it, eh? Paranoia. *It's everywhere, it's everywhere.* People are paranoid about everything from the Ayatollah to the Mounties crack barn squad. We shut down entire schools because we're paranoid about asbestos in the ceilings. We call international conferences because we're paranoid about acid in the raindrops that keep falling on our lakes, doo wah doo wah. There are entire magazines devoted to everything from basement mildew to jogger's nipple.

People are buying Dobermans . . . taking kung fu lessons . . . Oh no, we're paranoid all right. It's not my imagination. And don't get me wrong. I'm not suggesting that we shouldn't worry about all those things. It's just that . . . well . . . I feel we've got our priorities

wrong, that's all. I mean it's all very noble to knuckle one's forehead over the Palestinian autonomy question, or man's inhumanity to the planet's ozone layer . . . but what of problems much closer to home? What, for instance, about the scandal of our public washrooms?

There, ladies and gentlemen, is something to properly knit your brow over. *There* is a subject worthy of your mental anguish. The public restrooms of this country are an outrage and a disgrace.

And let's face it . . . Not to be too paranoid or anything . . . but . . . if *you* were a sinister foreign power bent on sapping the will of a young and vibrant nation . . . could *you* think of a *better* place to begin your work than in the public restrooms of that nation?

Let us examine a typical Canadian public restroom. Through the door with the funny little humanoid stick man on it . . . Ummm hmmm . . . Here we have a row of sinks . . . in front of a long mirror. Reasonable. Adequate. Let us approach Sink A, in the manner of a citizen seeking to use same . . . Here is the hot water tap. Good. Turn it on . . . Fine . . . Now to move the hands to avail oneself of the copious flow of hot water coursing from the faucet.

Aha. But the instant you lift your hand from the tap, the water . . . stops. Move your hand back to the tap, the water flows again. Ah ah . . . but then you are shy one hand under the faucet. This is the tundra conundrum . . . Our answer to Chinese water torture. Canadian Zen: the sound of one-hand washing.

But why not simply fill the sink? Just put in the plug, fill the bowl and dabble your flippers in a mini-pond of your own making?

That's when you discover phase two of the Great Canadian washroom subversion scheme. There *is* no plug. There's a metal doohickey thing that theoretically falls and rises out of the drain like a miniature levitating manhole cover. But it doesn't work. Ever seen one that did?

Hey by gol but yer a Canuck eh? I mean . . . yer resourceful . . . yer usta things breakin' down. You can fix the Evinrude in a rain squall an rotate yer tires while yer waitin' fer the lights to change. Yer not about to be buffaloed by some dumb sink fer cryin' out loud. Whatcha want here is one o' yer homemade drain plugs. Good wad o' paper towel oughta do the trick . . . just jam 'er down the drain there . . . Where's the paper towel dispenser . . . ?

Welcome to Phase Three of the Bathroom Bolshevism Plot. There *is* no paper towel dispenser. In its place is a large white nodule on the wall, featuring a shiny button, a chrome jet . . . and a neat printed legend telling you that this is a sanitary hand dryer. Shake excess water from hands, it says; push the button it says; rapidly rub your hands together under the jet it says; and hey, presto! — your hands will be clean and dry the new sanitary way.

It's a damned lie. The machine will howl like a banshee. You will look like a committable idiot who is trying to shake hands with himself. When it is over you will wipe your still-dripping hands on your thighs and leave the restroom a broken person, praying that no one wonders about the stains on your slacks.

I haven't even mentioned that most inconvenient of all the conveniences found in public restrooms . . . Yes. Them. That line of cubicles ranged against the back wall. Toilets. Yes. But *pay* toilets. *Pay toilets.*

What can you say about a form of life that would inflict the concept of pay toilets upon itself?

Mark Twain once observed that man is the only animal that blushes. Or needs to.

I like to think that when that thought struck him, Mister Twain was standing in a public washroom, fruitlessly trying to find someone with change for a dollar.

MOOSE

I'D LIKE to pass along a few tips for the moose hunters in the audience. I know it's a little out of season, but what better time than the dead of mid-winter to retreat to an easy chair in front of a fire and review our moose strategy and tactics . . . sort of mentally 'psyching ourselves up' for next year's hunting season.

I suppose I should lay my credentials right out on the table as far as moose expertise goes. Won't take too long. Shucks I've seen a couple of moose in my time. In fact, exactly two, now that I think of it. One was in Newfoundland, he was browsing along the shore of a lake — or pond — as they call them in Newfoundland, and he was only about a mile and a half away. Actually I'm not perfectly positive that it was a moose. The motel operator at the place assured me it was, but now that I think of it it could have been a couple of kids standing under a brown rug as a tourist attraction . . . Sort of Newfoundland's answer to the Loch Ness monster.

Ah, but the second moose I saw . . . there's no doubt about that one. It was a moose all right. I snuck right up to within oh, 20 to 30 feet of him (or her). Actually . . . the moose sort of snuck up on *me* to tell the truth. I was driving along the north shore of Lake Superior for the first time in my life, I was about halfway between Nipigon and Schreiber, when suddenly this moose sauntered out on the highway in front of me. Right in front of me. I didn't know it was a moose at the time . . . all I saw was two big eyes and an acre and a half of brown hide. I hit the brakes and as the car went into a four-wheel skid, I remember thinking that although the north shore scenery was undeniably breathtaking, it hadn't done a thing for the horses in the area — that was the homeliest Clydesdale I'd ever seen.

That's about the extent of my moose expertise . . . and some veteran hunters out there might grumble that I'm a little short on experience and a little long on gall to be offering moose hunting tips — but I think I've inadvertently stumbled onto something that even long-time moose snipers might have missed.

See, from what I understand of the pastime, one of the biggest problems in moose hunting — or in hunting any large antlered animal — is getting close enough to the critter to take a shot. Well there's this fella in Alaska, a research biologist by the name of Anthony Bubenik, who's been working on the problem . . . and he's come up with a way that allows him to get within 10 yards of bull caribou . . . or a full caribou herd, pretty well any time he feels like it.

What's more, Mister Bubenik says his method works with any member of the deer family — including moose. What he does, this Mister Bubenik, is he straps on a specially made false caribou head, complete with antlers . . . antlers suitable to a large bull caribou. Then, slowly, cautiously, he approaches a standing caribou herd. He's found that when it's done right, he not only gets menacing glances from the biggest bull in the herd . . . he also gets come-hither glances from the cows. What happens if the bull caribou charges? Well, Mister Bubenik has discovered he can *stop* charges by gesturing with the antlers in a particular way. See that's the whole point. Mister Bubenik has discovered there's a whole ritual among caribou and moose and all deer that revolves around the antlers. The animals take their behavioural cues from what the other animals are doing with their hat racks. In fact they watch the antlers so carefully that they don't much care if the antlers are attached to a caribou, or Anthony Bubenik.

Well okay for caribou . . . but does it work for moose? Mister Bubenik says it does . . . sort of. He says there's an extra problem with moose . . . and that is that they don't fool around. He says he's gotten to within 25 yards of a bull moose using his method but he wouldn't care to try it much closer. Because he says if you make one wrong gesture with a bull moose, he'll charge. And if you get charged by a bull moose, you are in serious trouble.

Apparently bull moose have a personal zone . . . like a hockey defenceman. It extends all around the bull, and the zone is somewhat longer in front than behind. Spanish bullfighters know this too — they call this space the bull's *quarencia* . . . and they're careful never to get inside that personal zone until the last possible moment.

Which brings us to the one insurmountable problem of adapting Anthony Bubenik's method of stalking to moose hunting. A false moose head with antlers attached would be so heavy and bulky to wear that you really wouldn't be able to carry your hunting rifle. So what would you do when you finally did get close enough to shoot the moose?

Worse still . . . what if you managed to use your technique to get within say 30 yards of some huge majestic browsing solitary bull. You get all the way up to him, well away from the trees, when suddenly he lifts his mighty head to look at you and . . . you suddenly realize he's not a he at all. He's a she . . . with a gleam in her eye.

JACKALOPES

THIS is definitely the quiet time of year in northwestern Ontario as far as tourism goes . . . Oh there's a good number of downhill skiers here in Thunder Bay . . . but for the most part they stick to the ski slopes and the chalets and lodges that wait at the bottom of the runs. Aside from meeting them in the airport lounge or seeing cars pass through with ski-racks abristle . . . a non-skier might never know they were in town.

Then too the hunting seasons are closed — moose, deer, duck. And most everybody with a Winnebago or a camper has abandoned it in the backyard for the winter — they sure aren't parked on the shores of our lakes. So as I say, it's the downtime of year for tourism . . A good time for reflecting on just what tourists bring north, to trade for our fish and game and our scenery.

They bring money of course . . . everybody knows that. But sometimes I think they bring in an even more valuable commodity . . . The commodity of . . . gullibility.

Now it's hard to put a dollar value on gullibility . . . but it seems to me that anything that can bring a chuckle to the lips of a northerner without fail . . . that can make him laugh and slap his thigh and fall to swapping tales with strangers . . . It seems to me that's a pretty valuable merchandise.

And the gullibility of tourists — especially tourists visiting north for the first time — does all of that in spades.

We in the north know for instance that next summer we can absolutely count on seeing several cars with American plates fighting their way through an 85-degree afternoon with skis on the luggage rack and a bewildered look on the driver's face.

We know that we're going to read stories in the newspapers of tourists disappointed because the OPP don't wear those cute red uniforms with the Smokey the Bear hats like Nelson Eddy did . . . and other visitors are sure to be downcast because they didn't get to see any Eskimos.

Of course northerners don't always sit back and wait for the tourists' gullibility to bubble forth ... on occasion northerners have been known to ... bait the hook as it were.

Which explains the fur-bearing trout that you can buy in many souvenir shops. It's a small run-of-the-mill speckled trout mounted on a plaque ... with one major difference ... It's covered with soft white fur. The accompanying pamphlet explains without a suggestion of a smile ... that the water in some Ontario lakes gets so cold, the fish in those lake have grown fur out of self-preservation.

I also know one tourist outfitter who stopped carrying the fur-bearing trout souvenir plaques, because she got tired of explaining to customers that it was really a hoax, and no, they couldn't go and catch their own.

Still, Canadians have got no corner on the weird-trophy business. I was reading in the paper the other day that down in the town of Douglas, Wyoming, souvenir stands are doing a brisk business in mounted Jackalope heads. Jackalope? It's a cross between a jack rabbit and an antelope. Way back in 1934 a taxidermist in Douglas happened to place a recently caught rabbit beside a pair of antelope horns on the floor of his shop.

Maybe he had a couple of drinks, I don't know ... but next morning, staring back at him out of a handsome wall plaque was a rabbit with antelope horns ... thus was born the Jackalope.

It started out as a joke ... but tourists took to it and it became the number one tourist item in Douglas, Wyoming. Nowadays, the Douglas Chamber of Commerce issues thousands of Jackalope hunting licences every year (valid only June 31st, between 12 midnight and 2 A.M.) And there are even signs on the highway outside Douglas that read 'Slow ... Jackalope Crossing.'

The scary thing is ... a lot of the people who buy the mounted Jackalope heads, and the Jackalope hunting licences and the Jackalope postcards ... don't ... know ... it's a joke. They even get angry if you tell them not to take it seriously.

Ah well ... I guess P.T. Barnum wasn't far off the mark when he suggested there's a sucker born every minute.

There's certainly a plentiful enough supply to guarantee yarn spinners and truth stretchers in northwestern Ontario a bumper crop of incredulous audiences ... I'm thinking particularly of folks like the famous Doc Skinner of Longlac, who's taken more than one tourist along for a gentle ride in his lifetime.

Never forget the first time I met the famous fishiatrist at Skinners Acres in Longlac. Doc for some reason had a stuffed raven sitting on his counter.

I was fresh from Toronto at the time, and I asked Doc why anybody would bother to stuff and mount a crow. Doc didn't bat an eye. Just gently explained that that wasn't a crow I was looking at. He pointed out that crows are much smaller and have a yellow beak . . . and a completely different song.

Nope the doc explained . . . that wasn't a crow I was looking at. It was the weak sister in a family of Longlac blackflies.

Damn near sold it to me too.

BIKES

YOU know people can talk about the marvels of modern technology . . . about pocket calculators and talking typewriters, Anik satellites and atomic reactors . . . those things don't mean a thing to me. Mostly, I admit, because I haven't a clue what makes them work. I am a pre-industrial person. I still regard airplanes in the sky as something between an act of faith and an optical illusion. I've never been able to adjust the volume on my stereo, let along open it up and tinker with all the miniaturized wisps of tubing and transistorized gizmos within.

To tell you the truth, machines confuse and terrify me. From the Ottawa computer that sends me mechanical threats about my income tax, to this typewriter before me . . . I hate machines . . . I hate them all.

Well . . . almost all. There is one machine that I have not only learned to live with in peace . . . but which I must confess a certain amount of affection for. It is the lowly bicycle.

And I am heartened to see that the bicycle is not so lowly as it had been. There was about a 10-year period there, in the 60s . . . when it was hopelessly square to be seen riding a bicycle. But that time is past. Now the streets are no longer the private domain of the car and the truck. Cyclists are doggedly competing for that thin strip of pavement between the car fenders and the shoulder of the road.

Not the same bikes that everybody had when I was a kid. No, those old one-speed clunkers are long gone. Replaced by exotic thoroughbreds from France and Italy with tires the width of your thumb, and clamps to hold water bottles, low-slung, copiously taped handlebars and a multiplicity of gears that should allow the rider to go straight up the face of a cliff.

Now I don't pretend to understand the subtleties of the 10-speed gear ratios — I don't even like to glance at the back sprocket of my 10-speed with its spaghetti-like configurations of chain and wire and dials . . . but the thing is, I understand the broad concept of the bicycle. If you push your foot on the pedal the wheels go round . . . the pushing gets harder or easier depending on which gear you're in; if you pull the handlebars to the right, you will lurch to the right; if you repeat the action to the left you will lurch to the left. If you stick your heel in the spokes of your rear tire while you are cruising along it will have three basic effects . . . It will stop your bike, rip out several spokes and hurt your heel like hell. These are the kind of esoteric mechanical principles that I can grasp, you see . . . and that's what makes the bicycle so dear to my unmechanical heart.

Apparently I'm not the only one whose passion for biking has been kindled or rekindled of late. Cycling is experiencing a tremendous boom against all odds. Consider the odds against taking up the bicycle. Right off the top, it's expensive. The going price for a new five- or ten-speed of medium to good quality starts at about the hundred and fifty dollar mark. For the fanatic there are bikes in the seven- and eight-hundred-dollar league. Then of course you'll want a few accessories which probably won't come with the bike. A tire pump, tool kit, a tote bag, a light for night riding, maybe a horn. Don't forget you need a licence too, and it's always nice to have an odometer to see how far you travel . . . and maybe a speedometer to see how fast you're going . . .

Well, you get the message. It's not hard at all to blow an extra 50 bucks on what car salesmen like to call 'options' before you even get to sling your leg over the saddle. So there's a financial barricade that you have to overcome, if you want to get into cycling . . . Ah, but that's when you run into the big roadblock: the hostility of non-cyclists.

You think you live in a civilized country, madame? You believe there's a basic reverence for life here in Ontario? And that only criminals and maniacs would jeopardize the well-being of their fellow humans? Hah. You have obviously not cycled down a main thoroughfare during rush hour. That's when you discover how it feels to be an oppressed minority.

A few, very few, drivers are outright hostile. They'll honk at you, brush by you, even roll down the window and curse you out. But many more drivers are simply thoughtless. They don't seem to realize that it can be pretty terrifying to have a ton and a half of steel go swooshing by inches from your left calf. They'll make un-signalled turns right in front of you . . . or, when they're parked at the curb and you're bearing down on them, they'll throw open the car door at the last moment which gives you (the bike rider) the option of veering out into traffic or ploughing into a car door . . . A difficult choice to make on the spur of the moment.

Ah, but I'm dwelling on the negative. Obviously there's a larger positive side, or bicycling wouldn't be enjoying the popular resurgence it is. If I had another 10 minutes I could tell you about the positive things . . . But I've got a better idea. Why don't you . . . this afternoon, or this evening, or this weekend or the next sunny day . . . just borrow somebody's bike? Just for an hour or two, and find out about the positive side yourself.

Two tips tho' . . . don't wear tight pants . . . and avoid the rush hour.

THE SANDMAN

ONE of the enduring rituals of living in Ontario's North is winter-watching.

We don't have a lot of choice in the matter, since we spend nearly half the year bundled up and hunkered down, skidding and sliding, shovelling and cursing the Perpetually Lost Glove.

So we all have our own personal ways of realizing that the season is irrevocably upon us. For some, it's when the last leaf falls. Others mark it by the Putting On of Snow Tires. For still others, winter's here when you finally decide to move in the lawn furniture, curl up the garden hose and shuffle the lawnmower to the absolute back of the basement.

Not me. For me winter isn't really here until The Sandman comes. He arrived yesterday morning. Winter's here.

You don't have a sandman? That's probably because you don't live on a hill. I do. The street in front of my house cants at about a 60-degree tilt down towards Thunder Bay Harbour. In the summer during a thunderstorm, the water turns down that street like a mountain stream, tumbling, twisting and slooshing.

In the winter time, cars do the same thing.

It has its advantages. Watching the terror-stricken faces of drivers white-knuckling a nigh-useless steering wheel as they cascade past the living room window beats Hockey Night in Canada for thrills. It has its disadvantages too. You get to push a lot of cars when you live on a hill.

Then there's the sidewalk, which runs between the house and the street. It gets pretty slippery too, and the logistics of running a Works Department sand or salt truck up a sidewalk are obviously self-defeating.

That's where the sandman comes in.

Every year, about this time, a little mound of sand magically appears on the boulevard between the street and the sidewalk. And virtually ever morning, from now until the snow stops flying, I know I can walk out my front door early in the morning and see the sandman — some anonymous, be-parka-ed worker — throwing shovelfuls of sand down the treacherous slope of the sidewalk.

Sounds like a hellish job — getting up in the pre-dawn murk of a Thunder Bay winter morning to heave sand . . . but I don't know . . . Last year I had a sandman who sang while he worked. This year, a new sandman — Italian I think. He's cheerful too, and he never quits until the whole length of sidewalk sports a brown gritty coat.

And yesterday, when I was sitting in the driveway, late for work and my wheels spinning uselessly, he put down his shovel and gave me a push.

He likes to chat sometimes and from his thick accent and his round-eyed conversational fixation on the severity of our weather — 'Ver' col' today! Never feel so col'!' — I like to think he's a recent immigrant . . . from the sun-baked streets of Naples maybe, suddenly whisked away from the ocean and the vineyards and plunged into the breathtaking climate of a sub-arctic foreign city by a frozen lake.

I know, I know . . . he probably drives a Peugeot and takes Honours Anthropology at the local university — but student or *paesano*, I know he won't be my sandman next year. I'll have a new one. They turn over fairly quickly. There are more comfortable jobs around.

But not many more comforting ones — to those of us who reap the benefits . . . those of us who would spend our winters slipping and sliding, maybe breaking hips and spraining ankles if they weren't on the job.

It's a small thing, but small comforts are important when it comes to slugging it out through a Northern winter.

Thank you, City Works for your sandman system. It makes the winter a little easier.

And Sandman . . . even if you do mean that winter is finally and irrevocably here, thank you, *grazie, e buona fortuna.*

TOMATOES

QUIZ time for all northwestern Ontario tillers of the soil. Anybody out there who has ever tried to coax, cajole, bribe and wheedle the sullen tundra we live on into growing something edible can play.

The question: what's small, round, green and hard as a lump of Precambrian granite?

Answer: your tomatoes. It's fall once again, and once again those stubborn little mothers in your garden have resolutely refused to turn to bright cheery red. They hang there on your tomato plants, unrepentantly. Like so many emerald marbles, like so many jade squash balls and it's time you admitted something to yourself. Forget optimism. Never mind the surefire quick-maturing seed you planted. Don't dwell on the way you coddled those little seedlings last spring, trying everything short of an iron lung to give them an early start.

Face it.

They are Not. Going. To Turn.

Any day now, a killer frost is going to come down on your garden like a platoon of Cossacks. Those tomato plants are going to go down like dominoes and you're going to be left with a backyard full of green gravel.

Once again.

Statistics Canada doesn't put out any figures on it, but I'd be willing to bet a bag of Vigoro to three stale zucchini seeds that more northwestern Ontario gardeners have gone ga-ga over stubborn tomatoes than long winters.

Well, not to fear. Old Green Thumb Black is here with a solution.

No, I can't make your green tomatoes turn red, but I can give you something to do with the suckers, short of cruising the backroads on a moonless night looking for a sanitary landfill project.

Actually, I owe it all to Mom. She's about as good a gardener as I am. Which is to say not very. The only gardening award she ever won came from a miniature gourd she managed to harvest one year.

Beautiful tiny thing. Pure orange. About the size of a snow pea. Unfortunately she'd planted pumpkin seeds.

She had even worse luck with tomatoes. We finally had to show her a colour photograph in the *Random House Encyclopedia* to convince her that ripe tomatoes were red, not green.

But she wasn't impressed. I think she's still convinced that red tomatoes are vegetative victims of sunstroke.

She didn't care anyway. Because she had The Recipe.

A closely guarded family secret for generations, Mom Black's Green Tomato Pickle Recipe finally went public in these pages two years ago.

Partly because I felt I owed it to humanity. Partly because my mother forgot my birthday.

Mostly because I was strapped for an idea for a column.

Be that as it may, the response was instantaneous and gratifying. People tried the recipe and loved it. Cards and letters of heartfelt thanks inundated the newspaper office.

So, it being that time of year again, here it is:

MOM BLACK'S GREEN TOMATO PICKLE

INGREDIENTS

6 quarts green tomatoes
5 large onions
salt
2½ cups cider vinegar
1½ cups water
1½ pounds brown sugar (or less)
1 teaspoon each of curry powder, turmeric, cloves, cinnamon, celery seed, and pickling spice if desired.

DIRECTIONS

Cut tomatoes and onions into thin slices. Sprinkle with salt and let stand overnight. In the morning, drain the tomatoes and onions. Combine remaining ingredients in a large pan and bring to a boil. Add tomatoes and onions and simmer until thick, stirring frequently. Pour into sterilized jars and seal.

That's it. That's all there is to Mom Black's Foolproof Failsafe Green Tomato Pickle Recipe. Stone guaranteed to turn your annual garden disaster into a taste treat bonanza.

And even if it doesn't . . . The house will smell great for days.

ANIMALS

THIS is being written early in the morning.

Believe it or not, there are some good things to be said for hacking out a column early in the morning. For one thing, it's cool, which it probably won't be later today. I've tried writing in the heat of the midday sun but the pith helmet keeps slipping over my eyes.

And it's quiet. The buzz and beep of traffic hasn't wound up to the angry high-pitched whine you get in the morning rush hour.

There are no distractions. It's too early to dial up a friend and wile away a quarter hour in gossiping. There's nothing on TV aside from a clutch of test patterns and some owlish university professor trying to interest me in the Islamic Renaissance.

But there's a far better reason for writing in the early morning than all that. I get the privilege of working with a chorus. Yeah. Just like Ray Charles. They're singing right now. And they're better than the Raylettes. Instead of the throbbing monotony of 'Oooowah, ooh ooowah' I'm getting cheeps and chirrups and warbles and pweets.

Songbirds. They perform for free like this every morning. I like to think of them as a volunteer back-up group, but I know that's conceited. They don't even know I'm pecking away at my Olympia down here — and if they did, they couldn't care less.

So why do they? Sing, I mean. Come to that, why do wolves howl and cats in heat *miaoooowurl* and grouse thrum and bullfrogs *jugarum* and whooping cranes do a stately free-form pas de deux that would do Karen Kain proud?

Why all these free performances before empty houses?

Well, I'm indebted to the Thunder Bay Field Naturalists Club for providing at least part of the answer. In a recent newsletter the club cleared up some of the reasons behind a few of the animal antics that mankind has long theorized about.

Not surprisingly most of our pet theories are way off-base. Wolves don't howl because they're lonely or hungry. Wolf howls are actually one of the most sophisticated and complex 'languages' in the natural world. Howling is a wolf pack's way of communicating, keeping in touch at night when visibility is poor.

As for grouse thrums and pigeon pouts and peacock displays and all the other feathered *son et lumière* shows that go on out in the bush — they're just what they look like. Courtship rituals designed to establish and enhance the fact that the performer is pretty hot stuff who believes that he and the object of his affection could make beautiful music together.

You can catch clumsy, hairless, two-legged imitations of the same phenomenon down at Alfie's Disco on any Friday night.

And the crane dance? It's as important as it is majestic. If cranes didn't dance, there would be no little cranes come spring. Young cranes that have never mated are about as good at it as that gangly kid in *Summer of '42*. The courting ballet synchronizes the male and female sexually. There are 15 species of cranes around the world. They all dance to the same steps.

If we humans had a shred of decency and respect for privacy, we wouldn't even be watching.

Ah, but what about the also-rans of the bird world? Dumpy little sparrows, vaguely malevolent-looking starlings and that Soupy Sales of the northland, the whiskeyjack?

Well, they have their songs. And the purpose of their songs is closely related to mating and nesting. There are something like four thousand different species of songbirds in the world and each species has its own signature tunes — tunes to tell strangers who they are and where their property line extends to, and tunes to pitch a little woo when the mating season rolls around.

But lately, biologists have come up with an astonishing theory. A revolutionary theory.

They now suspect — only suspect, mind — that songbirds might not just be singing only for practical reasons of mating and nesting.

There's convincing evidence that they might occasionally sing . . . *just for the fun of it.*

Frightfully radical idea. But nice.

If you want to know how nice, get up with the sun tomorrow morning. Continuous shows, unlimited seating.

No admission, no cover charge.

SCIENCE

I REMEMBER when I first knew I was going to have trouble with Science. It was in a grade 11 physics class. The teacher gave us a problem to work out. 'A workman, weighing 160 pounds, is spreading gravel on the roof of a building which is 230 feet high. He loses his footing and falls over the side. Discounting wind velocity, calculate his rate of fall at point of impact with the ground.'

My less squeamish colleagues hunkered down with knitted brows and flying ballpoints. The teacher turned to the blackboard, laying down strings of numerals interspersed with division signs and decimal points in a flurry of chalk dust.

I just sat there. I wanted to stand up and yell, *Wait a minute! What about this poor sucker who's spread all over the parking lot! Who was he? What's his wife going to do? Did he have any kids?*

I didn't say any of that of course. Technological ignoramus that I was, I was still smart enough to know that my concerns weren't 'relevant' to the problem.

Practitioners of Pure Science never allow themselves to be sidetracked by murky considerations like emotion, morality or ethics. That's how we got the atom bomb. The nuclear physicists who gave us the bomb were just trying to get their equations to work out on the blackboard. They didn't intend to vaporize the men, women and children of two Japanese cities. Unfortunate by-product.

It's still going on, this myopic, one-step-at-a-time, Band-Aid-and-baling-wire approach to problem solving. Recently our federal Department of Northern Affairs spent 80 grand to kill two bears.

The scientists wanted to see what effect an oil spill in the Arctic would have on polar bears. Scientific solution? Get a couple of polar bears, dunk them in crude oil and stand by with a note pad.

They did. Less than amazingly, the two young bears tried to lick the oil off their fur, ingested the oil and died. Lingering, horrible deaths. I don't know exactly how long it took the bears to die, but the scientists could tell you. They took notes.

An average trapper or garage mechanic could have told them what would happen to a bear eating crude oil, for a fee of 20 bucks. The Department of Northern Affairs spent $80,000 on the experiment.

Somewhere north of Kenora this summer, scientists have plans to kill a lake. It's a small lake. Landlocked. Unimportant. The scientists are going to systematically strafe it with chemicals until there's no living thing left in it.

Why? Well, they're concerned about acid rain, yet another unforeseen technological by-product that is killing our lakes. They want to see exactly how acid rain affects a given body of water, so they're force-feeding this little lake a concentrated dose of the stuff.

They will monitor the lake and find out how fast the trout die, and how quickly the walleye disappear and what concentration of poison it takes to wipe out the last sucker, the last frog, the last bullrush.

Well, who knows? They may pick up some valuable information that will slow down the death of larger, more important lakes. But I've got a hunch that what we'll end up with is a bill for a few thousand dollars, yet another never-read and unremembered government report.

And one dead lake.

And I keep having visions of that poor dumb clumsy sod of a workman in his screaming descent, watching the pavement coming up to meet him. Unaware that he had just become a problem in grade 11 physics class.

PAPER

IT'S SPRING. It must be. I put the Christmas tree out in the garbage last week.

That's a spring ritual around my place that's every bit as traditional as the first robin and the Bush-Boots-to-the-Basement Routine.

I know, I know . . . it's a shade past the usual Yuletide season and I never quite get over the flush of embarrassment I feel when the Disposal Truck screeches to a stop in front of my place one April morning, and every guy on the truck including the driver gets out to peer incredulously at the Christmas tree up until April.

Fact is, I don't keep it up — not in the house anyway. It goes out the door about a week after New Year's, but it doesn't go in the garbage. Instead I jam it upright in a snowbank beside the house.

And there it stays, through January blizzards, February freeze-ups and March maelstroms — a pine-scented pit stop for shivering sparrows, starlings and chickadees caught with their pinfeathers down between bird feeders.

And a pleasant change for these human eyes too, peering out of frost-rimmed windows over a dreary landscape daubed in shades of grey, to suddenly see a patch of sturdy upright green.

The illusion melts away come April of course — along with that once white and mighty, now brown and gap-toothed snowbank in the side yard. Each succeeding April dawn breaks on a tree listing a little more to starboard. One morning finds it on its side, and that's the end of the line for my once-proud shrub. Next garbage pickup day finds the tree slumped forlornly in among the Glad bags by the curb.

The reason I bring all this up is that I noticed a funny thing, dragging my Christmas tree out to the curb this week. It was a little white tag on one of the bottom branches.

I hadn't seen it when I bought the tree at the Kiwanis Christmas Tree Lot last December.

It didn't catch my eye when I put the tree up in the living room and decorated it.

But I sure noticed it last week. It told me where my Christmas Tree came from. The tag read Alliston, Ontario.

Alliston, Ontario is maybe 20 miles beyond the boundaries of Metropolitan Hogtown.

I live in Thunder Bay. In the bush, practically.

And my Christmas tree comes from the outskirts of Toronto?

There is something seriously screwed up about an economy that can grow a Christmas tree on land best suited to raising bumper crops of townhouses and condominiums, nurture it, cut it down and put it on a truck and sell it to a guy like me, who lives smack in the middle of several *thousand square miles* of Christmas trees.

Sure I'm a sucker for not going out and cutting my own. I admit that. I also confess that I did cut my own tree once a few Christmases back . . . and I wish to report that wading through navel-deep drifts in search of the perfect spruce and trying to chop through its frozen trunk with numbed fingers is not the heart-warming, character-building experience it's cracked up to be.

But that's not even the point. The point is, that somehow — crazily — it makes economic sense to sell southern Ontario Christmas trees to northerners. Like selling refrigerators to Eskimos.

And I can't figure it out.

Stew Brydges is having a hard time with 20th-century economics too. Mister Brydges is the editor-publisher of the Geraldton *Times-Star*.

The *Times-Star* has been rolling off the press in Geraldton for years with only the usual minor problems of a small town weekly.

Suddenly last September Mister Brydges ran up against an all-new problem.

He couldn't buy newsprint.

Go look up Geraldton on the map. You will note that it sits smack in the middle of miles of northwestern Ontario bush. It is surrounded by major timber-cutting operations on all sides. It is just a few miles up the highway from Domtar, Great Lakes Paper, Abitibi and Kimberley-Clark — some of the biggest mills on the continent.

And the *Times-Star* couldn't buy *newsprint*??

Money wasn't a problem. Mister Brydges pays cash. There just wasn't any newsprint to be had.

Well, the *Times-Star* weathered the drought. At the moment it's sitting on enough newsprint to satisfy its needs for the foreseeable future.

But how far that future is foreseeable I'm not sure.

Not when a northwestern Ontario newspaper can't buy newsprint.

Nor when Lakeheaders celebrate Christmas around a tree that grew up on the outskirts of Toronto.

HORN

YOU'LL never guess what the hottest new international growth industry is.

Horns.

You read right. — And I don't mean car horns, truck horns, trombones or bugles. The horns I'm talking about are those roof racks that all little Bambis get when they grow up. Antlers. Fortunes are being made on the International Antler Market.

Most of the fortunes are being made by Kiwis — New Zealanders, and that's a double boon for them, because the biggest pest in their semi-tropical paradise is the deer. It has no natural enemies in New Zealand and ever since the day in 1851 when a dozen red deer were imported for the hunting pleasure of Scottish settlers there's been a very real danger that the animals would overrun the island. The New Zealand government was forced to adopt emergency control programs, including sharpshooters in helicopters.

Now that grisly chapter of New Zealand deer management is pretty well closed. Authorities have discovered that their overabundance of deer are worth a lot more to them alive than dead.

Why? Because a dead deer is worth somewhere between 250 and 300 Kiwi dollars as venison, but a young healthy stag can grow about a thousand dollars worth of antler in one year. And he'll do it all over again the next year and the next and the next and the next.

Who pays such outrageous prices for these bony skull out-growths? The big market is in the Orient — Korean, Hong Kong, Japanese and Taiwanese buyers jostle for the privilege of buying all the New Zealand deer antlers they can get their hands on. But not just any old antlers. They want the soft velvet-covered young horns.

A new breed of New Zealand 'deer farmer' is only too glad to oblige. There are about 600 such entrepreneurs in New Zealand right now, each running herds of about a thousand head. Come round-up time, the deer are penned, relieved of their young horns under anaesthesia and veterinary supervision, then released to do it all over again. The horn — the 'velvet' it's called — is then shipped to the buyers for processing.

And it's big business. Last year one buyer alone — Johnny Wang — shipped 20,000 pounds — 10 *tons* — of flash-frozen New Zealand velvet all the way to San Francisco where it was meticulously processed according to a closely guarded formula.

The processing of horn is always a big secret. It may involve boiling, slicing, drying and pulverizing.

If New Zealand farmers are doing all right financially in the velvet market, the buyers are giggling hysterically all the way to the bank. The latest quoted price for dried velvet on the Hong Kong Retail Market was 40 to 60 dollars an *ounce*. Figure out how much Johnny Wang makes on each 20-ton shipment.

Even if he does have to pay his own OHIP.

Which brings us rudely back to home. I wouldn't say that deer are anything like a nuisance here in northwestern Ontario, but I do know for sure that their antler potential is being ignored. Aside from getting nailed up once in a while over a garage door or a fireplace, deer antlers are treated with complete disdain in these parts.

And if deer antler is fetching such handsome prices on the Hong Kong stock exchange, I can't help wondering how much they'd pay for the same commodity from the deer's homely cousin, the moose.

By gad, we could become the economic heart of this country yet . . . with little sheikdoms in Kenora and Hornepayne and Nakina . . . exporting black fly steaks and playing the international moose velvet market . . .

Jeez.

I just read this over and I realize for all I've told you about the

international velvet market, the New Zealand economy and how much you can get for an ounce of deer horn in Hong Kong . . .

I never mentioned *why* Asians are so keen on the product.

It's because they think it's an aphrodisiac.

Makes them feel horny I guess.

FISH

I KNOW it's not a popular thing to say, but I sure hate to see the ice go out.

Not that I'm any fan of winter. The only white I want to see between now and next Christmas Eve will be on golf balls, tennis shorts, seagulls and maybe the odd fleecy cloud way off on the horizon.

No, it's just that when the ice goes out each spring I start to get silly. It happens every year. I start dreaming. About leaping northerns, tail-walking muskies and that first tentative pluck of tension that travels up your line, along your rod, through your wrist, up your arm — all the way to the tiny hairs on the back of your neck, telling you that some finny, fairly large denizen of the deep is gumming the goodies on the end of your fishing line.

Don't get me wrong. I am some light-years removed from the Compleat Angler. I'm lucky if I get to cast my line three times running without ending up with enough backlashes, snarls and tangles to make my reel look like a work of macramé done by an acid freak.

Somebody once described fishing as a jerk at one end of the line waiting for a jerk at the other end.

He could have been talking about me.

Ah well . . . I can dream with the best of them. And I do. But I'd have to go some distance to top the fish story that came out of Sioux Narrows recently.

Did you hear about it? It didn't get all that much attention at the time, for reasons which I can't begin to fathom. If I ever landed a fish like Frank White landed I'd demand an Order of Canada medal at the very least.

Frank White is a commercial fisherman in Sioux Narrows. Last July he chugged back to the dock with his boat riding a little low in the water.

Well it might. On the deck was a scaly behemoth exactly seven feet five inches long. It weighed 250 pounds, give or take a kilogram. Its girth was 37 inches.

I've never even caught a fish 37 inches *long*.

Frank White didn't have the fish mounted. He probably would have had to sell his boat to pay for the stuffing. Instead, he and a friend filleted the fish on the dock. Using two knives and a wood-axe. Observers say the backbone was three inches in diameter — bigger than a fair-sized moose.

What was this fugitive from a Hollywood horror movie? *Acipenser transmontanus* if you want to get fancy; a dirty great sturgeon if you prefer it plain.

A 250-pound fish. It blew my mind — until I started checking the record books. Turns out Frank White's sturgeon was practically anaemic. Back in the late 1800s, sturgeons measuring upwards of 24 feet in length were regularly being hauled out of the Danube and Volga rivers in eastern Europe.

With block and tackle, one presumes.

On May 11, 1922, a female sturgeon was caught in the estuary of the Volga. The *head* weighed 633 pounds, according to the *Guinness Book of Records*.

Sturgeon run a bit more modest on this side of the ocean. Still, there are reports of 1,500-pound monsters being caught in Washington and Oregon around the turn of the century. The official authenticated North American record is a 12½-foot female taken in the Columbia River, near Vancouver, Washington, in the summer of 1912. It crushed the scales at a mere 1,285 pounds.

All of which is not to belittle the accomplishment of Frank White, the Sioux Narrows fisherman. After all his wisp of a 250-pounder did yield some 20 pounds of caviar and Lord knows how many fillets.

And it makes my dreams of wrestling four pounds of pulsating pickerel into a canoe seem positively pathetic.

PEAT

Well for Peat's sake, who'd o' thunk it?

In my continuing search for a new and vital economic base for northwestern Ontario (You remember my plan to harvest moose antlers for the international aphrodisiac industry? My scheme to have black flies certified under the Migratory Birds Act?) — in my unending endeavour to find some new overlooked and under-exploited resource that will put a few bucks in our pockets without turning the north into a desert or making us all glow in the dark, I think I've come up with a winner.

Dirt.

Well, not dirt exactly. My *Random House Encyclopedia* calls it 'dark brown decayed organic material with a high carbon content built up in bogs.'

That's what the book calls it. Most folks call it peat.

People in Europe have been using peat for fuel for centuries. Russia, Finland and Ireland run whole generating stations on dried peat.

In Canada we put it in geranium pots.

It's really absurd. The Russians claim that their peat-powered plants produce six thousand megawatts of power *per hour*. That's the equivalent of three nuclear reactors *á la* Pickering.

Somebody please explain why we're putzing around with multi-billion-dollar Strangelovian death traps that leak radioactive poisons — and ignoring the stuff that's lying out in the back yard?

The technology is as near as a long-distance call to Helsinki. There's a picture of Finnish 'peat-harvesting' in a recent issue of *Maclean's*. From a distance it looks like harvest time in a wheat field outside Brandon — with one difference. In the peat business, the crop grows down, not up.

What they do is drain a bog, then cut the peat fuel to a depth of about five feet. The loosened peat is sucked up by a gizmo that looks very much like a Massey-Ferguson harvester, and blown into a big rolling bin that runs alongside the harvester. The peat then sits in the sun for a few days to let most of its water content drain off.

Pretty simple stuff. And how far along the road is Canada in developing its peat potential?

Not even at the starting line yet.

Quebec is making moves though. Hydro-Quebec has a committee that's at least looking at the possibilities of peat power to generate electricity. It looks like this country's first peat-fired electrical facility will be set up on Anticosti Island, in the Gulf of St. Lawrence.

But it's pretty small potatoes — especially for a country like this, which after Russia, possesses the biggest collection of peat bogs in the world.

And as anybody who's spent any time in the bush knows, an awful lot of those peat bogs are right here in northwestern Ontario. We have particularly massive peat concentrations.

Would it be a good idea economically? Would there be environmental backlashes — pollution, destruction of habitat — that make the whole idea a non-starter? I don't know. But the point is, nobody in government seems to either.

As near as I can determine, nobody in these parts is looking at the idea of Peat Power very seriously.

Ah well... in the meantime, I can dream.

I foresee a golden, glorious destiny for northwestern Ontario — thumbing our noses at those Prairie sheiks as their oil finally dribbles down to a trickle and we're sitting on entire townships of the fuel of the future.

I see brand new and mighty metropolises speckling the Precambrian Shield . . . cities like Peatsburgh, Peaterborough, St. Peatersburgh . . .

I predict subtle name changes for old northwestern Ontario hamlets as this energy source transforms us into Saudi Arabia North.

Rosspeat... South Porcupeat... Big Peat Lake... Peatico Provincial Park... Peat Arthur...

It's all right officer, I'll come quietly.

WENDELL

TOM WOLFE once wrote a profile of Canada's most famous philosopher, Marshall McLuhan, entitled: What If He Is *Right*?

What an appropriate title that would be for a story on northwestern Ontario's least-famous philosopher.

Have to be an obituary I guess. Wendell Beckwith died last week.

He died on Best Island up in Whitewater Lake where he'd lived like a hermit for the past 18 years. He died amid his revolutionary ... well, 'cabins' is hardly adequate — 'monuments' would be more like it. He died surrounded by the Indian artifacts he'd collected from the vanishing culture he found when he went there back in the early 60s.

I don't know for sure, but I like to think that Wendell died in his 'Mole.' That's what he called the last structure he built. It was a cabin. An underground cabin. It was, like everything he made, a work of art. All inlaid wood, meticulously fitted. It had the warmth and intimacy of the captain's quarters on a 19th-century schooner.

Especially the warmth. Wendell had designed the Mole to be so heat-efficient he could keep it warm with a hearth fire of a few small branches.

He did most of his theoretical work in the Mole. A set of *Encyclopaedia Britannica* stretched across one wall. Reference books of every description shored up the encyclopaedias. Every hand-crafted nook and cranny in the Mole held papers or experiments or equipment for Wendell's work.

What was his work? That doesn't fit into any cubbyhole. Wendell worked on new improved cedar shingles and he worked on interplanetary relationships of space and time. He devised a contraption that used the concentric rings of a tree trunk to record barometric changes and he carved a breathtakingly beautiful Indian head at the front end of the ridgepole of one of his cabins. Rose Chaltry, a lovely woman and Wendell's friend, who knew him as well as anyone could, said: 'He's a philosopher, a scientist, — there was nothing he couldn't do. If there was something he needed, he would build it. Or invent it.'

To appreciate the phenomenon of Wendell, you have to understand that he did all this in the wilderness. Two hundred miles north of Thunder Bay. No electricity, no phone, no roads. The only way to get to Wendell's was by bush plane or canoe.

And it wasn't easy to find. Wendell and all his creations blended into the rock and the black spruce of Best Island. You could fly at treetop level over his retreat and never guess it was there.

But genius puts out a strong magnetic field. People found him. *National Geographic* magazine tracked him down and did a story on him. And every summer the canoe bows of more and more Outward Bound trippers nosed into the small sandy beach below his place and camped to hear the man talk and see his work.

Eighteen years ago, Wendell went to a faceless island on an obscure lake to get away from people. In the last years there were some summer days when he could have had fewer distractions in a glass-fronted office in Victoriaville Mall.

He handled the intruders with grace though. He was full of grace, this wild-haired man with eyeglasses that looked like Coke-bottle bottoms and a smile that never seemed to leave his face. I have a hunch that he really didn't like all the idolatry and intrusion. But he probably didn't like winter either. He just learned to go with it.

There are a million stories about Wendell. Did you know he designed Ogoki Lodge? Not the bloated white elephant that stands today — Wendell designed one that could have been built from native timber. One that would have blended it in with the surroundings. One that would have provided a completely different, almost totally authentic wilderness experience for its visitors. One that would have afforded employment with a maximum of dignity and a minimum of dislocation for the Indians in the area.

Wendell's idea for Ogoki Lodge was totally integrated — structurally, sociologically, environmentally, historically and aesthetically. Then the government whiz kids took over. They copped one or two of Wendell's ideas, ballooned them out of recognition, trucked in some B.C. fir and put up a structure that, aside from being unusually grotesque, offers nothing a visitor couldn't find anywhere else.

Aside from a spectacularly inefficient design, Ogoki could be the Bigwin Inn in Muskoka or Joe's Fly-in Fish Camp on Lake Witchapatootie.

Except that Ogoki loses more money.

But none of that is Wendell's fault. He drew up the plans for free, because it was a project that intrigued him. When the government botched it, I like to think that Wendell just shrugged and went on to some other mystery.

But why Whitewater Lake? Why Best Island? Why didn't Wendell set up shop on the campus of Harvard, or Yale or the U of T?

Well, Wendell had a theory about that. According to his calculations, this world isn't long for . . this world.

I don't pretend to understand the theory. It involves plate techtonics, numerology and massive shifts in the earth's crust. But what it boils down to is that sometime around the year 2026, Wendell expected the world as we know it to be largely destroyed.

Earthquakes, tidal waves and natural disasters like that.

One of the places that would weather the catastrophe, according to Wendell's calculations, is a small chunk of Precambrian Shield about two hundred miles north of Thunder Bay. Best Island, in Whitewater Lake, would be right in the centre of it.

Well, Wendell's gone on to larger mysteries now. And what he's left behind is being squabbled over by a millionaire who doesn't need it and a government that will never comprehend it.

His prediction is pretty easy to fathom though.

Twenty twenty-six he said. That's less than 35 years away.

And I can't help thinking: What if he is *right*?

WALKING

I HOPE when I get old and creaky that my kids are still interested enough in me to ask me what age I grew up in. I've got the answer all worked out. I won't say anything profound like the Age of the Atom or the Age of Psychotherapy. I won't claim to have throbbed through the Age of Rock or been programmed during the Age of Computers. Nope. I'm gonna tell them I survived through the Age of Exercise.

Really. All my life seems to have been spent watching earnest, slightly damp fanatics rush by me in tennis whites or warm-up suits, clutching a variety of athletic aids and crutches ranging from squash racquets to ski poles; from aluminum paddles to the handlebars of a 10-speed, magnesium alloy bicycle with an unpronounceable Japanese name.

This country is exercise crazy — and it has been for years. I can't decide whether it started with 5BX and 10BX — those puff and pant programs invented by the Canadian Air Force — or the crushing revelation a few years back that most Johnny and Janie Canucks were less fit than a 60-year-old Swede.

Maybe it was Expo. Maybe it was having a prime minister who could do a one and a half gainer off a motel diving board. Perhaps it was just a kind of national pre-menopause — I don't know what it was . . . All I know is that a country that used to get fashionably pink-faced and slightly out of breath at the prospect of taking on anything more strenuous than changing TV channels suddenly went berserk. Muscle tone was all. Everybody was jogging, biking, hiking, herringboning or making appointments with a chiropractor to deal with bruised muscles from doing same.

I don't mind telling you I sneered. When jogging appeared and books on jogging and courses on jogging and whole philosophies on 'the runner's high' . . . I scoffed. It was a fad, I said. Soon to go the way of the passenger pigeon, Joey Dee and the Peppermint Lounge. I gave it two years.

Well, I was wrong. Jogging is still with us and in fact there are more joggers hauling their protesting bodies up and down our streets and around our high school tracks than ever before.

And not just jogging. Squash is epidemic. Bicycle riding. Cross country skiing — Lord, cross country skiing. Do you know back in the late fall I had to pull my car over to the side of the road one day — I saw these . . . apparitions . . . swinging and lurching along the shoulder.

It was a family of cross country skiers. Mom, Dad and kids. Except it was 60 degrees and there was no snow on the ground. Wouldn't be for a couple of months. They had, so help me, skis with little wheels on them and they were *practising* for heaven's sake.

It was about that time that I realized that the Exercise Fad wasn't a bandwagon — it was a parade. And if I wanted to be in it at all, I'd better grab onto something that I could handle.

Fortunately my timing, though accidental, was perfect. The newest entry in the Exercise Sweepstakes is a bit of a sleeper. It's actually been with us all along, but there was no special warm-up routine for it, no hardcover how-to manuals. People just did it. It's called Walking.

Yeah. Just walking. Down in the States, the President's Council on Fitness and Sports did a national survey on forms of exercise. Everybody put down what they did to stay in shape — running, jogging, tennis, 20 lengths of the pool and so on. But the statisticians noticed something that kept cropping up in the 'Other' column. Walking. They found that nearly 35 million American adults walk for exercise every day. Another 18 million do so two or three times a week. They also discovered that walking as an exercise has staying power. It's the only form of exertion in which the rate of participation does not decline in the middle and later years.

If the President's Council on Fitness and Sports' seal of approval was not enough, the publishing business has responded in a manner guaranteed to enshrine walking as an authentic form of physical self-improvement.

Been to your local bookstore lately? Take a look at the Sports section. You'll find a minimum of one shelf devoted to the walking cult. *How to Condition for Walking; How Much, Where to Walk; How Walking Conditions Your Body; Who Should Avoid Walking;*

The Advantages of Walking Over Jogging and Running; and of course, *The Psychological Benefits of Walking*.

If you're lucky you may even be able to pick up a book about great walkers in history (Diefenbaker, Lincoln, Truman, Dickens) and quotable quotes about walking. ('Man's best medicine': Hippocrates. 'Two or three hours of walking will carry me to as strange a country as I ever expect to see': Henry David Thoreau.).

It's all there, down at your friendly local book store. Go and check it out for yourself.

But . . . walk, don't run.

THUMBS

Y OU worry? Of course you worry. We all do. We worry about whether the car will start. We worry about Aunt Agnes jetting to Florida and whether her flight will be diverted to Cuba by a bushy-haired fanatic in a flak jacket. We worry about high mortgage rates, mildew in the basement, hardening of the arteries, softening of the dollar. We worry about Western Separatists and Eastern Séparatistes . . . and all that head swivelling without forgetting to worry about the prospects of a shotgun marriage with our big, bear-hugging brother to the south. Anxiety is the theme song for the times we live in. Anxiety is just a 25-cent word for good old-fashioned nail-biting worry.

Not surprisingly in a worrisome world like this, the Worry Business is doing well. Mothers who used to aim their sons and daughters towards the medical and legal professions now have their sights exclusively honed in on Psychiatry. And why not? Psychiatrists make almost as much as plumbers and their fingernails are cleaner.

Yup, shrinks are doing swell. Pill makers are very bullish, as people pop tranquilizers the way we used to take One a Day Multiple Vitamins . . . Yogis, gurus, TVangelists and bartenders are all thriving in these nervous times . . .

People deal with worry in a variety of ways . . . For some it's two ounces of Wild Turkey, for others, it may be a nervous (*ahem*) clearing of the throat. Me? I twiddle my thumbs. Not very original I guess, but it's cheap. There's very little wear and tear on the body. And you don't have to dress up.

Besides there's something refreshingly *primitive* about twiddling your thumbs. You can do it on airplanes, in post-office lineups, at your desk or at a stoplight.

And you can work out your own individual programs with thumb twiddling. I'm particularly fond of seven thumb twiddles forward, a half revolution back, three forward again — then seven reverses. It's sort of my manual mantra if you will.

But you know what I always liked best about thumb twiddling? It couldn't be co-opted. Nobody could sell me 50-dollar thumb covers, or a colour coordinated warm-up suit or a special inclined plank with a naugahyde finish to twiddle my thumbs on. Thumb twiddling is incorruptible.

At least that's what I always thought. That was before I heard about Horace A. Knowles.

Horace is an information officer with the U.S. Department of Commerce. One of his tasks is to draft speeches for the Secretary of Commerce. A worrisome job I suppose . . . and one that occasionally would leave you with a little anxious time on your hands, listening to the Secretary mangle your finely tuned prose before a convention of chartered accountants in Tulsa.

In any case Horace Knowles is a compulsive thumb twiddler . . . and you'd think he'd be happy with that — being addicted to a harmless physical habit that dissipates anxiety without chemicals, hangovers or primal screams.

But no . . . Horace isn't just a thumb twiddler. He is also an inventor. And he's just taken out a patent on a bizarre little device made of plastic . . . with two parallel holes big enough to slip your thumbs into. He calls it The Twidd. Two 'ds' . . .

It is — you guessed it — an automatic thumb-twiddling device. Thanks a lot Horace. I can see it all now . . . a whole new growth industry. Pretty soon we will have Mark One and Mark Two Twidds. Organic Twiddle oil for lubricating the digits and reducing friction. And no doubt eventually a $12.95 fully illustrated hardcover manual called *How to Thumb Twiddle Like the Pros.*

Terrific.

In one ill-considered moment of inspiration, Horace Knowles has taken thumb twiddling out of the hands of the amateurs and placed it up there with all those trendy — not to mention pricey — pastimes like jogging, squash and tennis.

He'll probably make a mint.

And if there's any justice, it won't be enough to pay his psychotherapist.

DRESSING

D ON'T get me wrong . . . I'm not what you'd call a fashion plate or a clothes horse. In the summer, my clothes code leans to blue jeans and ratty old sweatshirts in which the armholes are still slightly bigger than the moth holes. In the winter I dress for warmth, which means that any random traces of chic stay firmly at the back of the rack in my cupboard. I will never be mistaken for Tom Wolfe or courted by Holt Renfrew to model a line of men's wear. My winter look is best described as neo-Sasquatch; my summer look as gothic beach bum.

But that doesn't mean I'm not *interested* in fashion. On the contrary, I love it. I still remember with fond delight the sack look of the 50s. The Empire Line. The Cuban hill guerrilla look that flourished in the 60s, in which stock exchange secretaries flitted up and down Wall Street wearing Che Guevara headbands with bandoliers of rifle bullets slung across their fashionably sunken chests.

Oh yes, fashion is hilarious . . . and not just for the sick jokes it plays on women. Season after season, men have risen to the bait and revamped their wardrobes according to the dictates of some obscure fashion arbiter of dubious gender in Paris or L.A.

Remember Madras shirts? Remember Ivy League and Mao jackets and that one incredible spring when every third businessman you passed on the street was wearing a sports coat of an astonishingly repulsive green pseudo-plaid? They looked like they were being consumed by some kind of jungle creeper. But it was In. For a season. Men bought them.

The game does on. Disco may be dead but there must be closets full of disco boots and silk shirts slashed to the navel and garlands of chains and Pisces medallions and brooches languishing in the backs of closets of male boudoirs of this country. And thanks to one forgettable movie — *Urban Cowboy* — it is now possible to meet a computer programmer in downtown Hamilton wearing a Stetson.

But that's really old hat. You want to know the latest trend in male fashion? What the smart set are wearing in the big fashion hubs like New York, San Francisco and Hollywood? You want to know how they're dressing these days?

Defensively. It's the very latest thing.

It's not so much a flight of fashion as a realistic response to hard economic times, and the fact that a lot of people on the streets of New York and San Francisco and Hollywood are a little more desperate than they used to be.

Quite simply, it's a bad time to look rich. And so . . . defensive dressing.

Look. Here is a lady waiting for the A Train in New York. She is wearing a wrinkled raincoat. She has on a pair of faded jeans. Scruffy, well-worn running shoes adorn each foot. She has a dollar-fifty-nine Woolworth's made-in-Korea kerchief on her head. She is carrying a shopping bag.

But do you know what's in the shopping bag? A silk dress. A pair of hundred-dollar-high-heeled-Guccis. There is a string of pearls and a cocktail ring in the inside pocket of her wrinkled raincoat. This woman is heading uptown to a very exclusive party in a very exclusive neighbourhood. She will change clothes at the party. Nobody at the party will consider her behaviour bizarre. She is just dressing defensively. If she were to get on the A Train wearing a silk dress, her Guccis and her jewelry, not only would she be behind the times, there's a very good chance she'd never get to the party.

Here is another man, *returning* from a Manhattan party. Doesn't he look swell? Stylish evening dress, black tie. He has about three blocks to walk from the subway to his apartment. But wait! He's taking off the jacket. And his watch, and his rings. He's stuffing his black tie into his pocket. He's opening his shirt buttons to the middle of his chest. He's slinging the jacket as casually as possible over his shoulder and warily strolling those three dangerous blocks, trying as much as possible to look like a tired, not very well-heeled waiter at the end of his shift.

Defensive dressing. It's not confined to the high rollers in big cities with big city crime rates. A recent National Study 'The Figgie Report on Fear of Crime' reveals that six out of ten Americans now dress plainly to avoid drawing attention to themselves.

Scary. Not so much for those of us who don't live in New York or L.A., I guess. Still less so for those of us who don't live in Toronto or Montreal or Vancouver.

And even less so for those of us who dress in a manner . . . well let's just say I'll never be mistaken for the illegitimate son of an oil tycoon.

All the same, I like to keep abreast of the fashion trends. Perhaps it's time to expand my sartorial horizons. I think perhaps I will make a small concession to fashion trends. A minor addition to my livery.

A CCM hockey helmet. In basic black.

CLUBS

ONE of the most humiliating experiences I had to put up with, growing up, was The Baseball Game. Games weren't organized then — no uniforms or car pools or earnest coaches or cheering mothers in the bleachers. There were no bleachers! No, a bunch of us would just be hanging around the schoolyard and somebody'd yell, 'Hey let's have a game.' And a little voice inside me would groan, 'Oh no, here it comes again.'

It was the *way* the teams were chosen, you see. The two best ballplayers became opposing captains of course. Then the meat market started. 'I'll take Koski' says one. 'McGregor' calls the other. 'Gimmee . . . Blakeley' says the first. 'Okay I'll have Mitchell . . .'

And so it would go, on down through the Millers and the McIlroys and the Agostinos and the Bouchards . . . and the little herd I was standing in dwindled and dwindled until one or the other of the flesh traders would end the misery by announcing . . . 'Okay you take Black.'

Well, what the heck? I was small, tangle-footed and I couldn't catch a ball with a washtub ... but it was humiliating all the same ...

Girls of course went through the same thing only in a different arena ... the school gym. Remember the dances, ladies? When the boys, strangling in their ties and suits, stood on one side of the gym and the girls, all primped and bouffanted and decked out in their best dresses, stood on the other ... each group pretending that the other side of the room didn't exist? Then the cross-overs began. The girls with steadies got rescued first; then the quarterback of the football team made off with the head cheerleader, then some other trembling male would pick the second most attractive girl in the school ... then the third would go, and the fourth ... and it was finally just like the baseball games ... three or four girls chatting in wretched animation as their paired-off peers shimmied around the floor.

Thing is ... you kind of thought you'd left all those humiliations behind once you escaped from high school. That was one of the pluses of growing up ... the freedom not to be centred out any more.

That's the way it should have worked out, but it didn't. We've got the sandlot baseball games and the high school sock hops all wrapped up in one single, sad institution of our time. The singles bar. You ever been in one? God they're ghastly. Everybody's *trying* so *hard* to look attractive and carefree and available all at once.

Of course the singles bars don't exactly hold out the promise of glories like being chosen to play first base, or being chosen to dance by the dreamboat in 11C ... Singles bars hold the promise of sex. And that's the saddest thing of all about them. Because I don't think the people in the singles bars want sex at all. I think they just want a friend ... and sad though it be, sex or the lure of sex has become the most fashionable way to say hello.

Well, there's a man in Calgary who's picked up on this. His name is Ken Turpin. He just moved to Calgary from Vancouver last year and he discovered a dismaying thing in his new home town. He could find lots of singles bars and party girls for one-night stands ... he could line himself up with female companions, male companions, bondage freaks and whole groups with a passion for Polaroids ... but he couldn't find somebody to go fishing with.

He wanted a fishing friend — that's all . . no leather, no booze, no drugs, no kundalini philosophy — just somebody to go fishing with — a friend. And he didn't know how to go about finding one.

It occurred to Ken Turpin (after talking it over with 15 psychiatrists) that he wasn't crazy, everybody else was. So he did a wonderful thing. He wrote a paperback. He called it *Friends*.

The book lists the names and addresses of 321 Calgarians who responded to Turpin's newspaper ads — ads that made it clear *Friends* was going to be just what the name implied — a publication designed to help link up people who want almost forgotten commodities like good conversation, sincerity — or somebody to go trout fishing with.

Did it work? Well the first press run of *Friends* ran to 25,000 copies. Fifty percent of them were snapped up within the first two weeks. *Friends* worked so well that Turpin already has a second Calgary area volume at the printers and he plans to expand into other major North American cities next year. Why shouldn't *Friends* work? There's nothing like it on the market.

Mind you Ken Turpin doesn't want *Friends* to be too successful. The publishing business takes up a lot of time. And he wants his weekends free. See, he ran his own ad in the first edition of *Friends*, found the somebody he was looking for, and they both can't wait for the trout season to open.

VIDEO

I THINK I'm suffering from Asteroids. You know Asteroids? It's one of those video games. You find it in pinball arcades, taverns, hotel lobbies . . . there's one at Toronto's Pearson International Airport that has about seven of my quarters.

Asteroids is a big upright box with a blank screen, four buttons and a slot to take your quarters. The buttons read Pivot Left, Pivot Right, Thrust and Fire. Put your quarter in an Asteroids machine and you are rewarded by a tiny isosceles triangle that appears in the centre of your screen. It is immediately beset by huge jagged video clumps — asteroids — that swarm at it from all corners of the screen. Object of the game: don't have your rocket ship totalled by an asteroid. You can avoid this by (A) moving your ship — that's your Thrust button, and your choice of left or right . . . or (B) turning your rocket ship towards the nearest asteroid, hitting the Fire button and blowing the asteroid to smithereens.

That's the basic game of Asteroids . . . there are additional niceties . . . a soundtrack for instance.

Insertion of the quarter also brings DOON GA DOON GA DOON GAH . . . noise that sounds a lot like the music from *Jaws* just before the hero moved in for a meal . . . that heightens the tension a little . . . And just to spice up the action, the asteroids get smaller and move faster as the game progresses . . . and every once in a while a flying saucer BEEP BEEP BEEP BEEP BEEPS . . . across the screen, spewing lethal bursts of fire designed to blast your little isosceles spaceship off the screen.

You get three rocket ships for a quarter, and the game lasts as long as you can avoid the pitfalls of marauding asteroids and malevolent flying saucers . .

It usually takes me about a minute and a half to lose all my spaceships . . . I'm predictably inept at the game . . . but I have seen nine- and ten-year-old Asteroid afficionados go on for a quarter of an hour, stroking their left and right pivot buttons, thumbing their thrust, all the while playing a deadly vibrato on the fire button which sweeps the screen clean of pseudo rocks and flying saucers — they look for all the world like Glenn Gould at a Steinway, these little space cadets . . . they sway and hunch and actually wince when their tiny ship gets totalled. As if they took the impact themselves.

Asteroids is a silly pointless waste of time and money. You win no prizes . . . You develop no negotiable skills. It's totally absurd. Also totally addictive.

The one down the street took 23 of my quarters yesterday . . . and if fate directs my feet past the blinking gates of that pinball arcade this afternoon . . . I doubt very much that I will be able to resist that DOON GAH DOON GAH DOON GAH DOON GAH siren call.

It's funny. I've never felt very close to computer technology and

I certainly never thought I'd get hooked by the trivia department of that technology — the video computer games. Remember when those first ones came out — the dreary little blips that you could play like a Ping-Pong game on your own TV screen? I thought 'What a boring way to spend your time!'

But now these sleek sophisticated consoles — not just Asteroids but Space Invaders and Rip-Off and a whole host of similar money eaters.

We used to joke about computers taking over our lives . . . but it really is happening . . . We've got video cassettes, home computers — do you know it's now possible to hook yourself into any one of several worldwide computer communication systems? Yes — and you can move around with it too! All you need is access to a telephone to plug your portable terminal into a computer complex with hundreds — potentially thousands — of terminals around the world.

And right on the horizon — Videotext — the capacity to press a button and receive an instant printout of newspapers, magazine articles, books, pamphlets or — well, you name it!

That's the high side — the low side if you will, are these video games . . . I have this uncomfortable feeling that in a few years we're going to wonder what we did for recreation before video games came along — the same way kids now look up at you like some aging, almost extinct species, and ask: 'But jeez dad . . . what did you *do* when there was no TV?'

Makes you feel a bit like how a wandering troubador must have felt when he saw his first copy of the *Gutenberg Bible*.

All I know for sure is that this silly game Asteroids is very popular . . . The company that makes them, Atari Corporation in California, says it can't turn them out fast enough. I even had to wait in a lineup for a turn at my Asteroids machine yesterday. There was a tall, rangy, casually dressed fella in front of me. Not a student. I could tell he wasn't a student because he had a paperback in his back pocket.

I watched him as he spun his little ship left and right and crisply gunned down asteroids . . . and I report absolutely without further comment that the paperback in his back pocket was a Penguin edition of John Milton's *Paradise Lost*.

TUBS

W E SEND rockets to Jupiter, right? We build 60-storey buildings, right? We have machines that can move mountains and others that can rearrange neutrons in a brain cell; we have microwave ovens and computerized checking accounts; we have earth satellites that can bounce a basketball game from Baton Rouge to Zimbabwe faster than you can say slam-dunk.

We have all that — so how come we have such lousy bathtubs?

These thoughts are not off the top of my head. As a matter of fact I'm reading them from a postcard the front of which shows the Town and Country Motel in St. Augustine, Florida. I wrote this postcard last month while I was folded like a human pretzel in the bathtub of Unit Nine, trying vainly to get the water level up over my chest. I don't have a big chest. Unit Nine of the Town and Country Motel in St. Augustine has a small bathtub.

But it's not unique. I have a bathtub that's too small at home. So do you. My question is: why?

The Finns have the sauna. The Turks have the Turkish bath. Even the Romans, who thought Jupiter was something you built statues of, not throw rockets at — the Romans had baths that make our pathetic tubs the sensual equivalent of one of those pre-moistened Qwik-Wipe serviettes the airlines give you. Why are our bathtubs so laughably inadequate?

Everything's wrong about them. They're way too small to start with. Only a child or a pygmy could as we like to say 'stretch out in a hot tub.'

They're too low, which not only means that they won't hold much water, it also necessitates a kind of linebacker crouch to get into the thing.

And most incredible of all, the controls are at the wrong end! Ever been having a bath, or worse a shower, when suddenly the water turns ice cold or blistering hot? What do you have to do? You have to dive through the water to get at the taps! Who's in charge here?

When you add on top of it all that bathtubs are slippery as the devil, studded with knobs and faucets and as hard as the knuckles of your average downtown bar bouncer ... When you realize that this year some eight thousand Canadians will fall in those slippery tubs and sustain some kind of injury, they begin to look like an insidious foreign plot, cunningly designed to make us fearful and cranky, and to mug us when possible.

Well, if it is a plot, I've got good news. The Mounties are coming to the rescue. Not the Mounties precisely ... actually it's a small firm in Seattle, Washington, run by a fellow by the name of Scott Bortz.

I humbly suggest that the name Scott Bortz be enshrined along with those other Giant Benefactors of mankind — the geniuses who invented the zipper, the safety pin and contoured bedsheets. For Scott Bortz has done a wonderful thing. Not only has he invented a bigger bathtub — (reason enough for eternal gratitude) Scott Bortz has gone one better. He has invented the soft bathtub.

The Soft Bathtub Company of Seattle, Washington has given the world a foam-cushioned, vinyl-clad fibreglass bathtub. It takes a little longer to fill ... but it's worth the wait. It is 60 inches long by 36 inches wide and it is 20 luxurious inches deep. He says the vinyl coating is actually less slippery than the conventional porcelain. The foam cushion under the vinyl not only gives your body a treat ... it retains the heat, so you don't have to keep toeing the hot water tap open every five minutes.

How long does the tub last? Not as long, admittedly, as the old-style tub — those cruel mothers are made for life. But the soft tub comes with a 10-year guarantee and should last you 20.

So much for the good news about Scott Bortz and the Soft Bathtub Company of Seattle, Washington ... now for the cold water. The price tag. The soft bathtubs start at about a thousand dollars U.S. and spiral all the way up to two thousand if you want fancy options like double width and whirlpool attachments.

I don't know. Edmund Wilson, the great American literary critic once wrote a paean to the American bathroom. He wrote: 'I have had a good many more uplifting thoughts, creative and expansive visions — while soaking in comfortable baths in well-equipped American bathrooms, than I have ever had in any cathedral in Europe.'

Hmmm. Well, I guess if it worked for a luminary like Edmund Wilson, I owe it one more try. But I can't help suspecting that Edmund Wilson — Giant of American Letters — wasn't an inch over five foot two.

WINTER

LOOK. I'm a patriotic Canadian. I'm as loyal, true and b-b-b-b-b-blue as the next frostback. Members of my family have been clinging to this unnaturally large ice floe for five generations. I know what being Canadian is all about. I also know what constitutes Canadian blasphemy . . . but it can't be helped.

You see . . . it's . . . well . . . it's about winter.

We're in the middle of another one, aren't we? And the truth is . . . well I'm not a kid any more. Truth is I'm a veteran. I've got better than three dozen winters behind me . . .

But I'm not getting any better at them.

I've tried . . . Lord knows I've tried. And I get the *little* things right. I no longer forget my mitts or my hat. It's been years since I fell for the fashion con — you know — the one perpetrated by men's wear designers who would have us make believe all of Canada is just a sprawling suburb of Fort Lauderdale and dress concessions to winter need consist only of a stylish lightweight gabardine topcoat and colour coordinated toe rubbers . . . ohhhh no.

I don't fall for *that* scam anymore. When I go out in the winter I'm swaddled in so many layers of thermal wear and wool and cotton and miracle fabrics and fur I look like a Finnish commando on Arctic manoeuvres. I'm so encased in protective clothing I've had to call the motor league to help raise my arms to the steering wheel.

I've tried the psychological approach too. The old Dale Carnegie option — you know — 'Hey winter's here! A wonderland! Let's get out there and enjoy it!'

Yeah I've got skis. Downhill. Cross country. I've got genuine Ojibway snowshoes and a toboggan and a pair of skates just like the ones Guy Lafleur wears.

At cocktail parties I can carry on at tiresome length on the perverse art of ski waxing . . . what kind of snow makes the best snow hut and the *eerie, haunting, silent unnatural beauty of a winter snowscape in the deep woods.*

'Unnatural' is the key word. Winter is not natural. There's a perfectly good reason it is silent out there. Anything with legs or wings and two brain cells to rub together has left — that's why it's silent. Robins, Canada geese, scarlet tanagers, canaries, monarch butterflies — do you hear them warbling about the eerie, haunting, silent unnatural beauty of a Canadian winter?

Of course you don't. Because to hear them warble about anything you'd have to go to Myrtle Beach or the Yucatan — that's where they beetled off to when the first eerie, haunting, silent unnatural snowflake drifted down in late October.

I know, I know . . . there are songs and poems about the glory of winter . . . but did you ever find yourself humming 'Winter Wonderland' while you were trying to shovel your left rear wheel out of a snowbank? Bing Crosby . . . 'I'm dreaming of a white Christmas.' Sure. Why not? Bing Crosby lived in California. I'd daydream about a white Christmas too, if I was standing by a sand trap on the seventh hole of the Palm Springs Golf Course wondering whether to go with a wedgie or a mashie.

I am told that the Inuit have some 60 words for snow . . . for different kinds of snow. That does not surprise me. They see a lot of it. I live considerably south of the tree line, but even I have 17 words for snow — none of them useable in public.

A few years ago there was talk on Parliament Hill of annexing the Turks and Caicos Islands as our 11th province. Do you know where the Turks and Caicos Islands are? They are the last wee pearls in a necklace called the Bahama Islands stretching languorously down into the Caribbean just north of Cuba and Haiti. Ottawa decided to curb any talk of such annexation. Wisely, I think. The Turks and Caicos are just tiny little buttons of coral, quite incapable of supporting 25 million snow-spooked northerners each winter. Besides, it would be internationally embarrassing to have a country in which 10 provinces were closed for the season three months of every year.

All of which leaves us with . . . winter.

And if I could, I would open my thermopane window, blow-torch the ice off my storm window . . . throw it open to the skin-searing, flesh-freezing, north wind that's beating against it right now . . . and bellow to that eerie, haunting, silent, unnatural, beautiful snowscape out there . . . I would bellow the ultimate Canadian blasphemy.

I hate winter!!!!!!

There. I said it. And I feel warm all over.